Vendetta

~ ~

Elizabeth Flaherty

Copyright © 2013 by Elizabeth Flaherty
Cover Art and Design copyright © 2013 by Stephen Gordon

ISBN: 0615780814
ISBN-13: 9780615780818

www.flahertybooks.com

From Little B's Briefcase

DEDICATION

This book is dedicated to the many who pray for justice after suffering at the hands of violent criminals. The criminal justice system is an extremely slow and somewhat imperfect process. Yet every day victims of crime handle their trauma with such grace and dignity that it almost seems unfair to use the word "victim" to describe them.

And to my beloved colleagues, the assistant district attorneys who work to bring the justice that the system promises. It is because of your hard work and strength of character that there is reason for hope.

~ ~

For six-year old Bethany Chase, life was perfect. It was a warm sunny day, and, like every day, her mom walked to pick her up after school.

When they reached the corner where they turned to head home, a perfect day got even better. Bethany's mom squatted down next to her with a very serious look.

"I'm wondering if I can trust you," she said.

Bethany giggled. Her mom was teasing her. She could tell by her voice.

With a pretend frown, she said, "If we take a quick trip to the park, do you promise you'll do your homework the second you get home?"

Bethany clapped her hands together. "The park? We can go to the park?"

"You have to promise."

"I promise! I promise!"

Her mom gave her a wink. "I think you and I need

a bit of fun this afternoon. Come on."

Bethany loved the park. Beautiful, gigantic Central Park. Now that it was Spring and it wasn't so cold anymore, it meant they'd be able to go to the park more often. And that was the most perfect thing of all. Because Central Park was Bethany's favorite place in the world.

She and her mom skipped together through the streets, laughing at the stern looking grown-ups they passed along the way.

The trees in the park were still bare, but Bethany could see the little buds, and she knew that meant there'd be leaves really soon. And the grass on their special little hill was greener every day.

Tiny crocuses poked their heads up everywhere. Bethany picked one of the little flowers and handed it to her mom.

"For me?" her mom asked. "You shouldn't have spent so much money!"

Bethany made a face. "I didn't spend any money! I picked it right here."

"Where? Right here?" Her mom laughed, picking her up and swinging her over the flowers.

Bethany would never forget the moment. The grass and flowers blurring by below. The trees ready to burst with spring life spinning by above.

The world suddenly lurched as Bethany fell from her mother's arms. She tumbled down a small incline and stopped harmlessly at the base of a shrub.

Laughing heartily, she stumbled to her feet, a little dizzy from the fall. The world tilted slightly as she tried to stand.

As things settled, she looked up to the top of the hill. At first she didn't see her mom.

She looked around a little, then she looked back up the hill. That was when she saw her mom lying up there. She was so silly, hiding like that.

Bethany cackled at the sight. "Mommy, I see you!"

She ran towards her mom and jumped on her.

Looking back, it was hard to say the moment when she realized things weren't okay. That her mother wasn't playing.

There was blood. Blood that clung to her tiny fingers. That stuck to her clothes.

Blood that would never be washed away.

~ 1 ~

Present Day

Bethany Chase stood in the shadow of the grandstand, one of the few spots that offered a reprieve from the day's relentless heat. But it was the sounds of laughter that soothed her more than the shade or the blasts from the industrial cooling fans.

This was what she did. Who she was. She needed these events to remind her of that. They were all that kept her from floating into the ether like a child's abandoned balloon.

Next to her, folded into a small chair, was Geoffrey Quinn. His head was down, studying note cards, preparing for his big moment.

This was who he was, too. This was what they did. Together. Their engagement made sense. Marriage would make even more sense.

Geoffrey looked up and smiled at her. He tucked his note cards into his suit pocket and stood, taking her hand.

"Almost time," he said.

She ran a hand over his always perfect hair, as if that could fix any hidden flaws. He straightened his jacket and the collar on his button-down shirt. He looked the part of the candidate – pressed, polished, but somehow casual, comfortable. He'd be a good mayor, a very good mayor.

Twenty-five years ago, she'd been placed on a path that led her to this point, made her into the perfect person to be in this place at this time.

Maybe that was why she still had doubts. How could she trust anything connected to that awful day?

She shook off her hesitancy. Today wasn't the day for those kinds of questions. She needed to be in character. Play the role she'd been cursed to play. The people in the audience believed they knew her. Believed that they'd somehow gained access to her life the day her mother had been stolen from her.

She let them see what they wanted and she hid the rest. She'd been doing it for so long now she wondered if even she knew where reality ended and the secrets began.

The sound system squealed to life and a voice asked for the crowd's attention. The sounds of the carnival rides, squeals of children, buzz of adults, faded.

"Welcome to the seventh annual Family Day here in Central Park. As always, we're sponsored by the Chase Family Charitable Foundation. I am happy to report we've broken an attendance record again this year and the park safety patrols are going to be able to expand their efforts even more than in years past! Thank you all so very much!"

The crowd roared in triumph and Bethany gave

Geoffrey's hand a squeeze. "You ready for this?" she asked.

He winked at her. "I was born ready for this."

His tone was pure sarcasm, but Bethany knew the truth. He'd known most of his life that this was his goal. Part of him did think this was some sort of birthright, something he was destined to do.

She gave him a kiss for luck before she approached the back stairs to the grandstand and prepared herself to do what she'd been destined to do.

The voice of the M.C. spiked again, quieting the crowd. "It's my honor to introduce the reason you're all here today. The president of the Chase Foundation – Bethany Chase."

The roar of the crowd was familiar, as were the flashing cameras. Bethany ascended the steps to the grandstand with the grace of a runway model. Sunglasses hid her eyes and a broad smile concealed the rest. She knew what the crowd saw and she played her part with finesse.

She saw there were news crews poised, waiting anxiously. Though her events always garnered at least a token cameraman from the network affiliates, this was different. Reporters were positioned by the cameramen, pads ready. And they weren't the people who did the fluff pieces. They were ready for the night's lead story. Clearly Geoffrey's campaign had leaked just enough to ensure the proper coverage.

She wondered if her staff had noticed the peculiarity yet. She wondered even more why she'd chosen to keep it from them – from everyone.

She flashed one final smile to the audience and waved again before she approached the microphone. It was time. There was no delaying it any longer.

"Thank you all for coming out. I know it's a little hot, but remember proceeds are all going to park safety. So help yourself to as many ice cream cones as you can eat!"

She paused, allowing them to cheer and raise their ice cream, taking strength from the normalcy of it all.

"I know you all believe, as I do, that it's important to create a safe place for families to play together, to remove the fears and anxiety we have to endure in this city. You've all helped make that possible, but there's still more work ahead."

She didn't see the news crews now. She saw a child, front and center, sitting on her mother's shoulders, holding a bright red balloon. She looked about six. So young. So innocent. Bethany knew better than anyone how quickly that could be stolen away.

She held that image in her mind as she continued, "Today I want to talk about the future. About what we can do going forward, what we as a community can stand behind. We can't allow our view to become myopic. We have to look beyond park. Look to the city. The entire city!"

Bethany paused for the cheers, and looked off to the shadows behind the grandstand. The glare of the sun shrouded Geoffrey in darkness, but she knew he was there waiting for her.

"I'm going to introduce you to the man who can lead us to that safer community that we're all striving to build. I think most of you know him already. He's an assistant district attorney here in Manhattan, a graduate of Fordham and NYU. And most importantly, he's a New Yorker!"

Bethany smiled at the roar from the crowd, allowing the momentum to build for Geoffrey. "I've gotten the chance to get to know him pretty well over the past three years. I've come to discover he's a man who thinks big, who dreams big, and who's big enough to make those dreams come true. And that's why I admire him so very much. Today I'd like to introduce him to you again. Not just as my fiancé, not just as a tireless prosecutor and servant of the people of the City of New York, but as a candidate to be the next mayor of this great city! Ladies and gentlemen – Geoffrey Quinn!"

Geoffrey bounded up on the stage with an energy Bethany had come to love. He waved to the crowd and then gave her a tight hug.

"You're the best opening act ever," he whispered in her ear.

"Knock 'em dead," she whispered back.

Geoffrey gave her a big kiss, much more for the audience's benefit than hers, and greeted the crowd.

"Isn't she the most extraordinary woman in the world?" he shouted.

He waited for the applause to subside before he began, "As you all know, I've worked hard for this city for my entire adult life. Many of you know me from my work in the D.A.'s Office, but I hope even more of you know me from my charitable endeavors. Like you, I love this city!"

Geoffrey glanced over at Bethany and then back to the crowd. "I could have chosen any event to make my announcement, but I knew that this was the right place. The perfect place. We're here today because we're trying to take our city back. Because we want to keep our loved ones safe. I have dedicated my professional life to making that a reality. And now, I'm asking you to let me serve as this city's mayor. Because together we can make this a place that we would be proud to call home!"

The crowd roared in unity, confirming what Bethany had also known. This audience, this place, was perfect for the announcement.

As the crowd quieted, Geoffrey continued, "Many people in this city are victims of violent crime. Many others live in fear. I know many of you've been touched by violence. I personally have seen the way it changes lives. I've seen it through my work and I see it every day when I look at the woman I love."

As he spoke, Bethany could feel the humid air begin to close around her.

The reference to her had been inevitable. Expected, considering his platform. But she felt her heart constrict at his words. Twenty-five years later, any mention of her mother's murder or its impact still felt like a punch in the gut.

As Geoffrey spoke of the way violence ruined people and communities, Bethany assured herself that he was speaking generally. He was talking about the victims he knew from work. Not her.

But she heard the accusation in his voice, the judgment. Maybe he did think of her as ruined. Maybe it was unrealistic to believe he'd see her any other way.

Her mother's death had defined her. Made her the woman she was today.

There were only a few people who saw her as more than that damaged six-year-old. But they weren't here today. She'd made sure of that.

Part of her had wanted them to be here. But she'd been afraid to hear what they'd think about all of this. Afraid they'd try to talk her out of it. Maybe even afraid they wouldn't.

Talking about Geoffrey's plans inevitably led to conversations about her plans with Geoffrey. It was a conversation she hated. There was nothing worse than the people that you loved pointing out things that you were trying very hard to ignore.

But the avoidance was ridiculous. Richard and Annie were her best friends in the world. Geoffrey wasn't some deep, dark secret. He was her fiancé. There was nothing to be afraid of.

Maybe her life was just so full of secrets now that she no longer knew how to be open. She no longer knew how to share what she was feeling.

Applause brought her out of her thoughts. And Geoffrey's tone told her he was wrapping up. He stood tall and proud, beaming.

"I'm going to keep this short. It's important you get out there and enjoy the activities that were planned. But I'll leave you with this one thought – Vote Quinn for a Brighter Tomorrow!"

Geoffrey waved vigorously at the cheering crowd. Taking Bethany's hand, he raised it with his in victory. As she stood there, her hand in his, Bethany realized they were inextricably linked.

She just wished it was what she really wanted.

~ 2 ~

Richard Marshall was stretched on his couch with the baseball game playing silently on the television. He wasn't waiting for her. He'd muted the game because the announcers were annoying. Not because he was listening for Bethany's return.

At the sound of the elevator bell, he was on his feet. He forced himself to walk slowly, casually, to the door. Her apartment was directly across the hall. It was the only other one on the floor. There was no way he could miss her.

Seeing her chestnut hair in the peephole, he swung the door open to greet his best friend.

"Not so fast," he said.

"Damn elevator bell," Bethany muttered to herself.

"Now don't blame the elevator. I would've heard your door open. I have ears like a bat."

Despite everything, he smiled when she turned to face him. She looked beautiful, as always, and her expression was not unlike when she was eight and had been caught trying to steal a pack of gum.

"Ears like a bat?" she asked. "The last time the fire alarm went off in the middle of the night I had to pound on your door for almost five minutes to wake you up."

He scowled in response, his square jaw set tightly, promising himself he wouldn't be charmed. "I'm a heavy sleeper. That doesn't mean I don't hear everything you're up to."

Bethany snorted at the suggestion. "I know you're going to let me have it, and you should, why don't you come in?"

He followed her inside and flopped onto his favorite side of the couch, propping his feet on the coffee table. He considered saying something to start the conversation, but he waited to hear what she'd offer first.

"Geoffrey's running for mayor," she blurted out.

He almost laughed. "Really?" He glanced at his watch sarcastically. "It's not as if I read that online twenty minutes ago or anything. Is that why you told us to skip the fundraiser this year?"

He wanted to grill her a little, get the real story. Frankly, with her and Geoffrey there always seemed to be the need to pry information out of her.

But she looked like a trapped animal. It was a look he'd seen in her eyes far too often recently.

His voice softened, in spite of himself. He patted the couch. "How about you sit?"

She followed his direction and sank down next to him.

She focused on her hands when she spoke. "I should've told you. I don't know why I didn't."

"I don't know why you didn't either," Richard replied. "I imagine you were keeping this huge revelation from your father, and I can't say I blame you for that, but I can keep a secret. I've never told anyone you made out with Jack McKee at summer camp."

Bethany rolled her eyes. "Does it always have to come back to Jack?"

"Hey, I'm willing to tell the world about good old Jack if you want. Tell them all about your attempt to convince very gay Jack that girls were better than boys."

"Fine, you've made your point. As you always do. You can keep a secret. I know that. I guess it's just a little weird talking about Geoffrey with you guys. I know you and Annie aren't exactly thrilled with him," Bethany said.

Richard searched her face for any clue as to what was going on. "Annie and I both love you. We just want you to be happy."

"Geoffrey makes me happy. He's a good man. This'll be a really good thing for him."

Richard considered giving her the speech again, reminding her that her near obsession with saving the world wasn't a basis upon which to build a relationship. But she looked too tired to listen and he had no interest in starting a fight.

"It's not just a big thing for him, Beth," he said. "It'll be huge for both of you. You'll have some power, too."

A buzzing from her purse distracted her. Without a word, she checked the caller ID and then dropped the phone on the coffee table.

"Reporter?" he asked.

She shook her head. "My father."

He ran a hand over her shoulder. "You know,

ignoring problems doesn't make them go away."

She offered a weary smile. "But it does give them a little time to cool off."

Aston and Bethany Chase had legendary fights. They were Tyson and Holyfield without the ear biting. As a rule, Geoffrey didn't bring out the best in them.

"Does Aston actually cool off? I'm not sure I've ever seen that side of him," Richard said.

His joke was rewarded with a more sincere smile. "I can hope, can't I?"

After a moment, she said, "I hate to cut this short, but I have a training session in about fifteen minutes. I need to start getting ready."

"Oh, so now you're choosing time with your trainer over me? I'm pretty sure the Karate Kid was never this disciplined."

"Ah, yes, the Karate Kid – a role model of mine." She stood, laughing at his comparison. "It's healthy to have a hobby, you know."

"A hobby? This isn't a hobby, it's an obsession."

Richard didn't entirely know what went on in the martial arts studio a block from their apartment building, and he was pretty sure he didn't want to.

He was heading for the door when he stopped. "I almost forgot. Annie called after the announcement hit the news. She's thinking we should grab dinner tomorrow, significant others included. Then we can congratulate you and Geoffrey."

Bethany's green eyes sparkled. "Are you going to be bringing a significant other?"

"Whoa, there. I'll be attending all on my own. There's no way I'm going to subject anyone to you and Annie."

"How is Trisha these days?"

"Tracey," he corrected.

"Whatever. If any of your girlfriends manage to stick around for more than a month, I'll make an effort to get to know her name."

He shrugged. "There's a lot of beautiful women out there. If I stick with anyone for too long, I could miss out on something."

Bethany gave him a kiss on the cheek. "Yeah, you'll miss out on something sooner or later, that's for sure."

Richard glared at her. "How did this suddenly get turned around on me? We were picking on you. Not me. So, dinner tomorrow night?"

"It sounds nice. I'll double check with Geoffrey and let you know."

"Perfect. I'll set it up," he replied, heading back to his apartment.

Richard left her to prepare to battle her demons, or whatever it was she really did over at the studio. He wished he felt better about the conversation, but she'd done nothing to put his mind at ease.

There was something wrong. The more Bethany talked, the more convinced he became. Richard suspected it had something to do with Geoffrey. But one way or the other he was going to figure it out.

~ 3 ~

Bethany hated the lies. But they were necessary. As necessary as breathing.

No one knew about her loft above Master Jung's Martial Arts studio. No one could.

In that room, with its blackened windows, she searched for peace. The peace that could only come from the truth.

Some journeys required sacrifice. And until she found the truth, she'd sacrifice anything.

But in this place, she didn't think much of sacrifice. She focused only on the quest.

Bethany had started investigating her mother's murder after her first year of college. She'd expected it to be simple: get some paperwork, review the files.

She'd deluded herself into thinking the answers would be there, it would merely take a fresh set of eyes. But instead of finding the answers she'd dreamed about for years, she found a new list of nightmarish questions.

She hadn't realized how effectively her brain had been protecting her, how much she'd repressed, until the pictures of the crime scene brought all the memories back.

The details, now refreshed, were pristine. She could replay the moment in her mind. Running up the hill. Finding her mother lying on the ground, eyes glassy and staring, just staring. Even as a child Bethany had understood that was a bad thing.

And then she'd seen the blood. So much blood.

Before her investigation, the memories had been lost. Little more than flashes in her nightmares. But now they were sharp, clear, and they would haunt her for the rest of her life.

What was worse was that she felt it all again – the utter panic, the total isolation. She'd forever remember how it felt to clench her dead mother's hand in her own. She could almost hear her own voice begging her mother to wake up.

The police files stoked the fiery rage she'd felt on some level since that fateful afternoon. And that rage led her to a life-changing decision. She promised herself she'd use her power, her money, and anything else it took to find the answers. And, no matter what, she wouldn't stop until she did.

When she turned twenty-five, Bethany was given full access to her trust fund, and the ability to spend her money without anyone looking over her shoulder. She was still careful of course, funneling the money through brokers and agents, and even a few shell corporations.

And when that was all done, she owned a loft just a few blocks from her apartment. Master Jung's studio provided the perfect cover. She spent so much time there already, no one noticed a few extra hours.

After a few renovations, the space was hers. A completely secret spot where she could work without fear of discovery.

In the loft, she stored a small arsenal of weapons, and all of her gear, her mask, and anything else she might need to force the reluctant to talk. She'd painted the walls a bright white and she used them much the same way the police would use a whiteboard. In thick marker, she tracked her progress on the case. She taped photos to the wall.

Alone in the loft, she was surrounded by her sins. The stark white walls spoke bold accusations, written by her own hand.

It was no surprise that the names on the wall created a web. In reality, the loft was itself nothing less. With each passing year it became less clear if she was the spider or the fly.

With gloved hands, she checked the backpack that held her gear. The thick black ski mask was on top, made of a breathable nylon that covered all but her eyes and padding that altered even the shape of her face. A thin mechanical device covered her mouth. It was the only part of the mask that was uncomfortable, but it was necessary. Without the distortion it provided, they'd hear her voice. And that would destroy the effect.

In the pack, underneath the mask, was a black handgun, nine millimeter. She didn't plan to use it. She never did. But she'd be a fool not to bring a safety net.

Next to the unloaded gun was the clip. She'd leave them apart until she was ready to proceed. She didn't want a loaded gun knocking around in her backpack.

The final piece was the knife. Its long blade glinted as it peeked from its sheath. The knife was crucial to the plan. As were the black plastic zip cuffs that she would use to bind his hands, and his feet if necessary.

In the dense vegetation just off the path, she was still as a statue, invisible in the night's shadows. The only sign she was still alive was the trickle of sweat that slid down her back.

He'd pass this spot. Just the same way he had every night for the past ten days. He was very predictable. Most people were. It made them easy to catch.

And once they were caught, their fear was a more effective weapon than any gun.

Fortunately for the world, most criminals were impulsive and stupid. They didn't stalk their victims. They didn't research, or plan, or wait for the right time.

She wished she believed that was evidence she was more than just a criminal, but she knew the truth. Outlaws went out with the wild west. No matter how noble her quest, how righteous the goal, she was a criminal – nothing more, nothing less.

But tonight she thought little of any of that. He was

coming. The sound of soft footfalls reached her ears. Expensive leather shoes, bought with money from killers. Soon he'd be so close she could smell the sharp cologne he practically bathed in.

Like most predators, he was far too confident. The cocky bastard thought his connections to the Timminolo crime family made him untouchable. He was about to find out that all the protection in the world wasn't worth anything if the right person wanted to grab you.

Under the mask, she felt her cheeks flush with rage. She embraced the anger, pulled it close. And as he came into sight, she pounced.

Before he even realized he was being grabbed, she had one arm around his throat, another pulling his briefcase out of reach. With his line of work, she knew there'd be a gun inside the case. It would be better if that was taken out of play completely. She tossed the briefcase into some bushes and pulled one of Manhattan's best criminal defense attorneys off the path into a secluded area.

Though he squirmed initially, his pudgy frame was now still enough that she eased off his throat. An unconscious Angelo Bria wouldn't do her any good.

At the edge of a small pond, she threw him to his knees. She waited for him to take a deep breath, but before he could do anything more, she shoved his head under the water. Pulling his arms behind his back, she secured his hands with zip cuffs. With the plastic tight around his wrists, she allowed him to surface for air.

He coughed and sputtered, gasping as his head broke the surface.

Before he could speak, before he could even think, she leaned close. Her electronically distorted voice threatened, "Don't pass out on me there, Angelo, we need to have a little talk."

He turned his head to look at her, the awe and fear obvious. She knew he saw barely more than a shadow. Dressed entirely in black, with a hooded mask, she could scare the truth out of anyone. And that wasn't just an expression. She knew it for a fact.

"I don't want to hurt you. We can do this real easily. I have a couple of questions I need you to answer. Do you think you can handle that?"

Bria nodded attentively, his flabby neck swaying. But he said nothing. Silence was good. Silence meant she had his attention.

"Good. That's what I like to see. Word is you've been running your mouth about the Rita Chase murder."

"Rita Chase's murder? What do you mean? That happened twenty-five years ago. Why are you asking me questions about that?"

She cut him off before he could say anything more, shoving his head back into the water, counting slowly to herself, holding him under just long enough that he'd begin to feel the desperate need for air. Then she pulled him back to the surface, slamming his knees back into the muddy earth.

"You answer my questions, Angelo. It's simple. No comments. No expounding. Just answer the question you're asked. You're a lawyer, you should understand the concept."

Wet stringy hair dripped in his eyes. "I got it, man. Just cool off. I got it."

He was still too unconcerned for her, but his comment amused her. It was amazing really. They never knew she was a woman. Never even considered it. Chauvinistic sons of bitches.

She knelt down behind him, shoving his face forward when he attempted to look at her. This was going to be a very satisfying conversation. One way or the other.

"You know, Angelo, I was just reading the other day about the complexities of the joints in the fingers. Fascinating stuff. The knuckles are kind of like a hinge. But like any hinge, you bend it the wrong way and it'll break."

As she spoke, she wrapped her fingers around his left pointer finger, slowly, methodically tightening her grip.

"Rita Chase's murder. What do you know about the guy that killed her?" she asked again.

"I don't know anything about the murder." His voice was high, almost shrill. He sounded scared now.

But apparently not scared enough.

"I'd like to believe that, but I've got a friend who told me you said you knew what happened. That means you're lying to one of us. You don't want to be lying to me."

"I can't tell you anything," he said without conviction.

She laughed at his assertion. Without a second's hesitation, she snapped his finger back, allowing the tip to touch the back of his hand, savoring the sensation of the snapping tendons. She quickly submerged his head, muting the inevitable scream.

When she let him up, he was choking back what sounded like a sob.

She let him look at her now. He'd see only black eyes set deep in the black mask.

"I can't," he finally said.

"Don't be afraid of the mob, be afraid of me." There was no threatening calm now, only vicious rage. She grabbed his middle finger and snapped it back.

Again, she muffled his cries with the water, but brought him back to the surface quickly to be sure he wouldn't choke.

Despite her efforts, Angelo's eyes looked unfocused when she pulled him up. A slap across the face brought him back. "It's not going to be that easy, you bastard. Look at me!" she ordered.

Bria shook his head, focusing.

"The right hand is next, Angelo. You're right-handed, so that's going to make work more difficult."

"Who the hell are you?" he asked, seemingly unable to say anything else.

Stupid lawyers and their stupid questions. Grabbing the final two uninjured fingers on his left hand, she snapped them back, muffled his cries, and then brought him back to the surface.

"I'm asking the questions. And we're now officially onto the right hand. That's unless you want me to go for the thumbs next. I was going to save those for last."

Finally, there was some clarity in his eyes. "Rita Chase was killed in Central Park about twenty-five years ago," he began.

She wrapped her fingers around his other pointer finger.

"It was a hit," he added quickly. "A paid contract. The hitman waited for her and her kid in the park. The order was a single shot to the head. And that's what happened."

"I know all that. Tell me who the hitman was."

There was a flash of something in his eyes. It almost

looked like relief. That wasn't the look she wanted.

"Gino Niccolini did the hit," he said. "He was a client of mine at one point. He told me about it."

"What do you mean he told you about it?"

"He was a hitman. On trial for murder. We were talking strategy. I think he was bragging. He figured he could brag because of the attorney-client privilege."

"Who hired him?"

"I don't know anything else. I just know that Gino said he did it."

The rage flared again. There was more. There had to be more.

She leaned in closer, again pulling his finger back slowly. He should be feeling real pain in the joint now. With the pain already pulsing through his other hand, he'd want to tell her the truth. "I think there's more to the story," she said.

His eyes were desperate again, pleading. "There was nothing. He was bragging. Just bragging about the hit. He wanted to tell someone the details. How he stood there in the trees waiting for them. How he got the shot off clean. And he told me about the kid. How upset she was. He got off on it. That was all he talked about. Nothing about the business side. I'm not sure he even knew who he did the job for."

She could see it all, and it didn't bring rage, it only brought pain. But she shook that off, focused on the task at hand. "Where's this hitman?"

Bria's voice was soft when he spoke. "He's dead."

She acted without thought, without consideration, without conscious awareness. She snapped two fingers on his right hand back, barely feeling the crack of the bone, not hearing the snap of the joint. She shoved his face into the water, not really intending on ever letting him up.

But she did let him up. He was choking when he finally broke the surface, his nose and chin covered in black mud.

"You tell me a half-assed story about this hit; tell me you don't know anything useful; and then tell me the guy who was directly involved is dead? That's pretty fucking convenient," she said.

"It's true. I swear. Gino died in prison. Early nineties. Stabbed in a prison fight. The word was that he got knifed because he was talking to the Feds to get his sentence lightened. The people he'd worked for, they didn't like that."

She ordered herself to calm down, to breathe. There might be something here. "Was there a particular Family he did most of his work for?"

"Gino was a freelancer. Worked for himself. No loyalties," Bria said.

The answer was too simple for her taste. "But you defended him?"

"Yes," he said cautiously, "but that was years later."

That meant Niccolini had to be connected to the Timminolo Family in some significant way. Otherwise the great Angelo Bria wouldn't have been made available to him.

She wanted to ask more, but she knew that was the end of it. She wondered where she'd go from here. "Niccolini? Died in prison early nineties?" she repeated.

Bria nodded.

She grabbed his throat, lifting him off the ground. "If I find out you're lying to me, I'll shove your face in that water until the pond fills your lungs and you never breathe air again. Got it?"

She was rewarded with a look of pure fear. "Yeah. I got it."

She threw Bria back to the ground. Before he could regain his balance, she shoved a sock into his mouth and slapped duct tape across his lips.

Pointing to the long sharp knife she'd driven into the ground not far from him, she said, "That's how you get out of here. You cut the zip cuffs, then move on with your life. Maybe you should have a doctor look at those fingers. I will be back if you aren't telling me the truth."

Then, as quickly as she appeared, she vanished into the darkness.

~ 5 ~

Bethany's day began with a ringing phone. At barely eight, she didn't need to wonder who was calling. She dreaded the call, but she'd avoided him long enough. Too long, probably.

"Good morning, Dad," she said, trying to shake the sleep from her voice.

Aston Chase's voice carried even more fury than she'd expected. "Good? What exactly do you think is good about it?"

Bethany sat up in bed, pushing the sheets aside and steeling herself for the fight she'd avoided the night before. "Do you want to talk about this or do you want to yell?"

Not surprisingly, the question did nothing for his mood. "I'm honored you finally decided to take my call."

"I saw you left a message last night," Bethany confessed. "It was just a busy night. I planned on calling you this morning."

"He uses the Chase name to launch his campaign and you don't think I deserve a call before the announcement?"

"How exactly did he use your name to launch his campaign?"

"Please. He announced at the biggest event of the Foundation's year. You introduced him. He used our family history to humanize himself. It was presented as a Chase family endorsement."

Bethany stood and started pacing, her frustration and anger growing, as it always did in moments like this with her father. "I run the Foundation. Not you. I decide what happens at the events. Not you. With his platform, the event yesterday was a logical place to announce."

"I'm the Chairman of the Foundation's Board," he snarled back. "Or have you forgotten that? You run things because I let you run things."

Bethany almost laughed at the threat. "Are you suggesting you're going to fire me because you don't like my boyfriend?"

"Have I not made my position clear about him? Maybe I need to say it again?"

"I'm not a teenager, Dad. I don't have to break up with someone just because you don't approve."

Aston snorted at the suggestion. "He's using you. Using your position. Your family. And, by extension, he's using *me* to gain his political footing."

"I am not going to have this conversation with you again. You know that isn't true. If you found even the tiniest bit of evidence to suggest that you would've barraged me with it years ago."

"What more evidence do you need? He's using your

event. The event sponsored by a charity that carries my name! *You* are practically his platform for God's sake. And you still think he isn't using you? You're smarter than this."

Bethany absorbed the words the same way she absorbed punches during training sessions – muscles taut, teeth clenched, breathing even. "Are you done?" she said with a calmness that concealed her anger.

"I am not even close to done! I won't have this!"

"I don't think you have much choice in the matter," Bethany replied.

She could almost hear a snap as Aston realized he'd been manipulated.

"You knew this conversation would go like this. That's why you didn't tell me until after he announced."

She made no effort to deny it. "And now it's done. Don't you see? It's done. There's nothing you can do about it."

"The hell I can't!" he roared. "If you really think there's nothing I can do about this, then you, my dear, do not know me very well."

"What're you going to do, oppose your future son-in-law's campaign?" she countered.

"He's not my son-in-law yet," Aston threatened.

She'd had enough. "That's it. It's barely eight A.M. I need to get ready for work. I don't have time for this."

"This conversation isn't over," he insisted.

Though Bethany knew he was right, she said, "It is for now," as she disconnected the call.

Clad in the t-shirt and shorts she'd worn to bed, Bethany shuffled out of her apartment and across the hall to Richard's. She pushed open the door without knocking. She knew it would be open. It always was.

Eyes half closed, wishing she could return to the sleepy state her father had stolen from her, Bethany took a mug from the cabinet and poured some coffee.

She heard his voice before she saw him. "Ah, if it isn't my favorite coffee thief. You're a little late this morning."

Bethany shook her head as she drank down the rich blend. No one in the world made better coffee than Richard.

"One of these days you're going to try to barge into my apartment and discover the door is locked."

She only laughed and finally looked up at her old friend. "You start locking your door; I'll start locking mine. No free coffee for me and no free food for you. Nobody wins there."

Richard finished knotting his tie. "You look like hell this morning."

"Thanks for noticing. I feel like hell. Woke up to a phone call from my father. Not the best conversation ever."

One of the advantages of having a friend who'd known you since you were four was that you didn't have to explain much. Richard would know immediately what had happened.

"He's going to warm up to him eventually," Richard assured her.

Bethany doubted that. She doubted that any of them would.

Richard poured his own cup of coffee and asked, "So, when Geoffrey moves in, should I expect that he'll be stopping by for coffee?"

She hopped up on the counter. "We haven't even set a date. I don't think you need to worry about your precious coffee just yet."

"You know, I find it very interesting that he doesn't stay at the casa de Bethany more often."

She rolled her eyes at the implied question. "Really? You're really asking me that at this hour of the morning?"

Behind Richard's cheerful grin was a glimmer of concern. "I figure you're so grumpy and disoriented before your coffee you might slip up and give me an honest answer about lover boy."

"I like my space. You know that."

"Isn't that going to make the whole marriage thing a little tricky?" Though Richard's tone was sarcastic, Bethany knew the question was a serious one. She also knew that Richard was the last person she could have this conversation with.

She laughed it off. "Look, bud, I came here for coffee. I'm now heading back to my apartment to find some smashing ensemble for work. I have a Board meeting this afternoon with dear old dad. It's going to be a rough day. There's no need to start it with a bad game of twenty questions."

Richard's expression quickly changed. "You have a meeting with the Board today? The timing really couldn't be worse on that."

Bethany tried to rub the sleep from her eyes. "Unfortunately, I don't set the dates for the Board meetings and I'm not running the campaign. You know, I can't help but notice just how powerless I really am."

Richard ignored her self-deprecation. "Aren't you scheduled to pitch that gun exchange program today? Aston isn't going to like that idea."

"Not even if he was in his best mood."

Richard took a sip of his coffee and then added,

"He's going to crucify you in front of the whole Board, isn't he?"

Bethany rubbed the back of her neck in a fruitless effort to release some of the tension that was already starting to build there. "I'm going to have to say, yes. It certainly looks that way."

Richard topped off her cup. "Have some more. Sounds like you'll need it."

She ran her hand over Richard's arm appreciatively. "What I'm really going to need is a drink at the end of the day. You said the reservation was for Alfelini at eight?"

"Annie says that's Geoffrey's favorite."

"Geoffrey's excited. He really appreciates you guys doing this for him."

Richard shrugged off the thanks. "It's the least we can do. But first, off to work with you. The sooner you start, the sooner it'll be over."

Bethany nodded and plodded back to her own apartment, wishing she could climb into bed and pull the covers over her head.

It was hard to say what was bothering her more, the impending Board meeting or Richard's unwelcome grilling about Geoffrey.

With Richard, there was a fine line that had to be walked. That had been the case for years now, ever since the day he'd kissed her.

Of course there'd been alcohol consumed – quite a lot of it. And of course Richard had blamed the whole thing on the drinking.

But Bethany knew better. It had been college. Drinking was a big part of what they did most weekends. And despite that, it had only happened the one time.

Richard moved on. He hadn't seemed bothered by the rejection. He'd almost shrugged it off. Bethany often wondered what had hurt more – turning him away or the fact that he hadn't seemed to care.

But she pushed such thoughts from her mind. She and Richard could never be. That was the way it was. The way it needed to be.

She forced herself to forget how perfect the moment had been. To forget the way everything else had faded away. Because it was only that – a moment.

And she knew all about moments. She'd experienced more than a lifetime's worth of loss in a moment. The haunting memory of her mother's blood on her hands was enough to remind her of that.

~ 6 ~

Twenty minutes later, Bethany's driver was waiting outside her building, ready to take her to work. In the backseat was her assistant, Emily, bearing a low fat muffin and the morning paper. Bethany was almost knocked over by Emily, who was even more energetic than usual.

"Congratulations! I can't believe he's running. That's just awesome. Awesome! He's going to kick Mayor Wilson's ass. Here's the paper. He's on the front page. And you standing right behind him… I think that's a great angle they took you from. You look so excited for him."

Bethany took the paper and, as was often the case, was speechless at the greeting. Emily was the perfect assistant. She anticipated everything and could make impossible mounds of red tape disappear with a phone call. But on days like this, Bethany felt tired just talking to her.

Instead of trying to look vigorous enough to keep up, Bethany scanned the article on Geoffrey. It mentioned everything it should have. Education. Career. His parents who'd adopted him at birth. Predictably, the article shifted to their relationship, followed by the standard rehashing of her mother's unsolved murder – her "assassination in Central Park," as they chose to call it. It was nice that twenty-five years later they could still find new and colorful ways to describe the worst day of her life.

Emily interrupted her dark thoughts. "Your father's assistant called me about an hour ago. He'll be issuing a statement later today about Geoffrey's announcement."

Bethany tore her eyes from the paper. "He's not very happy that my mom's murder is already becoming a building block for a campaign that he had no intention of supporting," she explained.

Emily didn't seem surprised. Though, Emily never seemed surprised. "Mr. Chase's people said they'll provide us with a copy of his statement before it goes out. They'd like the same consideration from us."

A preview of the statement was more of an accommodation than she'd expected. She was pretty sure Geoffrey's campaign staff wouldn't be given that kind of advantage.

Emily waited until Bethany started flipping through the rest of the paper before she continued with the morning report. As they did every morning, Emily summarized the items of note while Bethany scanned the headlines.

"The biggest news is about Angelo Bria," Emily said.

Bethany kept her attention fully on the paper as she spoke. "The mob lawyer? What'd he do this time?"

"It's more a matter of what was done to him. He was attacked in Central Park last night. He says some punks robbed him. Beat him up a bit too."

Bethany turned her attention to Emily. Crime in Central Park was always got a rise out of Bethany, but this was something different. "Bria's a scumbag. He's put more murderers on the street than anybody else in the city. Sounds like he may have gotten what was coming to him."

Emily gave her an odd look, but she continued on, "The police are all over it. They're thinking there's a shake-up in one of the Families."

"Why?"

"His injuries weren't consistent with a mugging. They think somebody was torturing him. Also, he still had his laptop in his briefcase and his wallet. He gave the police some stupid story about having cash in his pocket that he gave the mugger."

"Any leads?" she asked.

"My sources tell me there's nothing yet."

Bethany turned her attention back to the paper. "Anything else?"

"It's a fairly slow news day. The temperatures are supposed to hit record highs by the end of the week. The city is asking the public to help with their elderly neighbors."

Bethany nodded as she kept reading. "We should talk to the people at the Reach Out Campaign this morning, make sure things are okay. It's been a brutal summer so far. They may need additional funds to stay out in the community and run the shelters."

"I called them earlier and suggested an 11 A.M. meeting. That should give you enough time to get in and clear your desk, but not so much time that things will start getting busy."

"Perfect. Thanks."

Emily paused long enough that Bethany looked up from the paper.

"Something's wrong?" Though it was intended to be a question, Bethany really didn't need to ask. The look in Emily's eyes was enough.

"As you can see from the article, they're already starting with the gossip. I'm betting Mr. Chase's press release isn't going to help that."

Bethany sighed. This was the part of her life that she hated. Geoffrey's candidacy was about to change the rules in an already complicated game.

Emily ignored the sigh. "The vultures are looking for a family fight on this."

Bethany nodded. "I know. I'll be good, I promise."

"Also, keep in mind, the photographers are going to be all over you, especially early on. You and Geoffrey are going to have to decide if you want to feed them or send them away. If you want to avoid cameras, you're going to have to be even more discreet than usual."

"You don't think my typical approach of pretending they aren't there and then ignoring what they write will work?" Bethany asked with a sarcastic smile.

"I think it'll work just fine for you, but the future mayor's people might be a lot more worried about his image."

"The group of us are going to Alfelini tonight. Do you think that'll be a problem?"

"This is a bit beyond my skills – campaigning isn't my thing."

Bethany waved off the humility. "What's your opinion?"

"That's a classy place. The owner's not going to let

the press get near you. You should be able to have a very quiet, relatively anonymous dinner."

Emily gathered up the paper and the remnants of Bethany's muffin as they pulled into the dark garage in the bowels of the Chase Electronics building.

As they exited the car, Emily stopped for a moment, meeting Bethany's eyes. "He's going to be a great mayor. You're doing the right thing supporting him."

Bethany's heart pounded as she absorbed the sincerity of her statement. Before she could even answer, Emily had turned and resumed her brisk pace to the elevator. By the time she'd caught up, the moment had passed.

They entered the elevator in silence and rose to the thirty-fifth floor. Once inside her father's building, she felt like a traitor even mentioning Geoffrey.

Twenty years of martial arts training was the only thing that kept Bethany's anger at bay. As she walked from the boardroom back to her office, she focused on her breathing, visualized dinner with her friends.

She was mostly successful with the exercise until she arrived at her office door only to find her father standing inside. He was at her window, staring out at the city below. At six foot five, Aston Chase was almost always the tallest person in the room, and his signature double-breasted suits somehow made his thin frame look solid and intimidating.

But Bethany was in no mood to be intimidated. "I don't think this is a great time to talk, Dad."

Aston turned to face her, his eyes cool. "Would you prefer we wait until after the election?"

Bethany couldn't decide if his sarcastic tone intended to convey annoyance or humor. Knowing Aston, it was probably a little of both.

She considered yelling and generally doing everything that never worked in situations like this. But there was something behind her father's eyes that changed her mind.

Instead, she shut the door, and sat on the couch. When Aston joined her without hesitation, she knew she'd made the right choice.

"I'm sorry I didn't tell you before he announced," she said. "I was trying to avoid a fight. It was stupid. I knew there'd be a fight one way or the other."

Her father shook his head, but offered a slight smile. "You get that from your mother, you know. She was always delaying the inevitable. I used to tease her about putting off until tomorrow what she should've taken care of today."

Bethany smiled. "I don't remember that about her."

"There must be a certain magic to the way you remember her. When you're just a child your mom is still perfect in every way."

There was a moment where they sat quietly.

Finally, Aston said, "You need to tell me the truth – was this your idea?"

"You mean not telling you? Look, Dad, like I said…"

Aston interrupted. "No, the campaign, the platform. Is this your campaign?"

Bethany was surprised by the question. "Actually, no, it wasn't my idea."

Meeting her father's eyes, she paused to give him a moment to see she was telling the truth. "Geoffrey's always talked about getting into politics. I encouraged him. I think he'll do a great job. But it had always been one of those things that would be happening in the future. A couple months ago he approached me with the idea that he should run in this election."

Aston rose and began to pace her office.

Bethany continued, "I'm actually not sure the timing is great. But despite my efforts to play devil's advocate, Geoffrey was firm. And so am I. I support him. One hundred percent."

"You think some young punk with no political experience is what's best for the city? If he wants to run, if he wants to have power, tell him to run for D.A. That's something he has enough experience to do."

"The current mayor worked on Wall Street before he ran. He had no more experience in politics than Geoffrey does."

"Is that the campaign you've planned for him – Vote for Quinn, he doesn't have any less experience than the other guy?"

"It isn't my campaign," Bethany repeated.

"I find that incredibly hard to believe."

"What do you want me to say? I'm telling you the truth. If it was my idea, I would've waited another term. By then we'd probably be married. By then he'd be older. He could get himself more into the political scene. With the Foundation I've had the chance to watch a lot of New York politics. There are ways to do this. Ways to make him a lock to win. These ways? This moment in time? If I were pulling the strings, this wouldn't be the way I'd do it."

Aston's probing eyes locked on hers. "Bethany, it's bad enough he's running. Don't lie to me."

She returned her father's stare. This was one time when she had nothing to hide. "I'm not lying."

"But you support his candidacy?"

"Entirely. This can't be a complete surprise, Dad. You knew he had political aspirations. I never kept that from you."

After a few moments, Aston stopped pacing and rejoined her on the couch. His voice softer than it had been. This was less an issue of the political and more of the personal. "I don't like him."

"You've mentioned," Bethany replied.

"Now, you're getting mad before you let me talk."

"I'm not mad. Go ahead. Talk." Bethany spoke through gritted teeth.

"He's a hard worker. Great record in the D.A.'s Office. He's very well respected. He must have looked like a knight in shining armor when he convinced the D.A. to back the park patrols that the Foundation wanted to sponsor. Who wouldn't fall for a hero like that?"

"You're unbelievable," Bethany retorted, refusing to hear the sincerity in his voice.

"I worry you didn't fall for the man, you fell for what he does. What he did," he replied.

"I don't know what you're talking about. What does that even mean? What Geoffrey does is a part of who he is. It's part of what I love and admire."

"Love? I've seen the two of you together. Seen the way you look at him. I don't believe that love has anything to do with it." The softness of her father's tone did nothing to cushion his harsh words.

Bethany glared. "You don't know the first thing about my feelings. Of course I love him. Just because I'm not drooling over him, constantly ogling him, do you think that means I don't love him?"

"When I see you with Richard and Annie you're different. There's a calmness in you, a casual confidence. A look that tells me you feel completely comfortable being yourself. You don't have that when you're with him."

"He has a name, you know. You could try to use it occasionally," Bethany snapped, avoiding the well-stated point.

"Honey, what happened between you and Geoffrey was a natural thing. He helped you with your most precious cause. You've been championing crime control in the park for years, for obvious reasons."

"Don't talk about her death so flippantly," Bethany growled. "My relationship with Geoffrey has nothing to do with what happened to Mom."

"Then why does it make you so mad to hear me say it?"

Bethany was on her feet in an instant, pacing in the same way her father had done moments before. "Goddamn it! How dare you twist things around like that."

Aston sat back a little and watched her. Bethany knew what he saw. Her father knew about the rage, the anger. He was the one who'd walked a seven-year-old Bethany into Master Jung's studio for the first time, hoping that martial arts would give her an outlet for the outbursts that were happening more and more.

It had worked, at least a little. Training had taught her how to control the rage. But it had never taught her how to let it go.

Bethany lowered her eyes and slowed her breathing. She could feel her father watching, absorbing. Losing her temper wouldn't help her argue in favor of her relationship with Geoffrey.

Her voice wavered when she finally spoke. "Sometimes it feels like you wield her death like a weapon."

"Sometimes it feels like her death is still haunting

you," he replied in an equally soft voice.

"I think it still is," she whispered.

"Just remember that. Remember that it shades your decisions. I don't want it to control you."

Of course he was right; she was haunted by the past. She wished she believed she could escape, that vigilance could somehow loosen the bonds tying her to that day.

But Bethany knew the truth. She was too far gone to be saved.

~ 8 ~

Annie Beltz found Bethany sitting alone at the restaurant bar, staring into her martini as if it might be the solution to all of her problems. With all that was going on in Bethany's life these days, it was a lot to ask of one martini.

Bethany looked up as she approached, seeming to sense that someone was close. "You're early," she said.

Annie laughed. "I may be early, but you're already here drinking. What's your excuse?"

Bethany shook her head, but there was a small smile on her lips. "Rough day at work. I had to leave. I thought I'd seek refuge at the bar until you guys arrived. Where's Karen?"

Annie had shown up early on purpose, hoping to talk to her friend alone. She'd asked Karen to make sure she was a little late.

"She's stuck at work," Annie lied. "She'll be here soon."

Annie slipped into the seat next to Bethany and ordered her own drink.

As they waited, Bethany said, "I'm sorry I didn't tell you about the announcement."

Annie only shrugged. "It was his secret, not yours. I totally understand that you weren't able to tell us."

Bethany's sigh of relief was almost audible. "Could you explain that to Richard for me?"

Annie thought there were several things that probably needed to be explained to Richard, but, as always, she chose humor as her way out. "I could explain it, but he wouldn't listen, so I think I'd rather save my breath. He's known everything about you for decades. It's an adjustment for him to deal with another man in your life. I assume he didn't handle the revelation gracefully."

This time Bethany's sigh was audible. "He was good. Well, he tried to be. It seemed like it hurt his feelings though. You know when he gets that look in his eyes. Like a kid gives you when they open up a birthday present they don't like. They'll thank you and be polite about it, but they have this look – just this enormous disappointment."

Annie chuckled. "I try not to disappoint small children, so I'm a little fuzzy on the analogy. But I know the Richard look. It's a killer."

Still not liking the look on her friend's face, Annie added, "He'll get over it."

"I hope so," Bethany replied, her eyes returning to her martini.

"I saw the press coverage of the announcement. His candidacy seems well received," Annie said, hoping to get at what was really bothering her friend.

Bethany's smile was a little stiff in response. "My

father wasn't pleased."

Annie nodded, waiting.

"But I think it's going to be a good thing. Don't you?" Bethany asked.

Annie laid her hand over Bethany's. "I'm happy if you're happy. So, the only question is – are you happy?"

"Of course I am," Bethany said far too quickly.

"Is he pressuring you about moving the wedding up?"

Bethany shook her head. "No, never, you know Geoffrey."

Unfortunately, Annie did know Geoffrey.

"You know, there wouldn't be anything wrong with you not being hugely thrilled about this. A campaign will be intrusive. The press is going to be a pain in the ass."

And, of course, there'd be the constant rehashing of her mother's murder. But Annie knew she couldn't bring that up. She'd known that was an off-limits conversation almost as long as she'd known Bethany. Which was why she found it impossible to believe that she was okay that the decades-old murder would undoubtedly be the centerpiece of this campaign. There was no way that a mayoral candidate running on a crime-control platform wasn't going to use his connection to the most famous crime victim in Manhattan.

Bethany smiled weakly. "The press will be fine. They'll start focusing more on Geoffrey, more on the issues. I'm a one-trick pony – it'll play out."

Annie had been one of Bethany's best friends since their first day at Columbia. She knew how things worked. It wouldn't play out. It would never play out.

She'd seen the old newspaper articles. The photos of the tiny little girl draped in a policeman's jacket with what must've been a streak of blood on her cheek.

They'd called her the "silent witness." For months the press tracked the case, followed Bethany, her father. There'd been so many pictures that a little version of Richard had even made his way into a few.

The city had been predatory from the start. Circling, watching. Even after all these years, New Yorkers were enthralled by Bethany. They professed only loving adoration. But their type of love was more destructive than cuddling with an anaconda.

Instinctively, Annie leaned a little closer, blocking her friend. As she did, she noticed a woman staring more than the others. She was sitting on the other side of the bar. And, strangely, she didn't even turn away when Annie looked directly at her.

"Do you know that woman?" Annie asked.

Bethany looked in the direction of her gaze. "The one with the really Italian looking guy?"

Annie nodded. "Black hair? About fifty? Very, very well dressed? Lots of jewelry?"

"Never seen her before in my life."

"Obviously one of your fans," Annie said with an eye roll.

Bethany shook her head. "Don't let them bother you. This campaign is going to be much too long to worry about the gawking and the ridiculously watchful eye of the public."

"They should pay as much attention to the issues as they do to Page Six."

Before Bethany could respond, Geoffrey breezed in. He kissed her on the cheek before either of them even knew he was there.

"Hey ladies," he said cheerfully. Then realizing he startled them, he added, "Sorry, I thought you saw me coming."

"Clearly you just don't realize how stealthy you are," Bethany replied.

Geoffrey laughed. "I'm the sneakiest guy alive. If you only knew the things I had going on behind your back."

"Obviously," Bethany smiled back.

"What were you two staring at?"

Bethany pointed in the direction of the gawker. "The annoying public. Nothing to worry about."

Geoffrey put a hand on Bethany's shoulder. Pointing at her almost empty glass, he said, "If you order another drink for you, could you order me a vodka tonic? I'm going to run to the men's room."

Annie watched Geoffrey slip away and wondered, as she often did, why she disliked him so much.

~ 9 ~

Karen arrived as Geoffrey was heading to the bathroom. Bethany watched with a certain awe at the easy way she slipped an arm around Annie's waist and gave her a soft kiss on the cheek. There was just something amazing about the two of them. They were the dating equivalent of the yin and yang.

Annie was fair skinned, with deep blue eyes and a head of unruly blonde curls. Karen was more Mediterranean, with raven black hair, olive skin and shimmering light brown eyes that had almost a golden hue. They'd been together for close to five years, and Bethany was certain she'd never met two people who were better for each other.

After the bartender took their drink orders, Karen offered Bethany a broad smile. "You look like you've had a rough day."

Bethany shook her head and exchanged looks with Annie. "Is she this direct with you, too, or just your friends?"

Annie draped arms over both of their shoulders. "Trust me, she's far tougher on me."

Before Karen could say a word in her own defense, Richard appeared over Annie's shoulder, making himself a part of the circle.

"What're you three conspiring about?" he asked, a laugh in his voice.

Bethany scowled at him. "You're actually lucky I'm not conspiring against you," she said.

"Against me?" Richard asked in a tone that confirmed Bethany's suspicions.

"My cell phone rang earlier today."

"Really?" He barely contained a snicker.

"You can imagine how surprised I was when the sound it emitted was something so horrendous that it might cause a person to jump out a window just to get away from it."

Bethany pulled the phone out of her purse and pressed a button to make the cords warble forth.

"Catchy," Richard said. "Like a salsa of some kind, wouldn't you say?"

Annie smiled. "Yeah, if you tried to play a salsa with broken instruments. That's terrible."

Richard ignored her. "If I was naming that ring tone, I think I might call it Salsa Number Three. Is that the name of it, Beth?"

"You changed my ring tone," Bethany accused.

"Now why would I do that?"

"Change it back, please," she stated firmly, handing him the phone.

Richard put his hands in the air. "I think it's time you figured out how to use your phone. Beth, you've got a rep. I don't want people thinking you're a boring person with a standard ring."

"Change the ring, Rich," she ordered.

Richard let loose one of his most charming smiles. "If I did these things for you, you'd never learn."

"You're a pain in the ass." Annie laughed.

Richard grinned at the compliment and quickly changed the subject. "I see a vodka tonic, but I don't see our future mayor. Where is he?"

Accepting she'd lost the battle, at least for now, Bethany conceded the topic change. "Bathroom," she explained, realizing that he'd actually been gone a while. "There must've been a line."

"Oh, I almost forgot," Richard grinned, "how was your big meeting with Aston today?"

Bethany figured it was probably best to get the story out of the way before Geoffrey returned.

Annie cringed. "The gun exchange thing was today? No wonder you were here early drinking martinis."

"Did he go after you?" Richard didn't need to explain who "he" was.

Bethany shook her head. "He let me get through the whole presentation without a word, which, of course, made me even more nervous than I already was. I open up the floor to questions and my father stands up and, in that deep controlling voice of his, says – 'I know this is a little unorthodox, but I'd like to make my own presentation before you vote.'"

"He made his own presentation?" Richard asked, his eyes wide.

"That's bad?" Karen asked.

"Beth's the president, that means she presents to the Board, who review and discuss. Board members don't present the con side to her argument," Richard explained. "I can't believe he did that!"

She'd been just as incredulous hours before. "He had a full PowerPoint presentation."

"He planned on doing it all along?" Annie wondered.

"It sure seems that way," Bethany agreed.

"What did the Board do?" Richard asked.

"They're taking the week to think about it. We have a follow-up meeting on Friday for the vote."

"How do you think it's going to go?" Karen asked.

Bethany knew it was both naïve and self-destructive to be optimistic. "Probably not very well."

"It's got to be a good sign they didn't say no immediately," Annie pointed out. "Your dad must not have the control he thought he did. It sounds like he was really pushing for a vote today."

"He actually fought my suggestion to delay voting pretty vehemently, but I did win that."

"That must have aggravated the hell out of him," Karen said with a grin.

Bethany nodded. "I'm trying to focus on the small victory and tell myself the inevitable loss on Friday is less important."

Before the others could respond, Bethany saw Geoffrey making his way back from the bathroom. "Look, I don't want to rain on Geoffrey's night. So, let's just forget the whole thing, alright?"

Annie glanced over toward Geoffrey. "Beth, if you need to talk," she said in a hushed tone.

Bethany shook her head. "We need to celebrate. This is his night. My unpleasant afternoon will be a topic for another day."

Bethany could see that none of them wanted to agree to her conditions, but she didn't intend to give them a choice. Bethany already felt like the worst fiancée in the history of the world. She wasn't going to start adding to her list of transgressions.

~ 10 ~

Their meal was as festive as Bethany had hoped it would be. The others were excited about Geoffrey's candidacy and, for once, it seemed like everyone was fairly comfortable with each other.

After dinner, Annie and Karen took a cab back to the Village and Richard took his own cab back to his neighborhood. Bethany and Geoffrey decided to walk. Afternoon thunderstorms had cleared the humidity and the fresh, clear evening air was irresistible. A stroll through the park seemed like the perfect way to end the evening.

It was a familiar walk, quiet at this time of night. The path was close enough to the city's constant buzz that it didn't feel isolated, but far enough that it was peaceful.

"You're pretty quiet," Bethany said, giving Geoffrey's hand a squeeze.

He gave her a kiss on the top of her head and pulled

her closer. "Just thinking about all that's happening, all that's changing. I'm going to miss this."

Bethany laughed. "Quiet walks? I think we can manage to squeeze them in."

Geoffrey led her off the path to a little pond that was tucked behind some trees, a fantastic secluded spot he'd discovered about a year before. It was one of Bethany's favorites.

In the dark night his face was hard to read. "I mean, running will change a lot. A lot about who I am, who I've always been. It'll be different."

Bethany gave him a kiss. "It'll be fine. I promise."

Geoffrey sat on a mossy patch at the foot of a tree and Bethany nestled under his arm, her head resting against his chest. It was so quiet she could almost hear his heart beating. It was a perfect moment, after a day that was anything but.

"How's your trial going?" she asked, after a few minutes.

"Fine, I think. I'm still a little worried about that one eyewitness. It's looking more and more like he might recant. I think he's getting a lot of pressure from the defendant's family. I expect to get him on the stand tomorrow, hopefully he'll be ready."

"This is your last case before your resignation takes effect?"

"Yeah. I'm really surprised they let me go ahead with the case after I announced, but my boss is concerned about this witness. She thinks I'm our best chance to get the witness to cooperate, since he and I have been talking for months."

"Probably true."

Suddenly, Bethany could felt Geoffrey stiffen beneath her, pushing her to the side as he did.

"Did you hear that?" he asked.

Bethany straightened up, regaining her balance, listening for whatever it was Geoffrey had heard. He was turned away from her, looking at some nearby trees. She was about to ask what he'd thought he'd heard when a crack shattered the night.

Her reaction was instantaneous. She shoved Geoffrey to the ground before the smell of gunpowder reached her nose. As she laid on top of him, it was like she was reliving a nightmare.

She raised her head to look around. There was no one in sight. No sign of movement. No additional gunshots. They were alone again. She was certain.

As the terror faded, she realized something she hadn't before. Geoffrey wasn't moving. He was laying perfectly still on the ground.

Slowly, her mind registered another smell under the pervasive smell of gunpowder. Blood.

She knew the truth immediately, even as her mind denied it. There was blood.

It was on her hands. She could feel it more than see it in the darkness.

She prayed the blood was her own, but she knew the truth. She grabbed Geoffrey and shook him.

She reached up and touched his head. Blood clung to her fingers. Telling her the truth. Forcing her to see what the darkness concealed. His eyes were blank. It was already too late.

Decades later, nothing had changed. She was still as helpless as that child left to weep over a lifeless body, waiting for help that would arrive too late.

For a moment she saw her mother's face in Geoffrey's, felt the warmth of her blood, smelled the void of death, and she could almost hear her fragile world shatter.

~ 11 ~

He was dead. After a week and a half of press conferences and interviews, wakes and a funeral, it was over. Geoffrey was dead and gone. And Bethany was left to figure out what to do next.

Feeling lost and confused, she went to the only place she knew could provide her with answers. The loft.

It was a perfect place to hide. A place where she didn't need to pretend to be normal or rational. Here she could be completely herself, surrounded by a lifetime's worth of hatred.

Time had made her an adept actress. No one wanted to hear about the nightmares, know about the haunting memories. They wanted her to move on, to forget. But she couldn't do that. She could never do that. So, she'd learned to pretend, learned how to appear whole, normal. No one could know that the memories of her mother's murder stayed with her, that they would until the day she found the man responsible.

But in this room, there was nothing else. It was only her and the past.

On days like this, the loft was something more. It was a sanctuary. A place where she could be alone with her anger. This was the place where she'd find her way to the future. She was sure of that.

Losing Geoffrey in such a sudden and familiar way brought a whole new mountain of questions. A whole new universe of nightmares.

She stared at the crime scene photos of her mother's murder taped to the wall. She no longer needed to read the autopsy report to recite the biological facts of the crime. A single bullet wound, entered dead center from behind. It remained lodged inside her head. Death occurred almost instantly. No other bodily injuries.

She knew that Geoffrey's autopsy report would be similar – single bullet wound, the side of the head this time.

Just like her mother's murder, everything pointed to a professional hit – the clean shot, the absence of evidence. No bullet casings were found at either scene. The killer had apparently waited in some nearby brush. There was little indication that he'd been there, but the grass was matted down a bit, some branches broken.

It was possible it was a coincidence. But Bethany had been at this long enough to know the truth when it was staring her in the face. It was happening again. And despite years of searching, she still had no idea why.

She was staring, seeing nothing, when the buzz of an alarm clock brought her out of the trance. When she'd set the clock as a reminder she hadn't thought she'd need it. But she'd missed enough dinner dates over the years to know she tended to lose track of time when she was in the loft.

It wasn't a long trip to her appointment. A simple elevator ride from one secret to another.

~ 12 ~

Master Jung sat in a private training room awaiting his star pupil. Bethany had asked for a special session. Of course, her decision was a mistake. It was not the time to increase the chaos. It was the time to reach into training for balance. But that was not Bethany's way. It never had been.

He set up the session because he knew the environment was controlled. While there was the chance she could get hurt here, there was no chance it would be serious.

At precisely seven-thirty A.M., Bethany Chase emerged from her locker room. She was dressed entirely in black. Her sweatshirt and pants were loose enough to conceal her gender. The Kevlar vest she wore helped a great deal in that regard, as did the black mask that covered her face.

Only her eyes were visible and they appeared almost black. The Master assured himself her eyes were only reflecting the colors that surrounded them, but he knew it was untrue. Bethany was transformed into something else. There were times he wondered if the mask was necessary. Even her closest friends wouldn't recognize her, not when she was like this.

With perfect form, she bowed before him and then took her place. The Master snapped his hands together and two doors opened on either end of the room.

From one door two men emerged – both dressed in white – both several inches taller than Bethany and each at least a hundred pounds heavier. From the other door three men appeared – two in white, the other wearing red. The red was the capture. She would know that. He was to be restrained, not hurt.

The five men circled the concealed person before them. For them there was only one objective – take the masked individual out. The Master watched them as they sized up their competition. He knew what they saw. Their opponent was small, less than six feet tall and very slim, with oddly narrow shoulders. They'd expect agility, but not strength. They'd be wrong about the second part.

The tallest of the five men moved in first, while the other four hung back to observe the response and better evaluate the risks.

The scout was within two feet of Bethany before she moved, and the instant she did the others realized why. She moved like lightning. In a fluid blur, she fired off a kick to the head, and the scout went down like a rock.

The others realized simultaneously what they needed to do. They charged together towards their prey.

The ensuing fight took close to fifteen minutes. It ended when the man in red was hogtied on the floor and Bethany sauntered out of the room. Master Jung called one of his employees to take care of the situation and make sure the fighters were compensated. Then he left to join Bethany in her locker room.

Her mask was off, as was the sweatshirt and the Kevlar vest. She was sitting on a bench in the spandex she'd worn underneath. She was flushed and winded, and applying ice to her ribs.

As always, she appeared calm and almost normal now. It was an illusion that scared him, because he never knew how much of it was show and how much she believed herself. Conceit was a quick path to an early grave.

"You will help no one if you get yourself killed," he said simply.

The flicker of defiance in her eyes was a small comfort. She knew things had not gone as well as they should have, even if her words denied it.

"He kicked me in the ribs. He didn't come anywhere near killing me."

His response was as calm as hers was defensive. "I saw the kick. You struggled at that point. The other one came very close to punching you in the face. How exactly do you think you'd explain that to your public relations people?"

"I don't have public relations people."

He gave a small smile in response to her venom. "In a street fight, you would have lost. You cannot handle that many."

Bethany shifted the ice and allowed her eyes to drift from his. "I fight that many here. I'd never do it outside. I'm strictly one on one."

"And if someone caught you? If someone accidentally came upon you? What then? I have been against this from the beginning. You are becoming reckless."

"I am not," she snapped back. "I'm completely in control."

"You do not look in control right now."

Bethany took a deep breath, plainly going through the appropriate steps to gather herself, control her breathing, her heart rate.

Knowing that talking was the last thing Bethany ever wanted, he took a chance. At this point, it seemed there was no other choice.

"I have known you since you were seven years old. You know you are more than just a student to me. You also know you promised you would stop if you did not find any information. Ten years ago, you began your quest. Have you found any information?"

She spoke through gritted teeth. "I'm getting close."

Her eyes told a story that her words didn't. If he questioned her, she would leave. It had only been out of necessity for her training that she'd even told him her secret in the first place.

But the Master did not even consider letting it go. It was time.

"You are close? Is that why the boy is dead?"

Bethany's head dropped in shame.

"You started this to get justice. It was a noble task. But it has been long enough now. Now it should end. The price is too high."

Her voice was still soft, the rage still barely concealed. "I need to know what happened to her."

"You need to find peace. There are other ways."

Bethany met his eyes. "Not for me."

Master Jung examined the young woman who stood before him. He saw what the others did not – closely clipped fingernails, wiry muscles, and razor sharp dexterity. She was a warrior, and there was a certain nobility in her quest, but there was a certain insanity in it as well. He hoped she realized that.

Resigned to her choice, he pointed out the problems in the fight, points she needed to work on. They would meet again for training the next night to work on some balance and strength exercises.

"You must promise me one thing," he ordered in conclusion. "Wait at least a week before you go back out. Your focus is not what it needs to be right now. You could be easily distracted."

Bethany nodded in agreement. "I promise," she said.

He prayed that she would yield, that she would obey, but if he knew Bethany at all, he knew that such a passive existence was not possible for her.

~ 13 ~

Bethany returned to her apartment to find Richard sitting on her couch, reading her paper. At the sound of the door, he dropped the paper and looked up with a desperate expression.

"Where've you been? I tried your cell about ten times. Are you okay?"

Bethany brushed off his concern, and tried very hard to ignore the piercing pain in her side that seemed to get worse with each breath. "I do turn my phone off occasionally."

He didn't look amused. "It's not even ten yet. I wanted to surprise you with muffins from that place you like."

Ignoring the rest of his comment, Bethany headed straight for the coffeemaker. Grabbing a mug of the coffee Richard had been kind enough to make, she picked a muffin and joined him on the couch.

"Thanks. I'm sorry I worried you," she said. She

was sorry, but she had no intention of telling him where she'd been. Early morning training sessions would make her sound even crazier than usual.

Richard gave her a once over and said, "Seriously? You were at the gym? You were working out at this hour?"

Bethany could only stare in response.

He ran a hand through her hair. "Still damp."

Shaking her head, she replied, "So, I showered this morning. I do that on occasion."

"You use a different shampoo at the gym, more coconut, less flowery," he countered.

Bethany laughed. "Who knew you paid that much attention to my hair care products."

Richard mostly ignored the crack. Running a hand over her cheek he asked, "Did you get any sleep at all?"

"Are the circles that bad?" She knew they were. Every time she closed her eyes she heard the crack of the bullet, felt the blood on her fingers. Sometimes it was Geoffrey, sometimes it was her mother, every time it was agony.

Richard smiled. "Just eat your muffin."

Bethany settled back on the couch and nibbled, placing her coffee mug on the table. Though caffeine was typically a drug essential to her survival, she felt jittery enough already.

"You want to talk about it?" Richard asked after a few minutes.

Bethany looked at her friend. "There's nothing to say, but thanks."

"We're here. You know that, right?"

She nodded. "Always."

From the corner of her eye, Bethany watched Richard. He was watching SportsCenter with his feet on her coffee table, drinking his coffee, and trying to pretend he wasn't worried. The circles under his eyes didn't look a lot better than hers. Clearly she wasn't the only one losing sleep. She needed to beef up her acting skills, unless she wanted everyone worrying.

"I figured you'd be at work today," she said, trying to manage some level of polite conversation.

"The funeral was yesterday. We didn't want you to be alone today."

His use of the word we, sent a clear message. "When is Annie scheduled to arrive?"

Richard grinned, as he always did when he was pulling her leg. "Scheduled? Whatever do you mean?"

"I mean, when she called you last night and you two conspired about how to be my support system for the day, when did you agree she'd show up?"

"You know us too well." Then with a shrug, he added, "She should be here in about an hour."

Bethany smiled. It was nice for some things to be normal and predictable when the world was spinning so out of control.

"Well then, why don't you pass over the newspaper? I'd like to catch up on what I missed this week."

Bethany thought she saw a flicker of caution behind Richard's eyes. "Arts and Leisure okay?" he asked.

It took a moment to figure out what he was doing. She always read the front page first. It was never a problem; Richard didn't believe in reading much beyond the sports.

"There's coverage of the funeral, I guess."

He nodded. "I'll keep the papers for you, but it's nothing you need to look at this morning."

"I'd like to see," she replied, reaching for the paper.

"There are pictures. There are articles. There are

theories. It's insanity. You don't need to read it."

"Theories? Theories on the shooting? What kind of theories?"

Richard cursed under his breath, clearly realizing he'd said too much. "Ridiculous theories that have no basis in reality."

"If they had no basis in reality, they wouldn't be in the paper."

"That isn't really true."

Bethany responded with nothing more than a glare.

Richard sighed. "They're saying the police are looking into a number of angles – Geoffrey's career and his candidacy being the most obvious. But there's something else. They're reporting that the police are looking into whether you were the actual target."

"That's insane. It was one bullet. Clearly they were aiming at Geoffrey."

She could see that he considered lying to her, protecting her from whatever evil lurked in the paper.

She was relieved when he continued, "They're suggesting it's possible someone killed Geoffrey to get to you. He was killed in the park. Everybody knows about your work to keep the park safe. They're wondering if maybe somebody went at Geoffrey to get you to back off."

She was worried about the same thing. It shouldn't have hurt so much to hear him say it.

"See, this is why I don't want you reading the paper. Beth, it's a crazy theory, that's all. It's stupid."

Of course, it wasn't stupid. Someone had gotten away with murder for two decades. There was no telling the lengths they'd go to protect their secret. What better way to warn her off her investigation than to repeat the vicious crime?

The ringing phone pulled Bethany from her dark thoughts. The caller ID told her it was her father.

His voice was soft and supportive, even if he was obviously uncomfortable with the emotions. "I just wanted to make sure things were okay over there."

"I'm fine, Dad."

Aston paused, seemingly at a loss for what to say. "Are your friends there?"

"Richard's here. Annie'll be by later."

"Good. Good," he replied. "You should try and get out. Get some fresh air."

Maybe a walk in the park? her mind taunted. Bethany bit back against the sick feeling in her stomach. "Sure. I'll try and get out."

He hesitated again, but then continued, "Are you planning on going to work tomorrow?"

The question reminded her that more than a week had passed. "I hadn't really thought about it yet, but there's a lot I need to take care of. I guess I should go in for at least part of the day."

"It's a good way to take your mind off things. It helped me after," he paused, "after your mother died."

It was a good thing Aston didn't try to make her feel better very often. The blows she'd taken in the fight that morning hurt less than his words of comfort. "Thanks. I'll think about it."

There was silence on the other end of the line as Aston seemed to struggle for the words.

He finally said, "If you need anything at all, please call me."

Bethany promised and disconnected the call. She looked over at Richard who was trying to pretend he hadn't been listening to her conversation. After a moment, he looked up and gave her one of his most charming smiles.

"Sit," he suggested. And pointing to her muffin, he added, "Eat."

Bethany was certain she'd never been less hungry in her life, but she obeyed. It was easier. She lacked the energy to fight.

~ 14 ~

When Annie arrived at Bethany's apartment she was surprised to find her friend up and about and giving Richard more trouble than he could handle. Despite everything, it felt like life was more normal than it had been in months.

It was an odd thought, Annie knew that, but it was somehow true. It was just the two of them again – Bethany and Richard. And that was right, even if the way they ended up there was entirely wrong.

Richard stood defiantly, snatching the paper off the coffee table. "I am leaving and I am taking the paper with me. The whole paper. No Arts and Leisure for you!"

Bethany shook her head. "I didn't want that section in the first place, dummy. Couldn't you just take the front page and leave the rest?"

Seeming to be showing the softer side of his personality, Richard peeled a section from the paper and handed it her. He gave Bethany and Annie kisses on the cheek and headed out. He was already at the door when Bethany looked at the section he'd given her.

"This is the Car Buying section! Rich!" she called after him.

But Richard fled with a wink.

Annie settled onto the couch chuckling at the exchange. "Richard's protecting you from the big, bad newspaper?"

Dropping the unwanted section on the floor, Bethany leaned back on the couch. "He's hoping I'll forget it's a scary world out there."

"Any chance of that?"

Bethany closed her eyes. "Very little, I'm afraid."

Now that Richard was gone, Annie could see the strain on Bethany's face. As she sat there, eyes closed, the slightest wrinkles appearing at their corners, Annie thought that she'd never seen her look so very alone.

Annie cursed Geoffrey for the pain he was causing. She didn't blame him for dying, of course, but she'd always known they'd end up in this place eventually. She'd expected a messy breakup or an ugly divorce, but there was no way their story was going to have a happy ending.

Annie rubbed her friend's arm. "Anything I can do to help?"

Bethany shook her head. Clearly desiring a topic switch, she asked, "What's Karen up to today?"

Though she wished Bethany would talk about the things crashing around in her head, Annie knew there was no chance she would.

"She's at work. But, honestly, I wouldn't have seen much of her anyway, she started reading this book yesterday and hasn't put it down since. You know how she gets."

"You remember that summer we got the beach house? She must've read fifteen books that week."

Annie thought back to the vacation. She hadn't known Karen for that long. Bethany and Richard spent the majority of their time ignoring their own dates and checking out the new girl. Something must've told them she was the one.

"I was really afraid you guys weren't going to get along. As I recall, Richard warmed up to her more quickly than you."

Annie was happy to see Bethany smile. "Rich warmed up to the way she filled out her bathing suit more than anything else. I was a little less taken in by that. It was hard to tell if she was quiet or a total bitch."

"She likes to sit back and observe."

"And voraciously consume the printed word."

Annie grinned at the memory. "Who knew I'd end up with a nerd?"

"And a gorgeous nerd at that. It's funny, but somehow you two are perfect for each other."

"We're perfect opposites," Annie added in agreement.

"Well, you certainly aren't a gorgeous nerd," Bethany teased.

Annie punched her in the ribs in response, and she couldn't help but notice Bethany cringed more than she should have.

"A little sore?" she asked, trying not to sound concerned.

The distance returned to Bethany's eyes before she spoke. "I took a hit when we were sparring earlier. It's no big deal. Just a bruise."

At times like this, Annie wondered what really went on at the martial arts studio. Bethany pretended like her training was little more than a mundane hobby. But she spent hours secreted away in that big old building and she never missed a session.

They never talked about it, but they all knew Bethany carried an anger none of them could get near. To Annie, it seemed a therapist would've been a better way to have helped a child deal with her mother's death. The fighting didn't seem to ease the anger; it seemed to keep the fires kindled.

"Do you need to ice it or anything?" she asked.

"No, it'll be fine," Bethany replied, and then changed the subject, "Did you hear Richard is still dating that Trisha girl?"

"Her name is Tracey. You know, you could make a little effort to remember their names."

"She'll be gone in a month; why should I bother?"

"Have you met her?"

Bethany only laughed at the idea. "Rich hasn't let me meet a girlfriend of his since the Tiffany debacle."

"Oh God, I'd forgotten about that. You threw a drink at her!"

"She deserved it."

"He really liked her too."

"She called me a spoiled bitch."

"Only after you'd been hassling her all night about her 'intentions' with your best friend."

"I didn't use the word 'intentions.' Who says that?"

"Apparently you do when you're drunk, because you were totally grilling her. Trust me, Beth. I am certain my memory of that night is better than yours. As I recall, things started to unravel around the time you ordered your fourth martini."

"Was I wrong? She was shady. Very shady. She dumped him a couple of weeks after that, didn't she? She started dating some underwear model, right?"

"I think Richard would prefer if you never spoke of the underwear model, or the fact that she dumped him. For the record, you were totally right about her. Even Karen didn't like her. Though, we decided to express our displeasure in more subtle ways."

"I think the drink to the face got my point across well."

"One of these days he's actually going to meet someone with a little substance. When he does, you're going to have to figure out a way to give her a chance."

Bethany pushed the comment aside. "I gave Karen a chance. When it's the right one, I'll back off."

Annie didn't think she would. It was different between Bethany and Richard. She wondered if they'd ever realize that, or if they'd play this game forever.

"Well, Karen and I'll be there to clean up after you throw your drink at the next one. After all, a friend's work is never done."

"You know, speaking of work, my dad called to see if I was planning on going in tomorrow."

Annie rolled her eyes. "You don't need to be a workaholic just because he is."

"The weird thing is – I think I want to go back tomorrow. Is that reasonable?"

As was often the case, Annie wondered if Aston had any idea of the chaos he caused when he tried to help. The circles under Bethany's eyes told her that she needed a day off, probably more. On the other hand, Annie wondered if time alone might be self-destructive.

"Though I normally adopt an anti-Aston policy, I

can see wanting to get back.   Downtime would probably be tough right now."

"It's not weird if I want to go back? Is there some sort of etiquette here I don't know about? I don't want it to seem like I don't care."

"Beth," she said, laying a hand on her shoulder, forcing her full attention. "This has to be about what *you* want, what you need. Not what I think or what your father thinks or what the stupid newspaper prints."

There was a hesitancy in her friend's eyes, a deep pain that went far beyond the loss of her fiancé.

Annie continued, "What do you want?"

Before Bethany could respond, the doorman buzzed the apartment to tell them there were two detectives in the lobby.

When Bethany told the doorman to send them up, Annie assumed a protective position, perched on the edge of the couch. "This is what I was talking about. It's okay to demand some space for yourself, some time."

Annie knew Bethany had talked to the police almost every day since the shooting. Though she understood they had a job to do, she hated that they kept dredging this up.

Bethany stood to open the door.

"They're just trying to figure out what happened," she explained. "They've been respectful of my space when I've needed it. Besides, I know the two detectives from the Park Watch Program. We've worked together before."

Annie didn't think she'd ever seen such an amazing transformation in her life. Where there had been emotion only moments before, now there was nothing at all. There was no way this was a healthy response.

Bethany might not believe she needed help, but that didn't mean she wasn't going to get some anyway.

"If they're so charming you won't mind me hanging out while they bother you with more questions."

Bethany shrugged. "Whatever you want."

~ 15 ~

Moments later, Detectives Zapp and Heinrich appeared in Bethany's doorway. Annie thought they both looked very young. Too young, it seemed, to be investigating something of this magnitude on their own.

Zapp was short and stocky, with the beginnings of a receding hairline and a close trimmed goatee. He looked like the kind of guy you'd expect to find in a flashy nightclub wearing lots of gold chains.

Heinrich was taller, very blond, with wire rimmed glasses. He seemed more of a thinker, less of a nightclubber.

"How are you, Bethany?" Heinrich asked, taking a seat in the chair near the couch.

"I'm moving along," Bethany replied without emotion. "Do you have anything new?"

Not surprisingly, Zapp's voice was more brusque. "Nothing so far, but we're running down some stuff."

"I hate to ask again, but we'd appreciate if you'd run

through the night with us one more time," Heinrich said.

"Do you really need to do this?" Annie growled, sliding closer to Bethany on the couch.

"I know we've been through this, but sometimes after the initial trauma subsides people start to remember things."

Bethany put a hand on Annie's leg, signaling she was okay. "We left dinner around 10 o'clock. Everybody else took a cab home, we decided to walk."

Heinrich poised his pen over a small notepad. "Whose idea was it to walk?"

Annie chimed in. "I think Geoffrey suggested it, but you were commenting on how beautiful the evening air was. It was one of those mutual decisions. But I'm pretty sure Geoffrey did the actual suggesting."

"That sounds right," Bethany agreed. "I don't really remember."

"Did you usually walk home?"

Bethany shook her head. "It depended entirely on the night. The weather. Our moods. I wouldn't say it was a typical thing."

Flipping a page in his notepad, Heinrich spoke in a soft voice that seemed to be designed to prod the story along without interfering. "Tell me what happened next."

Bethany leaned back a little, closing her eyes. Annie shivered, realizing she must be seeing it all again.

"We were walking through the park. We decided to stop by the little pond. Just sit and enjoy the moment."

"You both decided to stop?"

Annie watched as Bethany's eyes closed even tighter. She couldn't remember, and it was driving her crazy.

The detective seemed to notice the same thing.

"That was a place you'd spent time before?"

Bethany's eyes opened now and the pain was obvious. "We went to that spot often. I kind of thought of it as our spot. Private and a bit out of the way, but not completely isolated."

"How were you sitting?"

Wiping quiet tears from her eyes, Bethany continued, "I was on his left side with my arm around his waist, my head was against his chest."

"Go on."

"Geoffrey seemed to hear something. He started to ask if I heard it and then there was the crack of a gun. I pushed him down, but it was too late."

After a pause, Zapp spoke. "We talked with Geoffrey's coworkers. The case he was working on was a rough one. The family of the defendant was putting a lot of pressure on the witnesses."

"Geoffrey mentioned that. I think he was worried one of his witnesses was going south on him. I can't remember his name. What was it?"

"It's Leo Snell. The trial resumes this week with a new prosecutor. She told us Snell won't return her calls. He sent her a letter. Says he never saw anything. He made the whole thing up. The police bullied him. The usual shit. Even says Geoffrey was leaning on him, if you can believe that. Anyway, the guy obviously took Geoffrey's death as a message. You better believe that's an angle we're looking at pretty close."

Heinrich added, "Bethany, we're checking everything and rechecking it. Geoffrey was a good guy and a great prosecutor. I have to believe this was about work somehow."

Zapp said, "I read that crap in the paper about this possibly being connected to you. That's total bullshit.

We aren't thinking that at all. Don't let them idiots mess with your head."

Bethany tightened up at the comment, but it was subtle. "Are you sure about that?" she asked. "Maybe you should be looking into my enemies?"

Heinrich leaned forward and, in a kind voice, he said, "This was a professional job. It's too clean not to be. They wouldn't have missed."

Bethany didn't seem persuaded. "Maybe they meant to hit him. Maybe it was some kind of threat?"

The detective sat back, looking more closely at Bethany. "Have you been threatened?"

She shook her head. "No, not directly, but…"

Zapp jumped in. "Well then it would be a pretty crappy threat, don't you think? The point of a threat is to get you to do something. Unless they tell you what they want you to do how can it be a good threat?"

Bethany sank back into the couch. "Maybe there was something about the way he was killed? Maybe the method was the message?"

Heinrich shot his partner a look that was clearly designed to get him to tone it down. Annie was pleased by his sensitivity.

"Bethany," he said gently. "This wasn't about you. You were just in the wrong place at the wrong time. They were going after Geoffrey. That much is clear. We'll figure out why. I promise you. It's just going to take a little time."

Though Bethany nodded, Annie was certain that she didn't believe a word. The reaction was a little surprising, but Annie knew Bethany well enough to know that she took too much on herself. Perhaps it wasn't strange to think she'd blame herself for what happened to Geoffrey.

Heinrich took her silence as a chance to move the conversation along.

"We're looking into his mayoral announcement. The timing on that seems very tight to be just a coincidence. Asking around, we're getting the impression there were some pretty strong views on his candidacy. Some Mayor Wilson haters seemed to think Geoffrey was the wrong guy. The Wilson supporters were, of course, not happy with such a high profile challenger. But at the same time, I'm not convinced someone would shoot him over that. Not a warning shot or anything, either. It seems too extreme to fit. But we're certainly exploring it."

Bethany asked, "Have you had a chance to talk to his parents? Maybe they can think of something else?"

Heinrich slipped his notepad back into his pocket. "We were out in Westchester the other day talking to them. Nice people. They didn't really have anything useful. I did ask them if they knew if Geoffrey had contacted his biological parents at any point. Maybe there was something weird there. But they were insistent he wouldn't have done that. Did he tell you anything?"

"He never talked about it," Bethany replied. "I think he really just thought of Natalie and David as his parents."

"Is there anything else we should be looking into?" Zapp asked.

Bethany shook her head. "Geoffrey was kind and thoughtful, sweet and caring. Anybody who knew him, loved him. I don't think he had any enemies."

Of course, they were wrong about that, Annie realized. Quite obviously Geoffrey had at least one enemy.

~ 16 ~

Bethany found a subdued Emily waiting in the car in front of her building the next morning. With little more than a good morning, she handed Bethany her muffin, without the newspaper.

Taking the muffin, Bethany glared at her assistant. "You need to keep this normal. Everybody else is treating me like a china doll. It's not going to be that way at work."

Emily's eyes were desperate. "Are you really sure you're ready to come back?"

"Yes," Bethany replied more decisively than she thought she could have. "Let's run through what's going on, which I imagine will take a little while since it's been a week. So, let's get started."

Bethany snatched the paper from Emily. She ignored the pain in her chest at the sight of Geoffrey's face on the front page. The murder was no longer the top story, but there was still a sizeable article on the continuing investigation. Bethany scanned it, forcing herself to read dispassionately. It basically told her things she already knew, except for a reference near the bottom of the article.

"It says there's a private hotline that's been set up to help police. And there's a five hundred thousand dollar reward for any information that leads to the killer?"

Emily's face told Bethany she was becoming more certain it was too soon for her boss to return to work.

"Your dad set that up. I think it was last Wednesday. He's paying for the hotline and the reward. There've been thousands of calls already. Nothing helpful. From what I've heard, he moved two million into an escrow account so the money would be easily accessible."

Bethany could do little more than gape at the revelation. Her father had hated Geoffrey. He'd made that abundantly clear. Now he was willing to pay millions to help find the man's killer?

Before Bethany could say anything more, Emily offered another piece of information.

"Mr. Chase was helping out at the Foundation last week. He stopped in mid-day Tuesday and, to be honest, I was a little defensive."

"Good," Bethany replied.

Emily shook her head. "He wasn't put off by that at all. In fact, he seemed to approve."

"He was probably impressed with your reaction. What did he do?"

"Actually, he did whatever I told him to. It was very strange. All week I was waiting for the other shoe to drop, waiting to figure out what the scam was. On Friday, he suggested the Board go ahead with the vote without you. That, I assumed, was his end game."

Bethany felt her heart pounding as she heard the story. "They voted without me?"

"I reviewed the bylaws and the charter and there's no rule that you have to be present for a vote. You aren't a member of the Board. You're only an officer. As Chairman, Mr. Chase can call a meeting whenever he wants. He doesn't even have to tell you."

Bethany couldn't believe what she was hearing. "I know. Though I have to admit, I never expected him to cut me out like that."

"I threatened to call you and tell you what was going on. That seemed to upset him. He practically begged me to allow you some space. He provided me with his note cards for the presentation and copies of the handouts. I kept a copy for your records."

Bethany told herself it didn't matter. She told herself that she was going to lose one way or the other, but it was like a punch to the gut. He was her father. How the hell could he do this to her?

Emily shook her head. "Bethany, it wasn't bad."

Bethany just looked at her. "What do you mean it wasn't bad? Of course it was bad."

Emily smiled. "He made your argument with flair and enthusiasm. He also presented some additional arguments on the con side. But then he wrapped up by explaining why he thought your position was more persuasive."

"What?" Bethany didn't understand.

"I wouldn't have believed it if I hadn't seen it myself. The Board was unanimous – one abstention. Lasiter Smythe didn't feel he could vote for such a radical idea, but he also didn't want to vote against."

"They voted in *favor* of the gun exchange?"

Emily nodded.

"Because my father told them they should?"

Again, her assistant nodded.

"Is it possible he was really just trying to look after things while I was out?" Bethany asked, as much to herself as Emily.

"He sure seemed to just be trying to help. It was like he was acting the way he'd expect you to act. It was bizarre."

Now it was Bethany who was wondering if maybe it was, in fact, too soon to go back to work.

"So, we funded the gun exchange," Bethany continued, trying not to appear surprised. "What else happened while I was out?"

Emily adeptly ran through things. Most had been handled promptly, but a few remained – things Emily felt required Bethany's personal attention.

The list of leftovers meant it was going to be a hectic day, probably a hectic couple of days. In a perfect world, work would be so busy it would envelop her from the moment she walked in the door and leave her exhausted at the day's end. If she was going to keep the promise she'd made to Master Jung and stay out of trouble for a week, she needed work to be overwhelmingly busy.

~ 17 ~

The day began as promised. The messages on her desk were a mountain. Her secretary, Debbie, had separated the messages into three piles – business calls that needed immediate attention, less urgent business calls, and personal calls. Without even a thought, Bethany dug into the pile of urgent messages. She didn't look up until close to noon when there was a knock on her door.

Debbie entered with a vase of two dozen purple roses. "These just came for you."

She carefully placed the arrangement on the corner of Bethany's desk and handed her the small card. Without another word, she slipped out.

The flowers were gorgeous. Bethany knew who they were from without even reading the message. Inside the card, she found Richard's familiar scrawl –

I FIGURED YOUR OFFICE COULD USE A LITTLE
BRIGHTENING TODAY.
HOW ABOUT DINNER AT MONIQUE'S
TONIGHT? EIGHT O'CLOCK?

– R.

P.S – ASSUMING THE FLORIST FOLLOWED
DIRECTIONS, IT'S NOON. THAT'S LUNCHTIME
– TRY NOT TO FORGET TO EAT!

Bethany smiled at the card, particularly the postscript. He knew her so well. Without the interruption she would've worked through lunch. At two o'clock, Debbie would've tried to force a sandwich on her, but she would've refused.

As ordered, she asked Debbie to call out for lunch and went back to her phone calls. It was close to five when she finally reached the bottom of the pile of urgent messages. She glanced quickly at the next two piles and realized that too many of the messages were about Geoffrey.

Before she could make a decision on how to proceed, Bethany's cell phone rang.

Happy for the distraction, she answered with a laugh. "Checking up on me?"

Annie stifled her own laugh. "I would never. Can't a friend just call to say hi?"

"My day was fine," Bethany replied, anticipating the question. "Not the best. Not the worst. It was fine."

"That sounds like the best we could've hoped for, wouldn't you say?"

Bethany smiled a little to herself. Annie was right. All things considered, it was a good day.

"Did you talk to the police today?" Annie asked.

Though her friend's voice should've sounded protective, it only sounded weird.

"No," Bethany replied cautiously. "Should I have?"

Annie answered much too quickly. "No, of course not. I was just wondering. I'd hate to hear that they were bothering you."

"Did you talk to them?" Bethany asked.

There was a pause before Annie said, "Yes, I actually did. Just for a minute. I thought it might be best. I figured your day was busy enough already."

Though her words made sense, her tone didn't. There was something wrong. Something very wrong. How could there be something wrong with Annie?

"Did the police have anything new?" Bethany asked, unsure what else to say.

"No, nothing at all. Pretty much the same thoughts they had yesterday."

Again, Bethany was overwhelmed by the sense that something was askew.

"I've gotta go," Annie said suddenly. "I'm meeting Karen for dinner in a couple minutes. I just wanted to make sure you were okay."

"I'm okay," Bethany replied, trying to keep her voice light, shaking off her paranoia. "Thanks for calling."

Annie signed off quickly and left Bethany alone again among her mountain of phone messages. She considered plowing through some more, but she turned her chair away from her desk and stared out at the city.

The streets were jammed with people in a perfect sort of organized chaos. That was one of the things she enjoyed about the city – it was always buzzing, never quiet. She was surprised to discover she felt less comfort in the bustle than usual. She just felt so tired, so worn down by life. There were so many questions and so few answers.

In her mind, she visualized her loft, considered the blank wall that awaited Geoffrey's name. She had investigators getting her copies of the police reports, but she knew what they'd say, she'd read it all before.

It was same the problem she'd faced ten years earlier when she began looking into her mother's death. There were no good leads.

The police had determined very early on that her mother's murder had been committed by a professional, but that was where the trail ended. Like most spousal deaths, her father had been questioned extensively. He'd volunteered to take a lie detector test. And, in the end, the police were satisfied that Aston Chase wasn't a murderer. They were mostly persuaded by his complete lack of motive. Rita Chase had no life insurance policy and there was no suggestion she'd been unfaithful to her husband.

But the suspect list began and ended with Aston, that was the problem. Frankly, decades later, that was still the problem. The police had questioned every one of Rita's friends. One way or another, Bethany had talked to all of them herself – some she'd blackmailed, some she'd approached under cover of night, still others she'd approached socially. No matter the approach, the answer was the same – Rita Chase was a fantastic woman who was loved by everyone who knew her. No one could think of anyone who'd want to kill her.

It wasn't a surprising revelation. Bethany knew her mother's story well. Rita Timmins was the only child of a working class father and stay-at-home mother who grew up in a crowded section of Staten Island. Her father died of an aneurysm before her high school graduation, her mother only a few months later — a heart attack. Despite the tragedy, Rita managed to hold herself together. She met the love of her life six months after her mother's death.

Bethany's mom would often tell the story. She was with a friend at a restaurant opening when she saw Aston across the room. He was so confident, sophisticated, handsome. She knew immediately she had to meet him. She introduced herself and they were never apart again.

It was the most outrageously romantic tale Bethany had ever heard. The type of romance that should never have had the tragic ending it did.

Though Bethany didn't share that kind of romance with Geoffrey, she knew neither of them deserved the tragic ending they'd gotten.

She was going to find out who did this to him. And she was going to make sure they paid.

But even as she swore vengeance, she knew the sad truth. Her investigation into Geoffrey's murder was unlikely to be any more fruitful than her investigation into her mother's murder.

The first person who should be questioned in a case like this was Geoffrey's fiancée. Of course, that should've provided her with a head start, but it didn't. Social background was a dead end. She knew all the answers just as well as she knew the questions. Geoffrey, like her mother, didn't have an enemy in the world.

The best place to start was with his work. That was a path to information they hadn't had with her mother's murder. Maybe work connections would provide her with the information she needed.

She thought of Geoffrey's witness who was so quick

to recant after his death. She'd purposely gotten his name from Detective Zapp the day before.

Though she'd promised the Master she wouldn't put herself in harm's way for at least a week, there was no reason she couldn't contact the guy. She could keep it simple, nothing like her usual approach. After all, there was nothing wrong with Bethany Chase going to talk to Snell and ask some questions. If she didn't get anywhere as herself, then she could come back later in full gear.

The more she thought about it, the more she thought it would be perfect. If she skipped her workout, she'd have just enough time to squeeze in a "conversation" before her dinner with Richard.

~ 18 ~

Bethany stopped at her loft over Master Jung's studio to pick up a couple of accessories before heading out. From a large locked cabinet, she extracted a Sig Sauer nine millimeter handgun – their smallest model – which fit perfectly in the small holster she attached to her ankle. She also grabbed a switchblade, which she nestled in her waistband.

Though she had no intention of making any trouble with Leo Snell, it seemed prudent to be prepared, in case he wanted to make trouble with her.

She slipped back out of the building as quietly as she'd entered.

She'd changed into a baseball cap, which was pulled low over her eyes, baggy jeans and an old t-shirt. In the unobtrusive outfit, no one on the subway even looked twice at her. Leo Snell didn't live in one of the better parts of the city, which meant a cab was out of the question, and Bethany's car would've been an open invitation to vandals and thieves. His house was less than a block from the subway. She could get in and out without any real trouble, which was key to the plan.

But she felt exposed knowing that whatever happened, Leo Snell was going to know Bethany Chase had been standing in his home. That was a piece of information she didn't like people knowing.

Despite her trepidation, Bethany found herself walking up the block to Leo's house. A few people were sitting on their front stoops, trying to find a little relief from the heat. They all noticed her as she walked up, but none made eye contact.

That was the way things were in this part of town. You always had to be vigilant, always aware of people in the neighborhood, but you never made eye contact. Eye contact with the wrong person could get you killed. She knew that if the police asked any questions later the answers would all be the same – nobody saw anyone walking up the street.

Leo Snell's home was even more dilapidated than his neighbors'. All the windows were open and numerous fans were inside. The front door was ajar, with only the screen standing between Bethany and the interior of the home.

Leo lived there with his grandmother. She was hoping to take care of this without ever dealing with the woman. That was why she was so pleased to see a man respond to her knock.

She recognized him from the photos her investigator had provided earlier in the day. He was a small man, listed generously on his driver's license at five foot five, and he couldn't have been much more than a hundred and twenty pounds. Thin, greasy, brown hair hung limply around his face. For the most part, his hair obstructed her view of his eyes, but Bethany could tell he was loaded. Crack was his drug of choice, and his breath revealed he was drinking cheap whiskey along with it.

He leered at the sight of her, his eyes lingering too long on her legs and her breasts. It was hard to bite back the urge to kick his ass.

Instead, Bethany smiled sweetly and asked, "Are you Leo Snell?"

"You're looking for me?" he slurred. "Who are you?"

"Can I come in?" Bethany avoided the question. She'd have more leverage once she was inside.

"Sure."

He opened the screen door to give her access to the place Leo called home. The smell of decay radiated from within, along with more pungent touches of mildew and smoke.

Leo pushed a stack of magazines, and what looked like a cockroach, off of the couch and offered Bethany a seat. Reluctantly, she joined him, promising herself she'd burn her clothes when she got home.

"Leo, I was hoping to ask you a couple of questions."

His eyes blackened with suspicion. "You a cop?"

Bethany kept her voice gentle and soft. "No."

"D.A.'s Office?"

"I'm Bethany Chase. I was Geoffrey Quinn's fiancée," she explained with her sweetest smile.

Her answer did nothing to put him at ease. He jumped to his feet and began to pace. "What do you want from me?"

"Look, I'm not here with the police or with the D.A.'s Office."

Leo looked her up and down. "They said on TV that you work with the police a lot."

"Not now, Leo. I'm just trying to figure out what happened to Geoffrey."

"He's dead. That's what happened. Take it from me, people die. You need to just let it go."

"Geoffrey told me about you before he died. Told me you were worried about testifying."

"I didn't want to testify. They made me. I told the judge. I won't lie on the stand. Quinn told me to lie."

Leo looked away as he spoke. Everything in his manner told Bethany he was lying now.

"Those thugs shot your best friend. You stood there and watched them shoot him. The guy's going to be a vegetable for the rest of his life. They shot two other guys too. Killed them. You're just going to walk away from that?"

Bethany was getting mad. She couldn't help it.

"I thought you said you weren't working for the police. Don't try to make me say things that I don't wanna say. I won't lie for the cops."

Bethany's eyes narrowed with rage. She didn't give a shit about his pathetic life. This was about Geoffrey, not him. Maybe she made a mistake not coming here to beat the information out of him.

"I don't care if you testify. I don't care about your friend or the jackasses who shot him. I care about why Geoffrey got shot. I want to know what you know about that."

"I don't know nothing about that."

"Bullshit," Bethany snapped.

She stood up and grabbed Leo by the shirt. In her boots she was half a foot taller than him. "What do you know about Geoffrey's shooting?"

"They said they'd kill me," he sputtered.

"Who said they'd kill you?"

"I can't talk to nobody. They'll kill me."

"I'll fucking kill you myself if you don't tell me what I wanna know," Bethany snapped.

Leo looked up at her, clearly starting to realize just how much trouble he was in.

"I don't know nothing about Quinn. I swear. The guys that shot my buddy Bobby, the guys that were on trial, they told me if I testified they'd kill me. Quinn convinced me to testify. But once he ended up dead, I couldn't do it."

"Did they shoot Geoffrey?"

"I don't know. I don't know," he stumbled. "But if a guy like that can end up dead, then a guy like me don't stand a chance."

"The letter you wrote after Geoffrey's death, the recantation, was any of it true?"

"Nothing. None of it."

Bethany let go of his shirt. She pulled a pad and a pen out of her pocket. "I want the names of anyone who could've been involved with Geoffrey's shooting."

Leo looked at the pad and then back up at Bethany.

"Who are you?" he asked, plainly trying to squint through the drug and alcohol haze that clouded his mind.

Bethany suppressed a smile. Maybe she didn't need to dress up all in black to conceal her identity. People were so certain they knew the real Bethany Chase, they wouldn't believe their own eyes.

"The names, Leo. Write them down. And any addresses or phone numbers you know."

Leo scribbled down a quick list and handed the pad back.

Bethany slid the pad into her pocket and then tried one more time. "Are you sure you haven't heard anything about what happened to Geoffrey?"

"Nothing. I swear."

"There's no buzz on the street?"

"People are saying those guys took him out. But I don't think that's true."

"Why's that?"

"They'd've killed me sooner than Quinn. I mean, why kill him? Stupid to kill a D.A. or a cop. There're a thousand more just waitin' to do their job. Just one me. Without me. No case. Without Quinn. New D.A."

"Yeah, but now you're not testifying. So, no case."

"I guess," he shrugged.

Bethany knew he had nothing else to say. She'd gotten what she'd come for. She'd gotten names and the truth about Leo's recantation.

She left him without another word.

As she walked back to the subway, she thought about what he'd said. He was right. Why kill Geoffrey? In these situations there was no value in killing the prosecutor. The value was in killing the witness. And a drugged out punk like Leo Snell had to be a lot easier to kill than a mayoral candidate. Which brought her back to the same dead end that had been torturing her her whole life.

~ 19 ~

Bethany was brought out of a haze of guilty, fitful sleep by a gentle hand smoothing over her hair. Her eyes slowly blinked open to find Richard squatting next to her and smiling down at her.

"Hey," he said sweetly. "You were sleeping so soundly I didn't want to wake you, but it sounded like you were looking forward to dinner. I hope it's okay."

Bethany tried to get her bearings. When had she fallen asleep?

As if to answer the question, Richard placed a hand on the very large bag of ice that rested on her ribs. She realized she was laying on her couch. She must've fallen asleep while she was icing down her ribs after her "interview" with Snell.

She didn't like the unspoken question on Richard's face. Avoiding it, Bethany asked, "What time is it?"

Unfortunately, Richard was as good at evasion as she was. "What happened?"

She sat up, trying to look strong, and silently cursed herself when the shifting ice on her tender ribs caused her to wince. "It's nothing. I took a hit when we were sparring the other day. I wasn't as focused as I should have been."

Richard helped her unwrap the ace bandage, and took the ice bag to place it in the sink.

"I am perfectly capable of doing that myself," she pointed out.

"You don't have to do everything yourself, Beth," Richard replied, meeting her eyes. "You can let me help."

"Let you help ice my ribs?" she joked, knowing that wasn't what he meant. "I think this is just another ploy to try and get me out of my clothes."

Richard laughed. "Yeah, it's my life's goal to see you naked."

"You've been trying since I was thirteen."

"If that's what helps you sleep at night, then sure."

"You're full of shit."

Richard mostly ignored the banter. "Are you okay?"

"I'll live," Bethany replied, not enjoying the serious look in his eyes. "Just give me five minutes to change and then we can head out."

Grabbing her arm before she could escape, Richard guided Bethany back to the couch. "Sit. Talk to me. Are you okay?"

Bethany could feel the tension building. This wasn't a conversation she wanted to have. "It's fine. What are you making such a big deal about?"

"If it's nothing, let me see."

Tension was turning to panic. The bruise on her ribs wasn't the type that would be easily explained. How had she gone through innumerable boyfriends and avoided this problem, but she was going to get caught because she'd fallen asleep on the couch?

She shook off Richard's grip. "Relax. It's nothing. Just a bruise. No big deal."

"If it's no big deal then stop making it a big deal and show me this tiny little bruise that's been bothering you since yesterday morning. I didn't like the way you were moving then and I like it even less tonight. How about you just put my mind at ease, huh?"

Bethany stood on instinct. "It's my thing, not yours. Back off."

"When you're hurt, that's my thing, make no mistake about it," Richard replied, standing to face her.

Mind darting, Bethany couldn't see any way this conversation was going to go well. She couldn't just blow Richard off and then avoid him indefinitely. He was Richard.

Her voice sounded more resigned than she would've liked when she spoke again. "Please just let it go. I don't want to get into this."

Richard stood firm, arms crossed, eyes solemn.

Reluctantly, Bethany raised her shirt, revealing the lower half of her rib cage. Unless things had changed dramatically in the past few hours she knew what he would see.

An enormous bruise ran the length of her ribs. It was an ugly shade of purple, with hues of green and yellow around the edges. The lowest point of the bruise was the darkest, it had a sort of circular shape.

A tiny defiant part of her hoped he wouldn't recognize it for what it was. But she knew that would never happen.

Richard's face darkened and he slowly bent over to get a better look. His fingers ran gently over the spot and traced the deepest point in the bruise.

"Is that a heel print?" His voice was a blend of awe and fear.

Bethany shivered a little. She told herself it was a reaction to his touch, but she knew there was more to it than that. She wondered if there was any way at all she'd be able to keep any of this from him anymore. More frightening was that she wondered if she even wanted to.

"Probably," she replied, struggling to keep her voice even.

"Jesus, Beth, this looks bad. Are you sure you didn't break a rib?"

"I'm fine."

"You aren't fine," he snapped. He looked at her now instead of the bruise, and there was a fiery anger in his eyes.

Bethany lowered her shirt and turned away from him. "It's a bruise," she growled. "It happens sometimes."

"So, Master Jung kicks you in the ribs on a regular basis?"

"It wasn't him. I don't always spar with him. Sometimes we use other people. And the Master monitors. Kind of like a tournament. Those times, it's full contact. Occasionally, I get a little banged up."

Richard grabbed her shoulder and spun her around. "What the fuck are you doing over there, Bethany? You're in a full contact fight the day after you bury your fiancé?"

The judgment was more than she could take, mostly because it was a question she'd asked herself innumerable times.

"What the fuck else am I supposed to do?" she

shouted.

The anger in Richard's eyes melted and he did what Bethany could never bring herself to do. He gave up the fight. Completely.

"I'm sorry," he said softly and he opened his arms to her.

Though her heart was still pounding, Bethany allowed herself the embrace. In his arms, she could feel the rage fade, the compulsion to lash out became a memory. Her head fit perfectly against his strong shoulder. She felt power and comfort radiate off him.

It had always been that way with Richard. He was her rock. Her best friend. The only person in the world who really understood her.

The first peaceful moment of her day was interrupted by the ring of her cell phone. She glared at Richard as she grabbed it. He offered his most adorable grin in response.

The caller ID told her Detective Heinrich was on the line, but his voice sounded strange. Almost giddy.

He wasted no time with formalities, getting right to the point. "We've got him."

It was all Bethany could do not to drop the phone. "You made an arrest?"

Richard hurried to her side.

"Vice found him. This guy was trying to solicit an undercover officer. He ran. They chased him into a building. Inside the apartment they found all kinds of weapons. There were two files on the coffee table. One of them had Geoffrey's picture inside and a description of the job. Ballistics is running the guns, but, Bethany, it sure as hell looks like this is our hitman."

"That's incredible."

"We've got him red-handed, especially if the ballistics pan out. I'm hoping he'll flip on the guy who hired him. We should know soon. We're interrogating him now. I thought you'd want to know."

"Can I come down?"

"Obviously you can't talk to him or anything, but you can watch from behind the glass during the interview, if you want."

"I'll be right there."

~ 20 ~

When they arrived at the police station, a uniformed officer escorted Bethany and Richard back to an observation room. Through the glass, Bethany could see the detectives, their backs to the mirror, and another man sitting at the table.

The tinny intercom system transmitted Zapp's voice. He was trying to convince their suspect that things were bad. But Tony, as Zapp called him, couldn't have been paying any less attention. He only stared at the tabletop.

"I'm supposed to give Detective Heinrich a high sign when you get here," their escort explained. "I know you already know this, but please don't touch the glass or the intercom system, please."

Bethany nodded in response, but failed to make eye contact. She was completely focused on the man at the table. This was the man who'd murdered her fiancé. Strangely, she felt nothing – no anger, no pain, just nothing.

Her mind assessed with icy precision. The man wasn't what she'd expected. He was perfectly average looking, almost plain. Somehow she'd thought he'd be bigger, stronger looking. She guessed he was about five-ten, maybe six feet, about a hundred and seventy pounds. He had black hair, clipped close to his head, and olive skin.

She wished he'd look up. She wanted to see his eyes.

Seeing the uniformed officer, Heinrich left his partner and joined Bethany and Richard in the observation room.

"I'm glad you came down," he said.

Bethany didn't turn to face him; she answered without any real thought, "Of course. How's it going in there?"

"It's not really. He hasn't said a word. I'm hoping once we get ballistics back it'll give us some leverage, but that won't happen tonight. He hasn't asked for a lawyer though, so that's a good sign."

"You're sure that's the guy?" Richard asked.

"One hundred percent."

"Does he have a record?" Bethany asked.

"Tons of arrests – mostly assaults, a couple robberies – only one conviction. He served two years upstate when he was in his early twenties, about ten years ago. Since then he's been brought in pretty frequently, but nothing ever stuck."

Bethany turned to face Heinrich. She knew enough about the system to know she didn't like the sound of that. "Why not?"

"It's hard to tell from what we have at this point. Seems like various things, but mostly witnesses failing to appear. He's a hitman, Bethany. We'd expect he'd use his connections to keep the witnesses away. This bust is different though. We don't need to rely on civilian eyewitnesses. Just keep your fingers crossed on those ballistics."

"If he's guilty, why hasn't he asked for his lawyer?" Richard asked.

"He wants to see what we have," Heinrich explained. "He's smart enough to sit there like a lamppost until we hit him with some real evidence. It keeps the communication open."

"So he can make a deal?"

Heinrich nodded.

Bethany turned her attention back to the man at the table. Detective Zapp was sitting opposite him. He wasn't saying a word. It looked like he was trying to wait the guy out. She thought it might be a while.

"I assume he doesn't look familiar?" Heinrich asked. "I thought about putting him in a line-up, just in case."

"I didn't see him," Bethany said absently, still staring at the murderer.

"I thought maybe you saw him around. Do you recognize him at all? Have you seen him in the streets? I just think he must've followed you guys that night."

The thought gave her chills. He was right. There was no way this man could've known the exact spot in the park they were going to stop. No way of knowing, unless he was following them.

Between the mayoral campaign, her father's temper tantrum, and, perhaps worst of all, her interrogation of Angelo Bria, she'd been distracted. She hadn't been paying any attention to the people who passed her on the street. In fact, nothing had been further from her mind.

Richard put an arm over her shoulder. "Staring at him isn't going to make him look any more familiar. Bethany, the guy gets paid a lot of money not to be noticed. It's no problem if you didn't see him."

Heinrich nodded. "I didn't mean to suggest you should've noticed him. I'm sorry. I just thought it couldn't hurt to give you a look."

Bethany finally tore her eyes away from the man at the table. She smiled weakly at the detective. "Thanks for letting me come in, but I'm sorry, I don't think I've ever seen that man before in my life."

"Is there anything else we can do?" Richard asked.

"We're going to keep talking to him as long as he lets us. We put a rush on the ballistics, but it'll take a few days. I'll call with anything new."

"Call anytime," Bethany agreed. "And really, thank you. Thank you so much."

Heinrich smiled. "This is the part of my job I really enjoy. We're going to get this one, Bethany."

Bethany returned his smile, hoping it looked genuine and not as distracted and guilty as she felt. In silence, she allowed Richard to lead her back outside.

The air was stale; the humidity still hung heavily over the city. Despite a substantial temperature drop from the afternoon, there was nothing refreshing about the evening. It felt oddly symbolic.

"What do you think?" Richard asked.

Her mind was swirling with questions. She wished she shared Heinrich's optimism, but a decade of disappointment had taught her that optimism was a luxury she couldn't afford.

Of course, she had no intention of sharing her dark thoughts. "They've captured the man who murdered

Geoffrey. I couldn't be happier."

Richard looked skeptical. "Are you sure?"

"What do you mean am I sure? Of course I'm sure."

But the truth was, she wasn't sure at all. Her gut told her this wasn't over, not by a long shot.

~ 21 ~

By the time they made it back to the apartment it was too late for dinner. Richard suggested they order in, but Bethany just wanted to go to bed. She needed time alone. Time to figure out what to do next.

Richard had been gone less than ten minutes when there was a knock on the door. Assuming Richard was checking up on her, she swung the door open with a bright smile and a snappy comment on her lips. But neither of the two large men who filled her doorway looked anything like Richard.

The men looked so much like mob enforcers they were almost a caricature. One appeared to be about fifty, heavy set, in a bad, but probably expensive, suit. His dark hair was combed back, accentuating his receding hairline. The other one was younger – probably mid-twenties, thick jet black hair, with a heavy stubble that no amount of shaving could ever diminish. The younger one was bigger, more fit looking.

Bethany's heart rate spiked, but her voice stayed even. "Can I help you?"

"Bethany Chase?" the older one asked, though it seemed very clear he already knew the answer.

Bethany thought the accent sounded like Staten Island, maybe Brooklyn, but it was hard to tell.

"How the hell did you get up here?" she replied.

"He asked you a question," the younger man said. His accent was thicker than his partner's, and his eyes more violent.

She wondered if there was a way she could take the two men out, but the dull pain in her ribs reminded her to be cautious. When she noticed the slight bulge of a gun holster under both jackets she realized she was most likely outmatched.

With what she suspected was supposed to be a reassuring smile, the older man said, "Maybe we discuss things inside."

That was the last thing she wanted.

"I don't know who the hell you are. Why don't you start by telling me that?" She wasn't going to take them on, but they didn't need to know that yet.

The younger one looked ready to bull-rush his way in, but the older one held him back. "It's a personal family matter. I think it's better discussed inside."

"A family matter? What do you know about my family? I think you need to leave," Bethany said, attempting to swing the door shut.

Without hesitation, the younger man barreled his way inside. With more dexterity than Bethany would've expected, he grabbed her and attempted to twist her arm behind her back. It was a basic move. The counter was instinctive.

Before he even realized what was happening,

Bethany had him spun around. The heel of her hand collided with his nose, spraying blood down the front of his silk shirt. She swept his legs out from under him, sending him face first to the carpet. When he hit the floor he was still conscious, and she would have left him that way had he not reached for his gun. A swift kick drove her heel into his temple, and she watched his eyes roll back as his body went limp.

Her back was to the other man at the door. Feeling exposed, she turned cautiously, expecting to find herself staring down the barrel of a gun.

What she found was even more shocking.

The older man stood in the doorway with a small smile on his face. His gun remained holstered. Next to him stood Richard, looking pale and more than a little afraid. When she met his eyes, he forced a weak smile.

"I heard some commotion. I thought you might need me. Jesus Christ, Beth, is he unconscious?"

Bethany turned to the other man in her doorway. She was very curious what was going to happen next, and very unhappy that Richard seemed to have walked into the middle of it.

"He underestimated you," the man said.

Bethany saw the unspoken words in his eyes – *I won't make that mistake.*

He stepped into her apartment and gave Richard a little shove to make him do the same.

"What the hell?" Richard exclaimed. "I don't think anyone invited you in." He looked at Bethany for clarification.

She shrugged and tried to appear casual. There was nothing she could do now, not with Richard there. The younger guy was already starting to come around.

The older man closed the door, and then gestured to

his colleague on the floor. "Sorry about that. He's a little hotheaded. We'll send someone to clean the rug."

It was a little like stepping into a scene from *The Godfather*. She was clearly talking to a member of the mob. What was also clear was that he didn't seem to have any interest in hurting her. Actually, he was treating her with more respect than really made sense.

"I can take care of my own rug," she replied. "What do you want?"

"I knew your mother from the old neighborhood."

The statement filled Bethany with both curiosity and fear, but she showed neither emotion when she spoke. "How nice for you."

The man smiled at her sarcasm. "Yous are more alike than I would've expected. From a distance you look more like your father. But, here, seeing you like this. Yeah, you're a lot alike."

As he spoke, the younger man slowly began to get to his feet. The blood was still running out of his nose.

The older man kicked him in the shins and threw a handkerchief at him. "You stay down. And stop bleeding on her rug. I'll deal with you later." The threat was growled in a thicker accent than he was using with Bethany.

"Who are you?" Bethany asked again. This time her voice revealed more curiosity and less contempt.

"Frankie Lioni. Your mother never told you about me?"

Bethany only shook her head.

"You was young when she died. Otherwise you probably would've heard more stories from the neighborhood."

Bethany doubted that. She'd asked a lot of people a lot of questions about her mother's life before she'd

met her father. The answer had always been the same –
Rita Chase never talked about her past. Bethany had
assumed it was because of her parents' deaths. She was
beginning to think she'd been wrong about that.

"Bethany, I need you to come with me. There's
somebody you gotta meet."

Richard jumped in. "She's not going anywhere with
you."

A ghost of a smile appeared on Frankie's lips. "If
I'd wanted to hurt yous, I would've already. There's
somebody she needs to meet."

"Richard's right," Bethany agreed, standing as firmly
as she could. "If you want me to meet someone, you
bring him here."

"Afraid that's not possible."

"Anything's possible," Bethany replied, her eyes
narrowing. "You seem like an okay guy. You pick a
place. I'll meet you there. You can bring whoever you
want me to meet."

Now Frankie did smile. "Sorry, I can't do that.
Look what happened to poor Vincent here. And that
was when we took you by surprise. No, I gotta worry
too much about concealed weapons if we don't do this
right now."

Bethany saw the sincere shock on Richard's face.
She spoke before he could defend her. "How do you
know I'm not carrying right now?"

"If you'd had a gun you would've taken Vince down
and turned it on me. You let me in because you knew I
was armed and you weren't. I can tell by looking at you
– you're a planner. I've got one advantage here –
surprise. I'm not giving that up."

Bethany considered arguing, but she knew it would
be pointless.

Richard was far less flexible. "Are you fucking kidding me? All we have to do is scream, you jackass. A building like this, people will call the cops."

Frankie gave Richard a close look and then turned his attention back to Bethany. "I like him more than I thought I would," he said without explanation.

Despite the strangeness of the statement, Bethany found herself suppressing a smile. Even though he was essentially holding her at gunpoint, Bethany was beginning to like this guy. He was very calm, very straightforward. And something about him told her that he held her in very high regard, out of respect for her mother.

The statement was very odd though, and it bore comment. "You sound like you've given him some thought before tonight."

Frankie gave a wink. "You're a lot like your mother."

Before Bethany could ask anything more, Frankie helped the younger guy to his feet. "You okay to walk outta here?" Frankie asked.

The bruised soldier nodded and glared at Bethany with a mixture of embarrassment and anger.

Frankie seemed satisfied with the response. He looked at Bethany and Richard and said, "Okay, let's go."

She'd been willing to go with this man, but this was completely unacceptable. She stepped between Richard and Frankie. "You can take me wherever it is you want to, but Richard stays here."

Richard responded before Frankie could. "Hell, no. If you go, I go."

"I'm afraid I'm gonna have to agree with Richie here. He's coming."

Bethany looked between the two men. Vincent looked pretty unsteady. Maybe she could take both of them out without Richard getting hurt.

Again, Frankie smiled at her. "I can't believe how much you're like your mother. You're right to think I might have a little trouble hurting you. But this guy, I've got no problem taking him down. That's why he's coming – a little insurance policy. And I think we both know Vince here wouldn't share my hesitancy to do you harm."

"Where are we going?" Bethany asked in resignation.

"Over the river and through the woods." Frankie chuckled at what was clearly an inside joke.

Bethany thought of the old song – *Over the river and through the woods, to grandmother's house we go.*

"What the hell does that mean?" Richard asked.

Frankie ignored the question. "Come on. He'll be wondering what kept us."

Vince led the way to the elevator, with Bethany and Richard in the middle and Frankie pulling up the rear. In the lobby, they found a third man standing next to their doorman, Wally. He appeared to be about the same age as Vince, with the same stature. He was chatting with Wally, trying to appear casual, but the look on Wally's face told a different story. His eyes were darting around the room, trying to figure out a way to escape.

Wally's expression changed when he saw them. He jumped forward with almost no regard for the beefy man who grabbed his arm to restrain him.

"Ms. Chase! Oh my God! Get your hands off her!" he shouted, despite the fact no one was touching her.

Bethany looked at the three men who were holding

them all captive. Getting Wally involved in this was the last thing she needed.

"It's okay," she assured him. Then looking at the third man, and trying to appear like she knew them and this was the most normal situation in the world, she added, "I hope my friends here didn't give you a hard time. They should've known better than to sneak upstairs like that. Please, take your hands off Wally, you're scaring him."

Frankie looked at her for a moment and Bethany worried he was going to do something crazy. She was pleasantly surprised.

"Come on, Joey," he said gruffly, "you leave him alone. We need to get going."

Fortunately, Joey was far more obedient than Vince. He quickly released Wally and hurried outside to start the car.

Wally stared at Bethany in surprise and then looked to Richard. "Mr. Marshall, are you sure everything's all right?"

Bethany was relieved to see Richard nod. "Everything's just fine, Wally. We'll be back later."

Leaving the doorman alone in the lobby, the four of them walked out to a huge black SUV with glistening paint and shining silver hubcaps. Frankie pushed Vincent toward the front seat and told Bethany and Richard to climb into the back, where he joined them. Once they were inside, Joey drove off.

"Since I don't want yous trying anything stupid and pissing us off unnecessarily, I'll tell you this now. The doors back here, they don't open from the inside," Frankie explained, pulling on his door handle to demonstrate. Looking at Bethany, since she was closest to the other door, he asked, "You wanna try?"

"I have no interest in jumping out of a speeding car," Bethany assured him.

"Great car, don't you think?" Frankie asked. "It's the new Cadillac. Pietro only sends the best for you."

"Pietro?" Bethany asked, her concern rising. There was an infamous mobster named Pietro. He was an old man at this point, but he was still very powerful.

Frankie smiled. "Didn't your father tell you nothing about your mother's family?"

"My mother told me about her family. She told me her parents were dead."

As Bethany watched, a shadow seemed to fall across Frankie's face. He almost looked sad. "She told you her family was dead?"

"Yes. She told me that expressly. That was why she never went back to Staten Island to visit anyone."

Frankie sat back in his seat, breaking eye contact. He sighed deeply before continuing. "What did Aston tell you?"

"What the hell do you think he told me?"

Frankie only shook his head. "I just didn't know what you'd been told, that's all."

Clearly, Frankie was wishing he'd never started this conversation. The strangely friendly man who'd abducted her was gone. Now he seemed distant and withdrawn. And that was the reason Bethany continued to question him.

"Are you saying that this Pietro is from my mom's family?"

"I think I better let Pietro talk to you himself."

"Why so cryptic? Won't it be easier if..."

But he interrupted before she could finish the question. There was a fire in his eyes when he turned to face her. "No more questions. You sit back and wait until we get there. Got it?"

Bethany nodded, appreciating that Richard was the one sitting closest to the angry mobster. In an effort to avoid eye contact, she began to stare out the window. It looked like they were headed for the Battery Tunnel. That meant either Brooklyn or Staten Island were their most likely destinations, probably Staten Island – where her mother grew up. That would be logical.

She found herself trying to remember exactly where Pietro Timminolo lived. Was he the reason Rita Chase didn't talk about her childhood?

~ 22 ~

Bethany and Richard were led into an enormous home with a beautiful cathedral entryway.

Frankie put a heavy hand on Richard's shoulder. "This is as far as you go."

Richard clenched Bethany's hand. "I go wherever she goes."

"Afraid not. She's going in there," Frankie stated, pointing to a set of heavy oak doors. "You're gonna sit in that chair next to them doors. Joey, you stay with him. Vincent, you're with us."

Richard, however, held his ground. "No."

Frankie smiled. "Look, kid, we need to have a little talk. You need to stay here. Pietro's gonna be pissed we brought you this far."

Realizing Richard wasn't going to budge on the issue, and also understanding that none of these men would hesitate to separate them by force, Bethany put a gentle hand on his arm.

"It's fine. I'll be fine. Please wait here. Let's just get this over with."

Richard looked back and forth between Bethany and Frankie. He was clearly unhappy, but he could see the realities of the situation as much as she could. He gave her hand a gentle squeeze and took his place by the door.

Frankie nodded with approval and led Bethany into a cavernous study. Despite the ornate woodwork and paintings, the focal point was the solitary man sitting in the shadows behind a large desk.

He was old. There was no kinder way to describe him. He looked short – no more than five foot four – with boney shoulders and a bald head. Despite his frail appearance, his eyes revealed his power. They were a vivid crystal green, and they were fixed on Bethany the moment she entered the room. It felt like he could have read her mind if he'd chosen to.

Frankie stood at his side and murmured something inaudible. The old man merely nodded, and Frankie took his place standing behind his chair.

In a sandpaper voice he said, "I am Pietro Timminolo."

His accent wasn't the same as the goons who brought her in. His was an Italian accent, with just a touch of New York.

She would've recognized him anywhere. He looked older than the photos she'd seen on television, but it was undoubtedly him. She'd known from the moment she walked through the door.

If he was disappointed that she didn't respond, the man didn't show it. "It brings me great joy to finally meet you."

Part of her knew where this was heading, but the

idea was so ridiculous Bethany refused to even acknowledge the possibility.

"Why did you bring me here?" she asked.

"Frankie says you do not know about the Family. Is that true?"

Bethany knew avoiding the question was impossible. "Were you related to my mother?"

"Would that be such a bad thing?"

"Apparently my mother thought so, because she never told me about you."

The old man smiled a little at her response. "Your mother was a very stubborn woman. We did not get along so well. But do you think our fighting should mean I do not meet my granddaughter?"

Bethany thought of Frankie's offhand remark – *over the river and through the woods*. "You expect me to believe you're my grandfather?"

"It is a shock, I know. But it was time. Too many years have been lost."

Bethany could feel her temper rising. This was preposterous. Absurd. She was sitting in the office of an infamous mobster and he was trying to convince her he was her grandfather.

"Is this really the reason you dragged me here? Who the hell do you think you are?"

There was temper in the old man's eyes too, but he chose not to challenge her. He said only, "Yes, this is why I dragged you here – as you say."

In all her years of searching for answers about her mother's death, Bethany had considered every option. She'd checked and rechecked every fact, or so she had thought. Sitting here, in this room, with this man, she realized she'd made a fatal error.

She'd never checked her mother's story. She had

believed everything Rita Chase had said. Bethany had never considered, not even for a moment, that her mother had been a liar.

But that didn't make her hate the man behind the desk any less. "You expect me to believe you – a criminal – over my parents?"

"The boss has never actually been convicted of anything," Frankie offered.

"That makes it better?" Bethany asked. "He's a mob boss. A murderer. The fact that nobody's ever proven it is evidence of his guilt. They're never able to convict the bosses. Isn't that right, Mr. Timminolo?"

"I understand your anger," Pietro replied. "But I am telling you the truth. Frankie, give her the album."

Frankie grabbed a photo album from the corner of the desk and handed it to her. Her heart fell. There were going to be pictures. They were going to show that this mobster was telling the truth and her life was a lie.

The first page revealed a sleeping newborn. A pretty, young Italian woman holding the baby in her arms.

"That is my Adriana," Pietro explained. "She died not so long after your mother. The strain of her daughter's death, it was too much."

Bethany didn't even look up. She continued flipping through the book. As she did, the child grew. And as she grew it became more and more difficult to deny the obvious. Occasionally, Pietro would interrupt with an explanation – the first day of school; her First Communion; their vacation to Florida; Confirmation.

The last page contained photos of a woman who looked almost exactly like the one who would marry Aston Chase only a few years later. She was formally dressed and with a young man who looked a lot like the man now standing behind Bethany's grandfather.

This time it was Frankie's turn to offer an explanation. "We was a couple in high school. She never wanted nothing too serious, always talking about moving to the city, getting out of her father's house. I never thought she'd do it."

"You were the guy she was at the party with, the night she met my father?" The pretty, romantic picture of her parents' meeting was being obliterated by his every word.

"Yeah. She was my girl in high school."

Despite the awkwardness of the situation, Bethany again found herself feeling at ease with Frankie. There was just something about him. Something that made her want to trust him. The old man in the chair, however, was another story entirely.

"You believe me now." Though it should have been a question, Pietro's voice allowed no room for discussion.

"Why did she lie to me?" Bethany knew he was the wrong person to ask, but she wondered if there was anyone else alive who knew the answer.

"I do not understand your mother. Maybe your father will know the reasons."

"He knew?" If it was possible, that revelation was almost more surprising than anything else.

"Not at first, but later, yes."

Bethany only nodded and looked back down at the photo album. The pictures seemed real. The stories seemed to match up.

She looked back up at the old man, this time looking more closely at his piercing green eyes. They were almost identical to her mother's. There'd been a softness in Rita Chase's eyes that was missing from his, but the color, the unique color, was an unmistakable match.

This was actually real.

"Why are you doing this?" Bethany asked.

"You are my granddaughter. I am an old man. If not now, then when?"

"The same could've been said a week ago. A year ago. Why now?"

Pietro sat back in his chair and looked more closely at Bethany. He seemed impressed.

"You think quickly," he said.

"You're trying to avoid my question with a compliment."

At that the old man chuckled and looked back at Frankie. "Can you believe how much they are alike? At first, no. She looks too much like her father, so thin and tall. But when she speaks, she is my Rita."

Frankie smiled at his boss and then at Bethany. "I was saying the same thing earlier."

Frankie's smile dimmed a bit, and he looked past Bethany to Vincent, who was still standing next to the closed door. "You okay over there, Vince?"

Bethany turned in her chair. The gangster was looking a little pale. His nose had started bleeding again and he was leaning against the wall.

"I'm sorry, Frankie, I just got a little lightheaded. I'll be alright."

Frankie looked to Pietro with an unspoken question. A nod of the old man's head gave him all the answer he needed. "Vincent, go ice that nose. Just make sure you don't get no blood on the furniture, okay?"

"I can stay. I'm alright."

"If that thing keeps bleeding, you're gonna need a

transfusion. Ice up. I'll need your help later."

Vincent reluctantly departed, leaving Bethany alone with her grandfather and her mother's ex-boyfriend, wondering if it was possible for her day to get any stranger.

Pietro quickly proved it could. "Frankie said you have a friend outside."

"Yes." Bethany wished there wasn't such obvious anxiety in her voice.

"Did he do that to Vincent?" Pietro asked. The question was directed at Bethany. Something in the way he asked it told her he already knew she'd done it, and he'd known for a while she was capable of something like that.

"Richard wasn't there when they barged into my apartment," Bethany said.

"You were to be polite to my granddaughter," Pietro said to Frankie.

"You know Vince; he finds it hard to resist a little physical persuasion."

"It looks like you taught him a lesson in keeping his hands to himself." Pietro's expression was that of pride, not anger.

"I was defending myself," she said more calmly than she would have thought possible.

Pietro turned his chair to get a better look at Frankie. "The stories are true."

"Yes, sir, it seems like it."

"You saw. What do you think?"

Bethany wanted to interrupt, to point out that they were discussing her when she was sitting right there, but her curiosity got the better of her. The Master was the only other person to ever observe her fighting skills without being a part of the fray. In spite of herself, she wanted to hear what they'd say.

"She took Vince down before he even knew what hit him. She knew I had a gun, saw she was cornered, didn't do anything stupid. Maybe she could've handled the situation in such a way as to use Vince to protect her from my gun, but for the most part, she's everything we've heard."

~ 23 ~

It took a moment to process what they were saying. To understand that they knew. They actually knew. How was that possible?

"Wait a second," Bethany said. "Everything you've heard? Heard from who? No one knows about…" Her voice trailed off – telling a mob kingpin her darkest secret was stupid, even if he was her grandfather.

Pietro turned his chair back to face Bethany. "Did you really think you could train that way and no one would know?"

Bethany could feel her jaw drop. She knew the astonishment on her face was confirming everything, but she was genuinely stunned.

"There are people who know. Not so many, but they know," her grandfather clarified.

"What exactly do these people know?" Bethany asked, trying to gather herself.

"You began your training when you were a small

child. You work every day. Once a month, there is a battle. It is with five or six men. They are sometimes armed. The men who compete are told to try and take out a masked man. They think he is probably Asian, because he is so thin. Some say he is very tall for an Asian, most say over six feet."

Pietro looked at her in that penetrating way of his and added, "It seems you look taller when dressed all in black."

"How the hell?" Was all Bethany could say.

"Your mother said I must leave her alone. I kept my promise, but it was necessary to watch. Many people do not like me. If they were to discover who your mother was…" Pietro paused. "I wanted to make sure you were safe."

"By spying on me?"

"My men, they guarded you from the day your mother took you home from the hospital."

Bethany took a deep breath. This was unbelievable. Absolutely unbelievable. "And that's how you know about the training?"

"About the training. And about the workroom in your loft."

The shock of the final part of his sentence drove her to her feet. "What did you say?"

Frankie took a small step forward, positioning himself between Bethany and her grandfather. "I understand this looks bad."

"You think?" Bethany snapped.

"I've been in charge of the project for fifteen years. I'm the only one who's been in the loft. I wouldn't've let one of them boys up there. But we had to make sure you was alright."

Bethany didn't hear any of the reassurances. She did

hear Frankie refer to her life as *the project*. That was enough.

"Let me get this straight. My mother hated you so much that she completely disowned all of you. She told you to leave her alone. To leave me alone. She hated you so much that she told me you were dead. And even with all that, you thought it was okay to stalk her only daughter? And you expect me to just say that's okay?"

"I let my daughter go. My only child. For all these years I protect her secret. I allowed her to have her freedom. But I must make sure the secret is kept. I must make sure you are protected."

"Yet here you are telling me everything. I'm sure my mother wouldn't call that keeping her secret."

Pietro sighed. "I always intended to honor my Rita's wishes. I did not expect to have this conversation with you."

"Then why the hell did you snatch me out of my home and drag me to Staten Island?" Bethany shouted.

"Your investigation into your mother's death has always caused me worry. But now some of Frankie's men are hearing whispers about you from other sources."

Bethany's anger melted away. This was about Geoffrey. This was her darkest fear.

She sank back down in the chair. "You think my poking around was making someone nervous."

"Yes. We were becoming concerned with that."

"And Geoffrey's death confirmed there was a problem," Bethany continued for him.

The old man looked at her closely, and with a surprising kindness in his voice, he told her the horrible truth. "The situation with the boy has us very worried."

Bethany could feel the tears, but she ignored them. "They shot Geoffrey in the head to warn me? I was sitting right next to him. Why not shoot me?"

"I do not know."

Bethany looked more closely at the old man in the chair. She realized that despite his criminal history she believed everything he'd told her. Until now. He had some ideas why they didn't shoot her. But he wasn't going to share them.

"Do you know who killed my mother?"

It was Pietro's turn to look away in shame. "I do not know who killed my daughter."

"Shouldn't there have been someone there that day? Shouldn't he have protected her?"

"We had a man with you that day. He was found in the alley near your school. Shot once in the head. We found him two hours after we received the news about my Rita's death."

Bethany sat back in the chair and tried to absorb everything. For years she'd been digging into this mystery because she thought the police weren't well-financed enough to be up to the task. She believed that with all of her money, and with a little encouragement that was outside the law, she could find the truth.

She was staring at one of the most powerful men in New York. He had money, influence, and he wasn't one to be restrained by the law. Undoubtedly he'd worked for decades to find her mother's killer. Yet he'd found nothing.

In a moment, the hope she'd held so tightly was snatched away. There was no way she'd find out what happened. No way at all. Geoffrey died for nothing.

Bethany's moment of despair was interrupted by

what sounded like a scuffle in the hall. She was at the door before Frankie could get out from behind the desk.

She had to blink to adjust to the bright light in the entryway as she swung open the heavy doors. Richard was standing nose to nose with Vince. An ice bag was laying at their feet, leaking onto the marble floor. Vince had a firm hand on Richard's shoulder and was ordering him to take his seat.

Unfortunately for Vince, the sound of the door opening gave Richard just enough time to land a right hook square into his bruised nose. The blow sent Vince sailing across the smooth floor.

Before Richard had even a moment to feel victorious, Joey emerged from the bathroom, gun drawn. "What the fuck do you think you're doing? Sit the hell down!"

Frankie stepped in front of Richard, his hands raised. "Calm down, Joey."

The young man lowered his gun. "Sorry, Pop."

"Take care of Vince." Frankie then turned to Bethany and Richard. "You two are trouble for Vince. You keep doing stuff like that, you're gonna piss him off."

Before anyone else could speak, the voice of Pietro Timminolo came from the doorway. "Is this the friend?"

Richard turned in surprise. It was obvious he recognized the mobster instantly.

Before Richard could ask anything, Pietro continued, "You have known my granddaughter a very long time, Richard Marshall. Are you here looking out for her?"

Bethany stared in amazement at the old man's attempt at casual conversation. Anyone who could be so relaxed in the presence of drawn guns and punches exchanged wasn't the kind of person she needed or wanted to be around. She'd talked. That was the deal. She didn't owe him anything else.

"I think it's time for us to leave," she said.

Pietro looked up at Bethany with an expression of pride. "You look too much like that father of yours, and you have every unpleasant characteristic your mother ever had. It has been a great joy to finally talk to you."

Bethany resisted the urge to shake her head in astonishment.

"Frankie will give you my phone number and his," he continued. "You will use both, if you need anything."

"You'll continue to have your people following me?" Bethany knew that should've made her feel safer, but the invasion of her privacy was too much to bear.

"For your safety."

The words made her realize that her overbearing security team had somehow failed to keep Geoffrey safe. It was a troubling question really. How was it that they hadn't protected him that night? It was a question she wanted to know the answer to, but to get an answer she had to stay. And that wasn't going to happen. Wally would have called the police by now. Her father was undoubtedly going ballistic. It was time to get back to the city.

~ 24 ~

Richard's head swam with questions on the drive back. He kept staring at Bethany, trying to read her expression, trying to figure out what the hell was going on, but the more he looked, the less he saw.

He'd known her most of his life. She knew everything there was to know about him. It was suddenly very obvious that he didn't know her at all.

The SUV slowed a few blocks from their apartment building. Frankie pointed to a no parking zone and told the driver to pull over.

The gangster turned to face them and, with the type of respect that could only be given a mobster's granddaughter, he said to Bethany, "I'm sorry we can't drop yous closer, but that doorman probably called the cops by now."

Bethany appeared to have expected this, though Richard couldn't understand how. She just nodded and said cryptically, "I suppose I'll be seeing you around."

The remark received a smile from Frankie, who said, "That smirk you got there. That's Rita. A hundred percent. Smart lady, your mother."

That seemed to take Bethany by surprise, and for the first time that evening, Richard thought he saw pain. Part of him wondered if her unflappable demeanor had only been an act, but he quickly dismissed the notion as wishful thinking.

Oddly, Frankie seemed to see the same pain. He grabbed Bethany's hand as she tried to leave. "You never made me before. I don't think I'll start catching your eye now."

Bethany cringed at his touch, quickly slipping from his grip and grabbing Richard's hand, as if for protection.

As they stood on the sidewalk, watching the car pull away, Richard wondered if it would have been less disorienting to be dropped off by an alien spaceship.

Slowly, he gathered himself. It was late, he realized, probably well after midnight. Most of the storefronts were dark, though there were still some people walking around the streets.

He looked to Bethany for some answers, but the expression on her face was a knife to the heart. She was still staring at the spot where the SUV had dropped them. Her eyes were blank, almost glassy. Though he was frustrated and angry at all she'd kept from him, when she looked like that, he just couldn't be mad.

As gently as he could, he led her to a bench and made her sit down.

Before he could say anything, Bethany started to get to her feet. "We have to get home. The police will be there. Wally looked petrified."

Richard put a heavy hand on her leg, forcing her to

sit back down. "We aren't going anywhere. Not yet at least."

Though he tried to keep the anger out of his voice, Richard heard the bite as he asked, "What the hell was all of that?"

Bethany looked away as she answered, intently focused on a discarded candy wrapper. "That was my grandfather. That was the reason my mother never talked about her childhood."

Richard ordered himself to ignore the pain in her voice. It was the only way he could figure this all out. "That was Pietro Timminolo, wasn't it?"

"Yes." She barely got the word out.

"He's your grandfather?"

Again, Bethany's voice was almost inaudible. "Yes."

Richard grabbed her shoulder and forced her to face him. "Stop saying yes! Talk to me! You're Pietro Fucking Timminolo's granddaughter? Was there a point when you were planning on telling me that?"

His anger brought the clarity back to her eyes and an expression of pure surprise. "You found out ten minutes after I did," she explained. "I never knew. My father never told me."

Richard immediately released the tight grip he had on Bethany's shoulder. "Jesus, Beth, I'm sorry. I didn't realize. I'm sorry. I just assumed. You seemed so calm. Are you okay? How are you okay?"

Bethany took a deep breath and seemed to consider the last question. She slowly shook her head.

Squeezing his hand, she said, "That was my mother's family. She was Rita Timminolo. Frankie was her boyfriend in high school."

Richard tried to look supportive, not overwhelmed and confused.

"My father," Bethany said, "he's known all along. I guess he figured it wasn't important enough to tell me."

"Aston knew? Are you sure?"

The darkness in Bethany's eyes told Richard that she was not only sure, she was furious.

Knowing he wouldn't get an answer to his last question, he asked, "Did you say you'd be seeing that guy Frankie around? Is he following you or something?"

Bethany's cheeks flushed at the question. Richard wondered if it was embarrassment or anger, maybe both.

"My whole life, that old man has had people following me. He had people following my mother, too. He says he's only doing it to protect us."

Richard heard the words Bethany didn't say – *a lot of good that protection did her mother and Geoffrey.*

"I'm sorry to have dragged you into this," Bethany said.

The expression on her face was familiar now. This was the woman he knew. This was his best friend. Richard tried to shake the feeling that he'd just witnessed a Jekyll and Hyde transformation. Simple shock and surprise didn't really explain all he'd seen that night.

"Don't worry about it." That was the least of his concerns. "I'm happy to be dragged wherever you are. Actually, I'm glad you weren't dragged alone."

Before he lost his nerve, Richard asked the question that had been bothering him all night, even more than anything else. "That guy – what was his name? Vince? You know the one with the broken nose? You took him down pretty easily."

Bethany tried to hold eye contact as she spoke, but

she failed. "I was pretty impressed with that right hook of yours actually."

Richard rolled his eyes at the evasion. This was typical Bethany. With all he'd seen that night, the skill seemed less like a cute quirk than it had before.

"Yeah, focusing back on you, Beth, I'm just wondering, how many other guys have you done that to?" He tried to keep his voice light, but failed to a great degree.

Bethany smiled, just a little too broadly, and dismissed the question. "It's a basic defense move. That's all. More than two decades of training, it's instinct now."

Richard thought of the ugly bruise he'd seen only hours before, thought of her remark about the tournaments. There was something more going on here.

"I don't mean in training. You didn't look like someone who was only used to sparring."

Bethany chuckled. "You have a very active imagination. Do you think I'm roaming the streets taking out would-be muggers?"

He was beginning to think there was a lot more to it than that. He considered pursuing the questioning, but he knew he couldn't. They needed to get back. He didn't doubt that Aston had half the New York City police force looking for his daughter.

But he wasn't done with this conversation. Far from it.

The lobby was chaos. Swarms of uniformed officers were milling about, talking among themselves. It was a little funny that no one even noticed them as they walked in.

Inside, the first sound that reached their ears was the voice of Aston Chase barking at Wally.

"What do you mean there are no security cameras on the other floors? What kind of half-assed security system only has one camera in the lobby? Of course they shot the camera out! Of course there are no useful pictures of the men who snatched my daughter! I want the manager. Now! I don't care where he is!"

Bethany had to raise her voice to be heard over her father's tirade. "Dad!"

Aston had her in an embrace before she could react. Richard couldn't miss the tears that were in his eyes, as well as the fear. Bethany had been right. Aston knew about her mother's family. He'd thought she'd been taken by gangsters, either her mother's family, or a different family. And with that thought, Richard suddenly wondered if the mobster's decision to have a "security team" on his granddaughter was actually a good one.

Aston finally stepped away from his daughter and looked at both her and Richard. "What the hell happened?"

Before they could answer, ten uniformed officers closed in. Richard's pulse began to race. It was like the inquisition.

They were police. They were trying to help. But he was quickly realizing he didn't know if they could tell them what had really happened. If they told the officers about Bethany's family, it would be on the front page of every newspaper in the city by morning.

He looked to Bethany for answers and again saw the unflappable expression he'd seen earlier. She was completely in control. No emotions. No fear. Just a disconcerting certainty. Richard had to remind himself that it had been a farce before and probably was again, but he couldn't quite believe it.

Detective Heinrich pushed his way to the front of the group of officers. Though his face looked relieved, his voice was professional. "Ms. Chase, Mr. Chase, Mr. Marshall, why don't we all go upstairs? It'll be easier to talk up there."

They all followed him, Bethany's mask firmly in place.

There was only one moment when Richard saw it slip. As they walked passed Wally, Bethany squeezed his hand and smiled gently. "Everything's fine. Please don't worry," she whispered.

The scene in Bethany's apartment was no less

chaotic. Crime scene photographers were snapping photos of the blood on the rug. Detective Zapp was on a cell phone shouting at someone. At the sight of them, he quickly signed off.

"I need everybody outta this room now!" he snapped. "Downstairs!"

Everyone filed out, leaving the five of them alone.

"Why don't we sit at the table?" Bethany's tone might have been more appropriate for a tea party.

Richard followed, fighting the urge to run back to his apartment and slam the door. His pulse was pounding, and from the look Detective Heinrich was giving him, it was obvious.

It was Heinrich who spoke first when they were all seated. "Are you alright? Do either of you need any medical attention?"

"We're fine," Bethany said. "I'm very sorry this caused such a stir."

Zapp jumped in. "Of course it caused a stir. Three big guys stormed your lobby, shot out the security camera, threatened your doorman, broke into your apartment and then took you with them. Did you think that wouldn't cause a stir?"

For the first time in his life, Richard watched Bethany act like an heiress, and a spoiled one at that.

"Honestly, guys, I'm afraid there's been a huge misunderstanding." She almost giggled as she continued, "People threaten me all the time. This wasn't like that at all. These guys wanted the Foundation to fund one of their projects. They've been calling. I've been working on getting the funding, but I guess not fast enough."

"They're blackmailing you?" Zapp snapped.

This time she did giggle. "Blackmail? No, no. It's

totally on the up and up."

"This is on the up and up?" Heinrich asked.

"Well, no, obviously this isn't what I'd call the appropriate way to conduct business. I had no idea what they'd done to the security camera. I'm happy to pay for that. They're some tough guys. You know, thick-necked, a little thick-skulled, but they're doing some fantastic work in Brooklyn with young kids. These guys are ex-cons that have made good."

"If they've made good, then why are they shooting out cameras and snatching you from your apartment?"

"I wasn't snatched from my apartment. Richard and I went with them completely willingly. Right, Rich?"

"Absolutely," Richard nodded, trying very hard to keep up with Bethany's insane story. He was becoming certain they'd end up in jail for impeding a police investigation before the night was over.

For the first time, Aston spoke, "Are these the guys from the Regional Alliance?"

Richard almost fell off his chair. What the hell was he talking about?

"That's them," Bethany said quickly. "Dad, I told them we were having trouble with Board approval, but we were working on it. I think we're close to the numbers for a vote."

Bethany glanced at the two detectives, and added in a conspiratorial voice, "The Board's a little on the conservative side. The Alliance's work is pretty rough around the edges. So, I've had trouble getting things through."

"So, they broke into your home and took you to this shelter, or whatever it is?" Heinrich asked skeptically.

"It seems they've left me a lot of messages at work, which is entirely possible. I took that week off after…"

she allowed her voice to trail off, and then continued, "I am so behind on my messages and work in general, honestly, I'm not sure I'll ever catch up. I guess the Regional Alliance was getting worried I'd forgotten about them. I told them it was the Board that needed convincing, not me, but they wanted to take me to their location. They're kind of a rough group, so I took Richard along."

"You expect us to believe that?" Heinrich said, once it became clear she was done.

Bethany smiled sweetly. "You don't have to believe anything. But it's true. Really, I'm so sorry. I would've called if I'd realized Wally would take things so seriously."

"They shot out the surveillance camera!" Zapp almost shouted.

"I can see how that would've freaked Wally out. If I'd known I'd certainly have called to tell everyone I was okay. Actually, if I'd known I probably wouldn't have gone with them."

Heinrich was looking concerned. Zapp was seething. Richard held his breath, waiting for the handcuffs to come out.

Instead, Heinrich said only, "This didn't have to do with Geoffrey's murder?"

"No," Bethany replied calmly.

"Who are these guys that took you from here? I'd like to talk to them."

Bethany smiled. "As angry as you are right now, I'd be totally awful to send you two after them. I understand your aggravation. I understand that manpower was wasted, and honestly, I am very sorry about that. They didn't mean any harm."

"What about the blood on the rug?" Zapp growled.

Before Bethany had a chance to answer, Richard spoke up.

He didn't know if it was the adrenaline or if epidemic lying was contagious, but he said, "That was me. I came across the hall when I heard Bethany talking to the two guys. I got a little worried. She was telling them that they should've had the doorman call up. I got a little jumpy, what with what happened to Geoffrey and all. I'm kind of embarrassed to admit this, but I punched one of the guys. Got him pretty good. I would've gone after the other one too, if Beth hadn't told me who they were."

Bethany placed an appreciative hand over Richard's and then looked back at the detectives. "Look, you guys know me. You know I wouldn't lie to you."

Heinrich nodded slowly. It seemed clear that he didn't believe Bethany wouldn't lie to him, but he was going to take her at her word anyway.

"Okay," he said reluctantly.

"What?" Zapp exclaimed. "Are you buying this bullshit story? Christ, Bethany, I expect better from you!"

"Genuinely, I'm sorry you wasted so much of your time."

"If the owner of the building wants to press charges about the scene downstairs, you're gonna have to turn over the names of those guys," Zapp threatened.

And that, Richard realized, was the reason they were giving up. There was no crime unless Bethany said there was. Without an abduction, all they had was a destroyed surveillance camera. If the owner was paid enough to fix it, and given some extra money for his trouble, this would all go away and there was very little the police could do about it.

Richard thought of Aston's rant about the security system when they arrived. Most likely, the building was going to be generously given a security system that would rival the one at Fort Knox.

Bethany obviously knew it too. "If they still want to press charges after we've had a chance to talk this out, then I'll be happy to pass that information on."

And with the final lie, Richard knew they were in the clear with the police. If only that made him feel better about the situation.

~ 26 ~

It was almost an hour before the police dispersed and the building owners had reached a monetary agreement with Aston for the appropriate repairs.

Bethany managed to catch Wally before he left and she apologized again for the confusion. The scared, shamed look on his face caused her more than a pang of remorse for her lies. He was a good guy. She'd have to do something to make this up to him. And with this problem, money wasn't going to be the answer.

She promised Richard she'd talk to him in the morning and sent him to bed. He looked like he'd been run over by a truck. Surges of adrenaline didn't seem to agree with her mild-mannered friend.

She hated the danger he'd been put in, but Bethany was secretly relieved that Richard had been with her; mostly because it meant he knew the truth. She knew herself well enough to know that if he hadn't walked into the middle of her family reunion she would've had one more enormous secret to keep from the people she loved. And of all the things that had happened to her in the past week, that would have been the worst.

Her father was sitting on her couch when she returned. He focused on the cover-up, instead of the more difficult issues that he had to know needed to be discussed.

"I took care of things with the Regional Alliance," he said. "The story's in place."

Bethany wished she had the strength to stand over him, but she just didn't have the energy. Instead, she sunk onto the couch next to him.

Aston continued, "I called my people right after the officers left. As you know, the Regional Alliance isn't above telling stories if it'll get them money."

"Okay," Bethany replied. Though she had a thousand questions, she didn't even know where to begin.

He gave her a moment to speak first, but when he was met with only silence, Aston asked the question they both knew the answer to. "I imagine it was him."

"Were you planning on telling me?" Bethany asked, in lieu of an answer.

Aston looked away. "No."

Bethany was relieved he'd decided to finally stop lying. But after the day she'd had it just wasn't enough.

"You didn't think I needed to know my grandfather is a mob boss?"

Aston made no attempt to meet her eyes. He was slouching slightly, his shoulders bowed. In that moment it looked like he would have been much happier being a small man, the type that could blend into the cushions.

"Your mother hated the life she'd left behind. She'd

left that man's house and she didn't want to ever speak of it again. I respected her wishes."

"She's been dead more than two decades! There was never a point when you thought it might be helpful to tell me the truth?"

"I thought Rita would've wanted it this way."

"Mom had no idea how things would turn out for us. With the public way I have to live my life? The public existence you lead? You didn't worry that someone else would tell me the truth?"

"It's a well-guarded secret," Aston admitted, looking more than a little ashamed.

Bethany thought of all of the fights she'd had with her father over the years, all of the relatively petty disagreements that had ended with her screaming at him and storming out of the room, slamming doors. She was almost shocked at her reaction now. She was beyond anger.

"I'd like you to leave now," she said in a cold, even voice.

Aston's head snapped up in astonishment. "I'm sorry, what?"

"Leave. I'd like you to leave," she repeated.

"Bethany, there's so much we need to discuss."

"You've never wanted to talk about it. I see no need to start now."

"Your mother…" he began, but Bethany stopped him.

"My mother has been dead for most of my life. Don't try to blame her for this."

"I was just trying to do what was best for both of my girls. Honey, please, with all that's happened I think it's essential we discuss this."

Bethany stood and walked to the door. She heard

the panic in her father's voice. She knew the anger that was coming. And for the first time in her life she didn't care enough to snap back. She was tired, drained. There was too much to process.

"You and Mom made a decision before I was old enough to participate in the process. I have no interest in changing the rules. Lying to me has worked for this long. Why stop now?"

"Bethany," he said, standing and hovering over her. "We will discuss this."

Bethany met his eyes with a look of dismissal she'd seen her father use any number of times on weaker businessmen. She didn't use the look often, but she saw Aston recognize the mimic immediately.

"Actually, we won't be discussing this. You should go. I wasted the better part of the night hanging out with a mobster while he tried to convince me he knew my mother better than I did. I'm done with family affairs for tonight."

And with that she opened the door. "I'll talk with you later in the week."

"You'll talk to me now!" Aston thundered.

Leaving the door open, Bethany walked over to the phone. "Shall I call downstairs and have you removed? I don't know, but I'm thinking the doorman would be pretty responsive to my needs after all that happened earlier. Do you want to check to be sure?"

"Don't you dare threaten me."

In an icy voice, she replied, "It's a promise, not a threat."

The cutting retort had more of an impact than she'd really intended. She could see it in her father's eyes. It looked like something was breaking inside of him. But he didn't say a word. Again, looking every inch a small man, Aston merely nodded and left, closing the door behind him.

For a moment, Bethany felt like she understood her father – forced to choose between lying to his daughter and breaking a promise to his wife. He'd loved her mother, and, even in their battles, Bethany always knew that he loved her.

But someone had to be blamed. Bethany couldn't let go of the perfect image of her mother that lived in her mind. She wouldn't let Pietro Timminolo take that away from her. And if it meant she'd have to blame the great Aston Chase for her injury, then she would.

~ 27 ~

Bethany was lost in her thoughts when there was a knock at her door. She wondered if after this evening she'd ever be able to answer the door to an unannounced visitor without shuddering. A look through the peephole revealed Richard, shifting uneasily from one foot to the other.

She opened the door to her best friend, and the smile that reached her lips was tired, but sincere.

"I heard your father leave. I thought you might need to talk," he said.

She could see he had hundreds of questions, but she could also tell he had no intention of raising them tonight. The offer was to listen, not to talk.

"My God, you're awesome," she said, taking his hand and pulling him into her apartment. "You do know it's like two A.M. You've done more than your fair share tonight."

Richard laughed. "I scoff at those who need sleep."

They both slumped onto her couch. It was only then that Bethany began to realize how much her side was hurting. Fighting with Vince earlier had been the last thing she'd needed. She considered getting an ice pack out of her freezer, but she realized she didn't have the strength.

Reading her mind as usual, Richard said, "You doing okay? I noticed you were sort of favoring one arm. Are your ribs bothering you?"

Bethany leaned her head on her friend's shoulder. "I'm doing fine," she lied. "Though, if I were you, I'd be running for the hills. Seriously, are you sure you want to hang out with the granddaughter of the infamous Pietro Timminolo? That could probably be hazardous to your health."

Richard snickered. "Nah, with grandpop trailing you all the time, I'm thinking the safest place in the city is right next to you."

Even as the words escaped his lips, she felt Richard tense. He'd realized the implications of his joke a second too late. But there was no taking it back now. Geoffrey. He'd probably disagree with Richard's assessment of Bethany's safety. Bethany simply sighed deeply and nestled closer in Richard's arms.

"Sorry, I shouldn't have said that," he said.

"That's one thing I wish I'd asked when I was there. What the hell happened that night? How did they lose track of us? How did they not see the shooter?"

"Beth," Richard began slowly, obviously reluctant to say it, "do you think it's possible they did it?"

That, Bethany realized, was a question she hadn't thought to ask herself.

"I guess anything's possible," Bethany replied. "It would be their M.O."

"On the other hand, why would Timminolo kill Geoffrey? What good could that possibly serve?" Richard pointed out.

"I don't know," Bethany admitted.

"You know, since we're already talking about it, I've got to ask you — do you have any idea at all why someone might want Geoffrey dead?"

She considered lying, but only for a few seconds. Between the fight about her bruise earlier and the trip with Frankie, it was beginning to seem pointless to try and keep anything from Richard. And she was quickly discovering that she lacked the strength to try.

It was time to tell the truth. At least a little of it.

"After freshman year of college, I decided to look into my mother's murder. I've been working with private investigators since then. Though I don't have much, I have to wonder, at least a little bit, if there was a link. If maybe the shot at Geoffrey was a warning shot for me."

Richard sat up and stared at her as if he was looking at a stranger. Her already bruised heart took another blow as she realized it wasn't the first time that night he'd done that.

"You've been investigating her murder?"

She could feel herself begin to panic. This was why she kept these things to herself. This was why she didn't let anyone near her secrets.

"Just asking some people to turn over some stones for me," she said stiffly. "You know, track down some leads."

"You've been doing this for ten years and you never told me?"

"I wanted to keep it very hush-hush. You know how the press can be."

"The press? Are you kidding?" he sputtered. "Did you think I'd go to the press?"

"No, no, of course not, it's just…" Her voice trailed off.

Richard stood. "It's just that you didn't trust me not to tell some reporter."

It's just that I didn't want to have to admit some of the things I've had to do to get the information I needed, Bethany thought. But those words would never come, she knew that. This was the best she could offer him.

"I'm sorry. It was just something I needed to do on my own."

She felt only fear as she watched Richard pace the room. She wondered what he was thinking, but knew better than to ask. Was it reasonable of her to have kept this from him? How would she have felt if the roles were reversed?

Unfortunately, she knew the answers to those questions. Richard was her rock, her constant, the person she could always rely on. If he told her he'd been keeping something like this from her, it would change everything. How could she expect him to feel any different?

His expression when he stopped pacing only made her feel worse. He was crushed, but his words carried no anger. "Are there any other secrets you're keeping from me?"

Anger, Bethany realized, would've been easier.

The question had an obvious answer, but it wasn't the truth.

She wished things could be different.

"Not unless I have some other sketchy relatives I don't know about."

Bethany hoped he believed her, but there was

something in his expression that told her otherwise. She pushed the thought aside as paranoid.

Richard sank onto the couch next to her. "You should've told me."

Now she did tell the truth. "I just didn't want you involved."

But Bethany was quickly realizing that no matter how hard she tried and how much she hoped to protect her friends, they were involved. And unless she figured out something soon, Geoffrey might not be the only one to get caught in the crossfire.

~ 28 ~

The dream was so vivid it felt more like a memory. It was summer. The dense shrubs and trees told her that as much as the heat did. Richard was at her side, holding her hand. They were in Central Park. The familiar scents of cut grass and earth enveloped her, but there was nothing soothing about them.

She quickened her steps because she could feel the presence, feel that they were being watched, followed, and the predators were closing in. She didn't know who they were, didn't know if they were circling for attack or if they were her grandfather's goons. Watching. Waiting. Protecting as only they could.

Looking at Richard she felt utter panic. They'd come after him just like they came after Geoffrey. She had to act. She had to protect him.

Bethany woke in a cold sweat, her heart pounding. She felt no comfort as she realized it had been a dream. It didn't matter. The reality was the situation could happen, probably would happen. She was living this nightmare.

In that moment, she made a decision she suspected she'd regret in the morning. Her body vibrating with energy, she grabbed the phone by her bedside. Reading from the card she'd promised herself she'd never use, she dialed.

The clock told her it was 3:45 in the morning. Still, she knew it wasn't too late to make this call.

A somewhat groggy voice answered the line. "Frankie here."

"It's Bethany." Her own voice was hushed, though there was no one around to hear it.

The sleepiness immediately vanished from his voice. "Is something wrong?"

"No. Sorry for calling at this hour."

"That's fine. Fine. No problem. What do you need, honey?"

The kindness in his voice eased Bethany's mind a little. Maybe this wasn't a huge mistake.

"Frankie, I need to finish what I started and I need to finish it before someone else gets hurt."

There was a long pause. "You want one of my boys to help you out?"

Bethany steeled herself. "No. I want you to help me."

"I can't do that. I work for your grandfather."

Of all the techniques she'd learned over the years, it was probably her father's stubbornness that best served her in times like these. "It's nothing permanent. Like I said, I want this done fast. Besides, my grandfather has you assigned to protect me already. This is really not all that different."

"Look, I don't know. I don't think that's such a

good idea."

"Meet me in my loft tomorrow at one o'clock. We'll discuss the details then."

Before he could protest, Bethany disconnected the call. She breathed out a deep sigh. Even the prospect of letting someone on the inside of her investigation was chilling. But, according to Frankie, he'd already made his way into her loft on his own. He'd already poked around and seen everything that was there. He was the only person she could bring in without having to reveal any new information. He was the perfect choice. He was the only choice.

Bethany stared out her bedroom window at the dense trees in the park below. The faint glow of the lights on the paths was barely visible, making the lush acres look even more foreboding.

Her park. Someday they'd reach a peace, but until then it remained a place of torture. Of fear. Of sadness. It was her nemesis.

~ 29 ~

Bethany had been looking forward to the paper in bed, along with coffee and a light breakfast. It was a vision that had soothed her weary soul. But it was another moment that wasn't meant to be.

The tinny electronic cords of Salsa Number Three pulled Bethany from a deep sleep, stealing any hope of a quiet morning. The phone had gone to voicemail before she could reach it.

She noticed the clock as she checked the message. Eight o'clock on a Saturday morning. Who the hell would be calling her at this hour?

The answer was even more disturbing than being awoken so abruptly. It was Heinrich. His voice was hesitant and almost sad.

"Bethany, I don't know how to say this… He's out. The hitman. The guy we brought in on Geoffrey's murder. We…" his voice trailed off. "I'm sorry. I can't leave this on your voicemail. Call me. Please."

Bethany sunk back into bed and returned the call.

"Thanks for getting back to me," he said simply.

"What happened?" Bethany asked, her voice wavering.

"The ballistics."

"They didn't match?"

The silence at the other end told her the truth. It was one thing if the evidence came back that this wasn't the guy. It was an entirely different thing if he was getting off on a technicality.

"Our people lost the bullet."

"Lost the bullet? How the hell does a bullet get lost?"

"The bullet's not in the locker it's supposed to be in. It wasn't properly checked out..." Heinrich's voice trailed off.

Though it was a naïve question, Bethany couldn't help but ask. "Do you think they're going to find it?"

"It's possible."

He didn't say anything more specific, but Bethany heard it all in his tone. This was a mob hitman. The bullet wasn't lost. It was gone.

Bethany had been around enough cases to know what that meant. "And without the ballistics you can't get the confession."

"And without a confession, we're not going to get the real story behind who ordered the hit."

"Will you still be able to get the conviction?"

Bethany could almost hear Heinrich clenching and unclenching his jaw. It was a habit with him and it never meant good news. "We've got the notes we found in his apartment. They're pretty detailed, but..."

"But that's all you have."

"The D.A.'s furious. We've dropped the murder

charges for now, while we try to build a stronger case."

"So, they released him?"

"We've still got the vice charges on him, but he's out on bail."

A sick feeling was growing in the pit of her stomach. The police had no leads on who hired the hitman and they were very close to actually losing the man who'd pulled the trigger. All of a sudden, the phone call she'd made in the middle of the night seemed less like a crazy leap of faith and more like an essential course of action.

"Bethany," Heinrich continued, "I can't tell you how sorry I am. This is just a setback. We're going to close this case."

"Thanks for letting me know what's going on. Please call me if anything else changes."

As they exchanged goodbyes, Bethany felt the tears pooling in her eyes. She put her head in her hands and cried.

~ 30 ~

Annie waited until close to noon before she made the call. She told herself she waited because she didn't want to wake her friend. The truth was she was dreading the call. But she'd made a promise. And more importantly, things were starting to look bad enough that she suspected she had very little alternative.

Bethany answered on the second ring. Though her voice sounded tired, it was clear she'd been up for a while.

"Are you psychic or do you just have my apartment bugged?" Bethany asked.

Annie laughed. "Can't it be both?"

"You do always seem to know when to call," Bethany replied. Though her voice sounded resigned, Annie was happy to hear there was still some humor in it.

More seriously, Annie explained, "A very worried police detective called me this morning."

The pause was long enough that Annie wished she was there in person to see her friend's face. "He told you about the ballistics?" she asked eventually.

"Yeah. The ballistics. He also mentioned your little field trip with Richard last night."

Bethany muttered a string of curses. "He didn't buy the story?"

Despite her nervousness, Annie laughed. "You thought he would? What the hell is going on up there?"

The story Bethany told was like nothing Annie could have imagined. Abductions. Gangsters. Family secrets. It had the makings of a Scorsese movie.

"Well it's not too hard to understand why you left the details out," Annie said.

"It's not that I don't trust the two of them, but there are leaks in the police department. Hell, there are leaks everywhere. If this got out…"

Though Bethany didn't finish the thought, it didn't take much imagination to know the truth. If this news broke, the spotlight that had been shining on Bethany for most of her life would become brighter than ever.

"This has nothing to do with Geoffrey's murder," Bethany finished. "They don't need to know about it."

Annie wanted to agree, to let the whole thing go, but the words came out before she could stop them. "Are you sure?"

There was a brief silence again before Bethany answered, "Of course I'm sure. How could my mother's family have anything to do with Geoffrey?"

Annie took a deep breath, voicing the worry that had been plaguing her since the moment she heard the details of Geoffrey's murder. "Beth, he died the same way she did. Like exactly. Same shot. Same place.

Same you sitting there through the whole thing. I mean it's downright creepy. It can't be a coincidence, can it?"

Bethany's voice broke a little when she answered. "It's a pretty extraordinary coincidence."

"If there's more information about your mother's murder, couldn't that be helpful?"

Annie could almost see Bethany shaking her head as she responded, avoiding the issue of her mother's death in the same way she had her whole life. "This isn't about my mother's murder. It's about her family. It's different."

Of course, her family was filled with gangsters and murderers, but Bethany knew that as well as Annie did.

Knowing that pushing the topic would only result in an argument, Annie said, "Can you promise me you'll think about it?"

Though Bethany agreed, Annie wondered if she would. Knowing she was already on thin ice, Annie wished she could avoid the rest of this conversation, but knew it was impossible.

"I have a confession," she began.

Bethany laughed uneasily. "Really? Because I've listened to more than my fair share of those recently."

"I called Heinrich the other day. I had some thoughts about Geoffrey. I considered going to you first, but, Bethany, you've had so much going on."

Bethany was silent on the other end of the line, waiting.

"I was thinking about their question. You know, the day after the funeral, when I was at your apartment. They asked if Geoffrey had any enemies." Annie paused, bracing for her friend's temper. "We both said he didn't and, honestly, I meant it at the time. But the truth is, there was one person."

Annie could hear Bethany shifting, probably sitting down.

"Beth, your dad hated Geoffrey. Like seriously hated him. You remember how he responded when he found out about your engagement?"

Bethany spoke through gritted teeth. "You think my father had something to do with Geoffrey's murder?"

"No, of course not. It's just, well, I realized we hadn't given them complete information. I mean, maybe it'll lead to someone else, you know?"

It was very clear that Bethany didn't know. "You seriously went behind my back and told the police you think my father had Geoffrey killed?"

Annie felt sick to her stomach. She'd known the conversation would go like this. Though Aston and Bethany had a volatile relationship, she adored her father. How could she not? He was all she had left.

"Beth, I can't stress this enough. I didn't tell them I thought Aston had anything to do with this. Actually, I told Heinrich quite emphatically that I didn't think Aston had anything to do with it. But maybe there's some connection? Maybe Aston's the link to the real killer? I mean, that could make sense, couldn't it?"

Annie could hear Bethany breathing more deeply, calming herself down. It was a move she'd seen often enough to know it meant her friend was furious.

"I understand," Bethany said, after a moment. "What did Heinrich say?"

Her tone was better, though the anger was still there. Fortunately, the conversation got easier from here.

"He said he knew about Aston and Geoffrey. Actually, he told me Aston volunteered that information the first time they spoke. Told him all about his history with Geoffrey. Aston told him that he had private investigators look into him. Did you know he did that?"

It sounded like Bethany almost laughed. "Yeah. I knew."

"Anyway, I wanted to make sure I told you what I did. I didn't want you to hear it from someone else."

By the time they exchanged goodbyes, Annie was pretty sure that everything was fine again. She'd considered telling Bethany about the rest of her conversation with Heinrich, but thought better of it.

Bethany didn't know that Annie had always distrusted Geoffrey. He'd been Ken-doll perfect, but the more they'd gotten to know him, the more Annie had suspected there was something off.

She wasn't sure what the detectives could do with that piece of information – most likely nothing – but she was sure Bethany didn't need to know the truth.

Bethany sat alone in the loft, trying to push Annie's call out of her mind. She couldn't think about her friends when she was in this place. She needed to focus on her mission, everything else had to be left at the door. But the darkness of the space was more haunting than usual.

She was pretty sure it was Superman who had the fortress of solitude where he'd depart from the world to reorganize and regroup. Originally, that was how she'd seen the loft. And she had to admit it was how she'd seen herself too.

When this had all started, she felt like a real life superhero on a quest for justice. It had been all she could do not to run out and buy a red cape.

But now, as she looked around, she wondered what you became when a quest for justice went wrong. She wasn't so far gone that she couldn't see just how crazy things had become.

Bare bulbs cast long shadows throughout the room. The light reflected sharply off the walls that she'd painted a stark, bright white.

On one wall, in its center, written in black marker, was her mother's name. Lines shot out from this origin, creating a complex web that led to other names. A web of leads, suspects, clues. More than she cared to count ended with a bold red X over the last name – a dead end. It was the chronology of a decade of failure.

The most recent chain led to Angelo Bria, and from Bria to the name Gino Niccolini with the word HITMAN under his name. To Bethany's frustration, Niccolini's name was covered with a red X. He was the man who killed her mother. She was certain of that. She'd heard it from too many sources for it not to be true. But as Bria had told her, Niccolini was dead. She'd have no chance to make him talk.

Bethany had begun her search for her mother's killer in secret – a masked woman on a quest for justice. But what had originally seemed heroic now only felt isolating.

With each new name scrawled on her wall she lost a piece of herself. Part of her feared what she'd become, feared she was somehow responsible for Geoffrey's murder. Maybe she'd asked questions of the wrong people. Perhaps her secret had been uncovered and Geoffrey's death was intended to be a warning to her, a message to stay away from the past.

She worried about her father, her friends. She wanted to stop. Actually, she wished that she wanted to stop. But she hated the questions more than she hated the fear.

She swore she'd be more careful, but she'd continue to move forward. She wasn't capable of stopping, not anymore.

So, on a new wall, dead center, was Geoffrey's name. Alone. Awaiting its own web.

She checked the clock when she heard the sound of the elevator rising to her floor. One o'clock, exactly. Frankie had obviously been telling the truth when he said he'd been in the loft before, and he was nothing if not prompt.

Bethany watched the elevator doors open to reveal her new partner. Her mother's ex-boyfriend. And hopefully the means to a very important end.

"You really did break in here with ease," she said. "I shudder to think how many others have done the same."

"I put a camera in a couple months after you bought the place. Knew it was too easy for people to break in – once they found out about it. So, I figured we'd monitor. You're the only one that's been up here."

"I guess I'm supposed to thank you for that?"

"Probably not. But the camera's just in the elevator. I wasn't spying on what you was doing in here. Just wanted to make sure it's safe."

Bethany sighed deeply at the reassurance. She hated that this was a part of her life, and hated even more that this man's help was exactly what she needed.

Instead of acknowledging her thoughts, she began with the necessary questions. "How long did you and my mother date?"

Frankie searched her face to determine what she was getting at, but seemed to find no clues.

"Rita and me, we was from the same neighborhood," he explained. "We were the same age. St. Alphonso School only had one class for each grade. So high school was the first time we didn't see each other every class. Your mother, she was a smart lady. And a really smart kid. All honors classes. I didn't do so well, myself. She offered to help me with my studying. I think I asked her out about a month after she started helping me. Musta been November – freshman year."

"You dated all through high school?"

"Yeah, she was my only girl. But we started having trouble senior year. I was working for her father more. I wanted to get married. She wouldn't have none of that talk. Said she was going places. Said she was getting out, going to the city. She was going to get away from her father. I didn't take none of that serious. Seemed crazy to me."

Frankie paused in the story. "I love my wife very much. I love my son. And I guess you don't understand this, but I got a good job, a good life. But there was something about your mother, something special. She was something special."

Bethany was comforted by the information, but she gave no indication.

Frankie continued, "I was sent to that party as a business opportunity, a chance to show what I could do. Mr. Timminolo thought I could handle it. He also thought Rita would love a night out.

"She had this dress. Cream. Kinda shiny, you know? Her hair was up and her ears sparkled with diamonds. She looked like a princess. I mean she was always beautiful, but that night was really something."

Frankie seemed lost in the memory. Bethany had never seen her mother in gowns and diamonds. They hadn't had that much money then. All that came later. But her mother had always been like a beautiful angel to her.

"The party went fine," Frankie continued. "I had to take care of some things, so I left Rita alone a while. I don't know how she met your father. I just know they was sitting together at the bar when I came up. She looked different than I'd ever seen her."

Frankie paused, as if he was unsure of the right words. He finally said, "She was really looking at him, you know, really listening to him. That's when I knew I'd lost her. I guess that's when I saw I never really had her."

Bethany let out a breath she hadn't realized she'd been holding. It was the story she'd always heard as a child. The story of love at first sight. The story of the beautiful woman who'd, by luck, met the handsome, brilliant man and was entranced. The story was true.

With all the other lies, Bethany knew this was the one thing that simply had to be true. She didn't think she could've handled it if it wasn't.

Frankie seemed to see the relief on her face. "Rita loved Aston. That I'm sure of."

Uncomfortable with his kindness, Bethany returned to her questions. "Did she tell my father who she really was?"

"No. I think she'd told him her first name, and she got his number instead of the other way around. She said her phone didn't always work so well, or something like that. I went along with it. We'd been friends too long for me not to. She hated being Rita Timminolo. I knew that. I got that."

Bethany steeled herself and stood. She slowly walked toward Frankie and gave him one final examination.

Stopping about a foot in front of him, she asked the only question that really mattered. "Will you help me, like you helped her?"

His deep brown eyes locked with hers, and Frankie spoke without a second of hesitation. "I'll do anything. You're all we got left of her."

"Good. Then I need you to help me hire a hitman."

~ 32 ~

Richard sat on the bench in front of his apartment building chastising himself. It was too dark to read his watch, but he knew it had to be after midnight. He was an idiot for sitting out here like this. A stupid, paranoid idiot.

Yet, he sat. And he knew he'd continue to sit until dawn.

He didn't know why he was acting like this. So what if Bethany had been weird all day. So what if she'd been acting strange all week. She just lost her fiancé and found out a whole bucketload of family secrets. The screw-up with the evidence in Geoffrey's murder investigation had to be brutal. That would make anyone act odd.

But it wasn't that. There was more.

She was avoiding him. She'd been avoiding him all day. It was like she was afraid to talk to him, afraid to tell him something. It was her "everything-is-fine-no-need-to-ask-questions" look that he was growing so very sick of. It seemed it was almost always followed by a huge revelation. A revelation like a nasty bruise on her ribs, her investigation into her mother's murder, or her ability to take down a man twice her size in less than a second.

She was his friend, his best friend. And she was up to something. He was sure of it.

The way he figured it, she must be sneaking out at night. It was a ridiculous conclusion to jump to, but he just had a gut feeling.

He'd prodded her a little earlier. Asked her about going somewhere for drinks. Suggested they stay in together, maybe watch a movie. There was something in the way she'd avoided him. It was nothing specific, but it was enough to convince him he was on to something.

He told himself he was sitting out there to protect her. If she was wandering around at night, she might need his help.

Even as he thought of himself swooping in to save Bethany, he remembered the stunned look on the goon's face when she'd dropped him like a rock. It was pretty stupid to think of protecting her. She could kick his ass. They both knew it.

But he was her friend. And clandestine trips in the middle of the night were dangerous. He wasn't going to let her do it alone.

Which, of course, he reminded himself, was all presuming she really was sneaking out of the apartment. Because the night was ticking away and it certainly seemed like Bethany was tucked safely in her bed.

As the reprimand was echoing through his mind, Bethany proved his paranoias well-founded. A figure cloaked entirely in bulky black clothes emerged from the side door of their building. A baseball cap covered her head and concealed her hair. She was entirely unrecognizable, but Richard knew it was her. He also knew he was probably the only person on earth who would've seen the truth.

Her normally curvy figure looked boxy and, with her hair hidden and her face shadowed, Richard was pretty sure that anyone who passed her would've sworn a man had just walked by. Even her walk looked different. It was aggressive, combative. Everything about her screamed get the hell out of my way.

Richard rose slowly from his darkened bench and began to follow from a distance. The nagging concerns that had been bothering him all day were growing worse by the second.

~ 33 ~

The hotel was seedier than Bethany had expected, and, frankly, she hadn't expected much. She could see Frankie knew what he was doing. This was a place where there could be sounds of a struggle and no one would think twice. It was a place where people went to remain completely anonymous.

The key she held was number 405. Bethany walked up four flights of shabby stairs, ignoring the stench of mildew and misery. As she walked down the hall, she could hear murmurs coming from the first room. It sounded like a fight. Cries escaped from a second room. Most likely they were sounds of pleasure, though Bethany found it very disturbing just how hard it was to tell. The third room was hers.

The key provided access to a room with peeling wallpaper and a sagging double bed. Two mirrors, one at the foot of the bed and the other at the head, were either trying to make the room seem larger or provide enjoyment. Bethany shook the latter image from her mind, though the sounds from the room next door made that difficult.

She managed to find a spot in a corner near the cracked, cloudy window where she was out of the line of the mirrors. It was then that she pulled the mask on. It was time to get into character. He'd be here any minute.

She was leaning up against the wall in the corner when there were two sharp knocks at the door. She braced herself and waited.

After a pause, the door opened and he entered without a word, closing and locking the door behind him.

She recognized him immediately.

He still looked a little small to her. Fit, but skinny. Shorter than her by at least a couple inches. His hair was combed back, much more neatly than the last time she saw him. It looked even darker now, a stark jet black. She took all of these features in almost automatically, but it was his eyes she fixated on.

They were a dark brown, almost black, so probing that it seemed he didn't blink. He stared back at her, clearly assessing her in the same way she was assessing him.

He was a killer. She could see that almost immediately. He was cold, calculated, vicious. He had no remorse. Possibly no feelings at all.

And this iceberg murdered her fiancé.

"You called me about a job?" Tony asked.

"Yeah, glad you could make it," Bethany replied. Her voice was the electronic voice of the mask, making it impossible to tell if she was a man or woman.

The killer seemed surprised, maybe even insulted.

"Masks? Voice changers? You can trust me. I believe in complete confidentiality."

As the words were escaping his lips, Bethany heard the sound of a key in the lock of the hotel room door. Both she and Tony exchanged accusatory glances.

As Bethany prepared for the worst, Frankie appeared.

"What the hell are you doing here?" she snapped, before she could stop herself.

"I was checking out the hallway. It's all clear."

"It was never the agreement that you be here for this," Bethany growled.

Tony's eyes narrowed in suspicion. "Who's this guy?"

"I'm just here to make sure business goes well. If there's no problems, I'll stay right here in the doorway."

Though the explanation seemed to be answering Tony's question, Bethany knew it was really designed to address her concerns. While she didn't want a partner, it didn't look like Frankie was going to give her much of a choice, which meant playing along.

Frankie closed the door and then leaned up against the wall, as if this whole scenario was the most normal thing that had ever happened. Of course, Bethany realized, in his work, maybe it was a normal situation. But that was a concern for another time.

She pushed on. "I think you were telling me about your confidentiality policy."

Tony looked cautiously back at Frankie. After a moment, he turned his back on the mobster to continue his discussion with his would-be employer. "My clients have the benefit of my complete silence. Nobody knows who I work for."

"That's a shame," Bethany replied. "Because I think

that's just the sort of thing that will make our friendship difficult."

As she spoke, she stepped away from the wall, approaching Tony. "You see," she continued. "I've got the money right over there on the bed. That's the price for a man's head. Only, here's the thing, I'm not entirely sure of the man's name."

"If you don't know the guy's name, how do you expect me to do the job?"

"I have a description," she explained, taking another small step closer. "And I'm positive you know who the guy is."

The hitman took half a step back. He was looking at her the way someone would look at a crazy person. He thought she was a killer. It was untrue, but she wondered if he was right about the crazy part.

"Look," he said, "I've already got some troubles with the police. It sounds like this job's got too many complications."

Bethany's eyes only hardened at his response. "I think you need to hear me out. There's no reason at all why you and I can't do business."

"Well, then, tell me the job," he replied, trying not to sound as nervous as he clearly felt.

"I'd like to know a little about your credentials first. Just confirm some rumors I've heard."

Tony nodded.

"You did the hit on the doctor who was killed in the hospital parking garage?" Bethany asked, using information Frankie had provided her earlier in the day.

He looked at her suspiciously. "What do you need to know about that for?"

Bethany inched even closer. "Just want to know what I'm paying for."

He shrugged. "Yeah. That was me."

"How about the killing in the park a couple of weeks ago? The mayoral candidate." Bethany struggled to keep her voice cold and even. It had to sound like she was interested in the work, not the details.

Tony ran a hand through his hair, clearly uncomfortable with how close she was standing. He took another small step back. "That's the reason for those legal troubles I mentioned," he replied with a chuckle.

Bethany laughed with him at first, but in a flash the laughter stopped. Before Tony could even register the change, she flew into action, twisting his right arm around his back and spinning him toward the door. She caught just a glimpse of her big bodyguard lurking. He seemed amused.

She swept Tony's legs out from under him and sent him chin first into the floor. Still gripping his arm behind his back, Bethany dug her knee into his spine. She pulled on the arm, just enough that he could feel the pressure. A separated shoulder was her next threat. By now Tony would be feeling enough pain that he'd be disinclined to invite more.

"I've got a simple question for you. You get one chance to answer," Bethany said, pulling his arm just a bit tighter. "You tell me who hired you to kill Geoffrey Quinn and I won't rip you into tiny pieces."

"You're assuming they wouldn't tear me into tiny pieces, too," Tony replied, trying to sound tough, but only sounding breathless.

"No, I'm assuming you'll have a head start to hide from them. And I assure you, he won't be alive long enough to make your life difficult."

"How do I know I can trust you?"

"You don't," Bethany snarled, pulling the arm further. She could feel the pressure building in the joint. It was just at the edge. He had to know that as well as she did.

"Tell me who hired you," Bethany ordered.

"It's not that simple."

"Make it that simple."

Tony cringed as she pulled his arm tighter.

"I got the call two weeks before the job," he sputtered. "I was told what night to do it. I was told how. The park. He told me where they'd be."

"How the hell did he know that?" Bethany asked. The growl in her voice was all but lost. She hadn't even known where they were going to be that night. She hadn't even known they were going out to dinner. Yet someone told him two weeks ahead of time.

"I don't know," Tony insisted. "He told me the park. Sent me a map with the exact location. Told me the time. It was supposed to be a single gunshot to the head. He was focused on that. It had to be done that way. It was significant to him."

Yeah, it was significant, Bethany thought sarcastically, but she kept the comment to herself.

"Who paid you?" she asked instead.

"I don't know."

"Don't lie," Bethany snapped.

"The money was wired to my account. I've got no idea who wired it. It was a big paycheck though."

"I don't fucking care how much you got paid. Who paid you?"

"Like I said, the money was wired."

Bethany snorted. "That can be traced."

"I tried to trace the money. It was the sort of job that I knew I'd want to know. But it was a dead end," his voice almost squeaked.

"The phone calls?"

"The number was one of those disposable cells you can buy. I couldn't trace who'd bought it."

"I want your account number. The account they wired the money to. How much was sent. And when." Bethany looked up at Frankie. "Do you think you can write this down?"

Frankie nodded, taking a pad and pen out of his jacket pocket.

"You want my account number?" Tony repeated.

"Don't repeat the question, moron. Answer it."

"What could that possibly tell you?"

"You said the wire was untraceable. I'd like a chance to make sure of that."

"Fine. Fine. No problem," Tony replied. He blurted out the information.

As he did, Bethany eased off his shoulder just a little.

"One final question, Tony," Bethany said. "Are you right-handed?"

"Yeah."

Bethany suspected he regretted the answer almost before he gave it, but she'd caught him off-guard.

He screamed in agony as she expertly pulled his arm back and fully separated his shoulder. She then dropped the arm, allowing it to flop to the floor. And with one swift stamp of her heavy black work boot, she crushed Tony's right hand.

"Sorry," she said, walking towards the door. "I just don't approve of the business you do. I have to make sure you're out of commission for a bit, even if it's temporary. Thanks for the info."

~ 34 ~

It had been too long since she'd gone into the hotel. The place looked shady, really shady. But Richard could see there was no way to get inside without risking running into her. And he was sure he didn't want her to know he'd followed her, at least not yet.

He was glancing nervously at his watch when he saw her. She was no longer alone. It was a moment before Richard recognized her companion and when he did his stomach lurched. Bethany was meeting Frankie Lioni at a seedy hotel in the middle of the night? This was bad. This was very, very bad.

As he watched Bethany and Frankie walking back toward her apartment, he slowly began to understand.

Bethany Chase wasn't who she appeared to be.

~ 35 ~

Bethany's Sunday morning began much the same way as Saturday. She was awoken by the sound of a ringing phone. The caller ID told her it was her father who was invading her sleep. She considered letting the call go to voicemail, but thought better of it. Might as well get this over with.

Her voice sounded thick with sleep when she answered, which yielded an unexpected response.

"I'm sorry, did I wake you? It's after eleven. I just assumed. I can call back later."

The tone of her father's voice was shockingly passive and apologetic. Bethany suddenly felt guilty for ignoring his calls.

She sat up in bed, shaking off the sleepiness. "No, Dad, it's fine. I just had a late night. I'm awake. I'm glad you called."

It almost sounded like Aston sighed in relief. "I'd like to talk about things."

Bethany was quick to agree. "I'd rather do it in person, though. Could you meet me for lunch today?"

This time Bethany was certain she heard a sigh of relief. Everything about her father's voice told her she'd put this off long enough. Maybe too long. It was time to discuss things.

It was a little over an hour later when she headed out of her apartment. She was surprised to find Richard in the hallway. He was just getting off the elevator, coffee in hand. He looked like hell.

"Hey, sunshine. You have a little too much fun last night?" she joked.

It was a few seconds before she realized the flat look in his eyes was for real.

"Are you okay?" she asked. He didn't look okay. In fact, she didn't think he'd ever looked less okay.

Richard nodded, but somehow, the gesture seemed sarcastic. "I'm fine. Just a late night."

"Are you sure?"

He only shrugged in response. "Where are you off to?"

Though his words were casual, there was nothing normal about the question. Nothing normal about him.

"To meet my dad for lunch," Bethany explained, resisting the urge to ask him again if he was okay. "I think I'm ready to talk to him about family matters."

"I'd like to talk to you later," he said abruptly, as if he'd just made a decision.

Bethany couldn't tear her eyes from his. So distant. So strange. "Of course. I'll call my dad and postpone. We can talk now. What's going on?"

Richard shook his head. "Later. Dinner," he added

absently. "Around seven?"

A sense of dread descended upon Bethany. What the hell was going on here? "Really, Richard, now is fine," she said again, reaching into her purse to pull out her cell phone. "Just let me call my dad."

Richard put his hand over hers. "No. Later," he said firmly.

And without further explanation, he slipped past her and into his apartment, leaving her in the hallway, holding a cell phone and wondering if she was having some kind of nightmare.

Bethany spent the entire walk to the restaurant trying to guess what was going on with Richard. She almost called Annie twice, but discovered she was afraid to. She didn't know what she'd do if there really was something wrong.

She pushed the questions to the back of her mind as she entered the restaurant. She had to discuss long hidden family secrets and mobsters. The day was getting better by the second.

The hostess escorted Bethany to a private room where her father was sitting alone at a large round table reading the menu. He looked up and smiled a greeting.

He looked so tired. His thin face looked more gaunt than usual and his hawk-like eyes clouded. He looked almost sick.

"Are you okay, Dad?" Bethany asked, the moment they were alone.

He smiled a weak smile. "I'm fine. Healthy as a horse. I think you'll be stuck with me for a very long time to come."

Bethany took his hand in her own. His hands were

broader than hers, but they had the same slender fingers that would make a pianist jealous. She studied them when she spoke, because the words were hard for her to say.

"You know I love you, Dad. I want you around for a long time. You're all I have."

Having said the words, she looked up and met his eyes. To her amazement, her strong, powerful father looked insecure.

Before he could pat her on the hand and dismiss her sentiment, Bethany pressed on, "I'm not saying you did everything right. I'm not saying we haven't fought constantly since the day Mom died. But you've always been there. And I know you'll always be there. I depend on that. I love you, Dad."

Tears welled up in his eyes, causing him to look away. But as he did, he said, "I love you too, honey. I'm so sorry I didn't tell you about the Timminolos."

Her anger all but forgotten, Bethany replied, "Could you tell me about them now?"

~ 36 ~

Aston knew it was time to let his daughter know the truth about her mother's secrets and her father's failings. Enough time had passed. Too much, in fact. The memories replayed like a movie, which made the story easy to tell.

"I'm not sure where to begin," he said honestly.

Bethany offered a supportive smile. "Why don't you just start at the beginning?"

"I was only a boy at the time. Fresh out of graduate school. My head filled with ideas and my pockets completely devoid of the money needed to make those ideas a reality. I was attending the party in the hopes of finding some financial backing so I could start my own company. I wanted a place where I could use my own ideas and not have to run everything by fifty small-minded executives before they could become a reality."

He looked at his daughter to be certain she was listening. She recognized the story of course. She'd heard it a hundred times before.

"It was late in the night, and there were two guys who liked my ideas. We hadn't discussed budget, but they thought it was worth talking things through further. So when I headed to the bar, I was looking for a Scotch, a nice Chivas Regal, to celebrate. And that was when I saw her. The most beautiful woman I'd ever seen. Raven black hair, beautiful olive skin and sparkling green eyes. You know, she was stunning."

"Yes, she was," Bethany agreed.

"She took my breath away." Aston closed his eyes for a moment, and he could still see her sitting at the bar, absently stirring the ice in her drink. "I knew right away that business was done for the night. I had to talk to her. I had to meet her. Something about her..." His voice trailed off. "It defies explanation. It was perfection. She was The One. I had no doubt at all.

"She introduced herself simply as Rita. We were lost in conversation when a burly young man with a thick accent joined us."

"Frankie Lioni?"

Aston smiled. "Did you get some of the story from him?"

He was glad to see Bethany nod in response.

"Frankie was very protective and more than a little jealous. I could tell right away he'd escorted Rita to the party. I didn't like him at the time, for obvious reasons, but Frankie's a good man. I don't think anyone in the world would've done more to protect your mother than him. You know, he's the only one she kept in touch with from the old neighborhood."

Bethany nodded again, but she remained silent.

"Anyway, I didn't notice much about Frankie at the time. I was so afraid he was going to take Rita away before I'd learn how to contact her. But she controlled the situation with that clever grace I'd come to expect from her. She patiently introduced us, pretending to be oblivious to the tension. And then she asked me for my business card. She promised to call. I think she said something about it being difficult for me to call her. I don't really remember that part. I understand now that was when the secrets began.

"As she was leaving, I realized I only knew her first name. I called after her to ask. That's the one thing I truly regret about that night. She lied, of course. Gave me that fake last name. I sometimes think if I'd only been more patient, she might've told me the truth in time. But once she'd lied there was no turning back. Or at least that's what she thought."

"You couldn't have known."

"No, I couldn't have, but that doesn't mean I don't regret asking the pointless question. I think I was scared she wouldn't call." Aston sighed. "But there's nothing I can do about that now. As you know, she called me. We got together a number of times. I asked her about Frankie. She said he was an old friend, nothing more. I know now they did actually date, and were dating when Rita and I met."

Bethany smiled. "He tells the same story you do, Dad. He knew. He understood."

Aston was relieved to hear the gentle support in his daughter's voice. The story was only going to get worse.

"We'd been dating about six months when she moved into the city. Not long after that I proposed. But you know all this. The whole time we were dating, she never mentioned her parents. I figured once we were engaged she'd introduce us. It was about a month after our engagement when I finally asked.

"I should've known it was a lie. I knew her well enough at that point to see it. There was just a little too much detail to the story. It sounded a little too polished. The pain in her voice, a little false. But I took her at her word."

"You had no reason to think she'd lie about her parents being dead," Bethany insisted.

Aston shook his head. "If I can impart upon you only one lesson it would be this – trust your instincts. Don't let reason get in the way. We're all born with lie detectors, and the mistake most people make is they ignore them."

"Some people just don't want you to know the truth," Bethany replied.

For a moment, Aston wondered if Bethany was speaking of herself as much as her mother. He answered, thinking of both of them, "Some people are eaten alive by the lies they tell."

Bethany avoided his gaze, instead focusing on her fork.

"Unfortunately, Rita wasn't the only one who was keeping secrets. The two men I'd met at the party that night – one of them turned out to be a dead end. But the second was more promising. He worked with a group of investors out of Brooklyn who had plenty of cash to get the business up and running. It would be my business to run as I pleased. They would just be the money men."

This was the part of the story that would be new to his daughter. As he'd expected, her eyes drifted back toward his, as if she could sense the foreboding in his voice.

"I knew it was too good to be true," he explained.

"How could I not? I have one guy who can't even front half the money I need and the other guy can give me everything I want and more. How's that not too good to be true? But I have this new girlfriend and I want to be a big shot, so I agree. I take the money. I quit my job. I spend my non-compete period setting up the new company. And when the six months are up I'm ready to hit the ground running. With the front money we're able to start fast. And, as you know, we had that new chip on the market within a year. The money starts flowing in and that's when my investors stop by for a little meeting."

The words caught in his mouth and Aston wondered if he really could finish the story. His beautiful, sweet daughter was staring up at him expectantly. Her face wasn't so different from when she was little, sitting with him reading a book, listening to the story, anxiously anticipating the ending, begging him to read just one more chapter. Though she said nothing, he could hear her tiny voice in his head. *Then what happened, Daddy?*

Reluctantly, he continued, "They had five duffle bags full of cash. I don't remember how much it was. Hundreds of thousands of dollars. They told me how excited they were that sales were up and now they needed to use their little investment property for the business. You see, they didn't care how I ran my business. They didn't care what my business did. They only cared that I provided them with a front. Then their cash could come through my business and back into their pockets."

"They were laundering money?"

"Not yet. They were telling me that was what they were going to do. They even had a scrawny little guy in glasses. He was my new accountant. They told me to consider it a gift. A prize for one year in the business."

"What did you do?"

"I didn't argue with them. You don't argue with guys like that. I considered just giving them the business, going back to my old job. I wondered if maybe they'd let me do that. But when I got home that night, your mother told me she was pregnant. That's when I knew I had to stay where I was. I was going to be a father. I didn't have the luxury of playing chicken with a bunch of mobsters."

Bethany stared at her father with an expression of confusion and surprise. He was actually just relieved it wasn't a look of judgment, at least not yet.

"I hate to admit this, but life pretty much went on that way for years. Eddie the accountant did whatever he did. And I ran my business. They were true to their word; my profits were my own. Whatever I made off the business was mine to keep, and the money laundering scam ran off to the side. But the more successful I got, the more concerned I became with their presence. We were the fastest growing electronics company in the country, and that meant the IRS was all over us.

"But even with that, things would've continued in the same way, if they hadn't started pushing me again."

Aston shivered at the memory of the day it all came crashing down. "I was visited by one of the original investors on a Wednesday night after the close of business. He told me they were going to be expanding the drug imports, and I'd have to allow him to have more of his men on site to take care of it."

"You were importing drugs for them?" Bethany gasped.

"It seems they were using the business to import

drugs. I had no idea. We were a huge outfit by then. I wasn't monitoring the boxes that came through our doors. It would've been simple to slip crates through, but they wanted more. I was furious. It was one thing with the money laundering, but this was too much. I had a little girl. I couldn't be supporting drug running. I told him that. And he laughed at me. Then I told him I'd turn them in. I'd tell the Feds. And he laughed again. He told me to stop whining and advised me that I'd have new employees the next day. They'd be his people and I should provide them with whatever they needed to deal with the shipments."

Aston put his head in his hands. He'd sat in his office staring out at the city for almost four hours that night, ashamed to go home. Four hours trying to decide what to do, what was best for his family. And after all that time he was no closer to an answer. That was why he knew he needed to talk to his wife.

He told the rest of the story with his eyes focused on his plate.

"I went home to your mother and I told her the whole story. The deeper this got the more certain I became that it would all end with my arrest. Likely the only way to stay out of jail was to come forward before I was discovered.

"I'll never forget the look on your mother's face. There was a deep sadness, a sort of resignation. It was well after midnight when I finished telling her the story. And that was why I was so shocked when she got up, picked up the phone and made a call. She said only one thing and it was so stunning I'll never forget it. She said, 'Papa, I need you to come.' That was all. Then she rejoined me on the couch and told me everything."

37

Bethany sat in amazed silence as her father's story unfolded. Three days ago her family had seemed normal. There wasn't even a shadow of this deception. Not even a tiny flicker. Though part of her begged for her father to stop speaking, she allowed him to continue.

"That was the first time I ever met Pietro Timminolo," Aston explained. "He was a heartier man then. Never tall, but a big man. Stocky, impressive. He has your mother's eyes – I guess you know that – those penetrating eyes."

He stopped for a minute and seemed almost confused. "I can't believe I never realized it before. You three have the same eyes. I mean, Pietro's are just so different. There's none of the softness, the kindness, but they're the same."

He paused long enough that Bethany wondered if he expected her to say something.

When her father spoke again, it was clear his mind was back in that night. "Your mother was respectful at first.   Practically kissing his ring.   Seriously, I was waiting for that. But Pietro would have none of it. He insulted her.   Called me a worthless fool, which of course I was."

Bethany tried to interrupt, but Aston stopped her. "No, honey. I was a fool. And she suffered for it. But she was amazing. Once it was clear he wasn't going to accept her reverence, she dropped the act. She met him with defiance, told him he was obligated to help us, if not for her then for you."

Bethany thought of all the times Frankie told her she was like her mother. She was starting to understand what that really meant.

"Pietro took issue with her reference to you. I think he was trying to use my mistake to maneuver his way into your life. Your mother was vicious with him. She told him he'd made his choices and she'd never allow you to be corrupted by them."

Aston shook his head. "You see, this is why I was so reluctant to tell you anything about her family. She hated them. She told him, and I remember this very distinctly, that she'd grown up in a world of deceit, blackmail and murder and she'd make sure you'd never know that world."

Bethany listened with a heavy heart, her mother's lost words hanging in the air. What would Rita Chase think of her daughter's life? What would she think of the hatred that consumed her? Of the violence she used to gain information? Of the web of lies she'd created in her name?

She knew what her mother would've thought. It would've broken her heart.

"Honey, I'm sorry, this is too much," Aston said suddenly.

Bethany looked up, his words shaking her out of her own internal battle. "What? No, please, go on."

Aston reached out and brushed tears from her cheeks. Bethany didn't know what was more bizarre – the sweetness of the gesture, or the fact she'd been crying and didn't even know it. Maybe Aston was right. Maybe this was too much. But she couldn't bring herself to admit it.

"Please, Dad, go on." As she spoke the words, Bethany heard the defiance in her voice. It was her mother's voice. She realized that now.

"Your grandfather took all the information from me about my investors. We drove to the office and went through the books together. He told me he'd take care of it. I had no idea what that meant. And, to be honest, I was just so relieved someone was dealing with things that I moved on with my life."

"What did Pietro do?"

"Rita told me later he bought the investors out, provided them with a similarly protected company to use as a front and paid them certain 'moving expenses.' That was the last I ever heard of them."

"That was it? They just let you off the hook?"

Aston shrugged. "I imagine Pietro paid them very well for their moving expenses."

"Pietro took this trouble off of your hands and placed it on another business?"

"Yes," Aston sighed. "I'm afraid that was exactly what happened. It was a smaller company, a company that was already indebted to the Timminolo family. Your grandfather basically gave it to my investors."

"You didn't care that you were just passing your

own trouble on to someone else?" Bethany accused.

"The guy was already in trouble. What difference did it make if the trouble was from Pietro or from these other guys? I didn't get him in trouble."

"Does that help you sleep at night?"

Aston looked away in shame. "No. It doesn't. But I believe I had no other choice."

Bethany considered laying into her father further. But before she could, a thought popped into her head. "How long before Mom's death did this 'buy out' occur?"

"Bethany, I know what you're thinking. There was no connection. I had people look into it. Your grandfather had people look into it. There was nothing. We would've found it if there was."

As much as she wanted to believe him, Bethany knew she'd need to find this out for herself. "How long?"

"Three months," he replied with resignation.

"Three months? Three months! And you really expect me to believe there was no connection?"

"You can believe anything you want, baby. Every rock has been turned over. There was no connection. Don't you think that was our first assumption? Don't you think we were praying that was the answer? It wasn't them. It was never them."

Bethany merely nodded. She'd believe it when she saw for herself.

38

Bethany spent the afternoon sparring with Master Jung. One-on-one, just the two of them. Sessions like this were her favorites. She could fight without the mask and all the heavy gear. She donned lightweight workout clothes that allowed complete freedom of movement. The result was higher kicks, smoother punches, and generally more fluid motion.

"Stop obsessing about your ribs," the Master ordered as he landed a punch on her shoulder. "You are losing your form. If you cannot fight without the injury controlling your mind, then you should not fight."

"I'm not obsessing," Bethany snapped back, though she knew the critique was valid. She forced herself to straighten up properly to keep her guard where it needed to be.

"Better. You keep hunching over and we'll see your picture with a big black eye on the front page of the

Post."

"That's not funny," Bethany replied, landing three rapid punches and attempting to sweep his legs.

The Master stumbled, but didn't lose his balance. "Good, good," he observed.

He responded with a kick near her injured ribs. Predictably, Bethany dropped her guard to protect the injury, leaving her face open. The Master followed with an immediate punch to the face. Despite the gloves, the blow was stunning. Bethany dropped back a step to regain her balance.

"Jesus, aren't you supposed to pull the punches when you have an open shot like that?" she muttered, shaking the cobwebs from her head.

"Aren't you supposed to keep your guard up? A clean shot to the head can be devastating. Consider that a little reminder."

Bethany attacked with vigor, driven by both the mistake and her embarrassment. A round kick to the head was swatted down, as were the series of punches to the face and midsection.

"Have the ribs been reinjured?" The Master asked, seemingly unfazed by the onslaught.

"Stop obsessing about my ribs," Bethany grumbled, dropping back to regain focus and balance and reconsider the method of attack.

"Not until you do," he replied, taking another shot in the direction of her ribs, followed by a quick shot to her head. This time Bethany reacted properly, deflecting both blows.

"Better," he critiqued. Then he repeated the question, "Were they reinjured?"

"They're just getting better more slowly than I'd like. I think working out might be aggravating the injury a bit. The twisting makes the pain worse."

"You've been icing?"

"Yeah," Bethany replied, unleashing another attack, this one beginning with a series of shots to the head and ending with a kick landed perfectly to the Master's right hamstring, causing his leg to buckle. When he fell to the floor, Bethany stood over him triumphant.

"Very good," he said, standing and bowing to his opponent. "Now we stretch and cool down. And then you go on with your life. Have you been fighting outside of here? Too much activity is probably worsening the injury."

Bethany joined her trainer on the floor and began to stretch out her legs and back. "I've had a couple of run-ins. Things that couldn't be avoided."

"Any problems?"

Bethany smiled. "No. Both encounters went well."

The Master nodded and turned his focus to the stretching. After a few minutes of silence, Bethany spoke.

"You don't approve of my decision to find my mother's killer." It was a statement, not a question. They both knew it was the truth.

"Nothing good can come of this obsession. Your mother is gone. Even your success in this will not change that."

"Someone should get justice for her."

Without looking up, the Master said the words Bethany didn't want to admit. "You seek revenge for yourself. Not justice for your mother. Your mother would not have traded your peace of mind for 'justice,' as you call it."

"Someone killed her, murdered her in cold blood."

"In front of her young daughter," he added.

"They've gotten away with murder for more than two decades. That's wrong."

"They may get away with murder forever. You may never find them."

"I'll find them." Even as she said the words, Bethany was surprised by the venom in her own voice.

Her trainer, however, showed barely a ripple of emotion. "At what price? The rage eats you alive. Your quest feeds the rage. Your mother would have wanted better for you."

"You don't know anything about my mother," she snapped. But she knew it was a lie. He was right. She'd been thinking the same thing since lunch. It was the reason she'd brought the topic up in the first place.

"I did not know your mother, but I know you. And I know your father. If you are so sure she would approve of your choice, why do you keep it from your father?"

Bethany tried to keep the shock from her face. "Why would you think I haven't told him?"

Her trainer offered a rare smile. "I am not a complete fool. You have not told your friends either. Do they even know about your training?"

It was obvious that decades of working together had taught the man more than she would've expected.

"They know how often I come here to work out."

"They think you are doing Pilates or some other foolishness. They do not really understand your training. They have no idea. If what you do is not wrong, why do you keep it a secret?"

Bethany considered avoidance, but realized she was just too tired. She thought of Richard's expression when he'd seen her take down Vince the thug, the look on his face when she evaded the police interrogation.

"They wouldn't understand."

The Master continued his stretching as if the conversation was insignificant. "They are your friends, yes?"

Bethany nodded, no longer able to focus on any of her own stretching.

"They care about you?"

Again Bethany nodded.

The Master stopped and looked her square in the eye. "Then they will understand."

After the whole fiasco with her grandfather Richard had come back to her. He'd clearly been overwhelmed, but he'd come back. And when she'd told him about her mother, about her search, he'd been upset, but not in the way she'd expected. He was upset she'd kept it from him. He didn't try to talk her out of it, didn't try to change anything. Maybe Richard would understand.

Bethany thought back to the night so many years earlier when he'd told her how he really felt about her. That night, she'd wanted to tell him the truth. To tell him her plans. To tell him she was going to find her mother's killer through whatever means necessary.

But it had been a moment to simply admit how much she wanted to be with him. To tell him she loved him. Just a moment. Not a soliloquy. And the truth was, someone like her could never have a moment like that. She'd either smother it with an avalanche of confessions, or she'd have to keep these enormous secrets forever.

Maybe it was time to reach out and tell Richard the truth. Maybe he'd understand. Maybe he'd still be willing to be a part of her life.

Or maybe he'd leave her forever.

He'd made a promise to her all those years ago. It

had been a crazy thing to say at the time. She'd always wondered if part of him actually knew the truth, understood that she was turning him down because of the secrets and not because of any of the stupid reasons Bethany had given him.

She wondered if it was true. And more importantly, she wondered if she was brave enough to trust that it was.

~ 39 ~

When Richard had called that afternoon to set up dinner, Bethany told herself the plans were good news. It was a fancy restaurant. Not the kind of place you went to if you were going to make a scene. Obviously, there was no problem.

And she'd almost believed it. That was until the hostess led them away from the main dining room to a private room in the back. In an instant, Bethany went from hoping things were okay to knowing they were anything but.

They were led inside the small room with a single table. Two martinis were already waiting. Bethany wondered if it would be inappropriate to down hers in one gulp and order another before the hostess left.

Once they were alone behind closed doors, Richard very formally pulled out her chair before taking his own seat.

He picked up his glass and offered a stiff smile.

"A toast," he said. "To old friends. There's nothing better than being with someone who knows everything about you."

Bethany suppressed a shudder.

"To old friends," she said simply, raising her glass.

The silence hung for a moment before she could bring herself to ask, "Rich, what's going on?"

Putting down his drink, Richard met her eyes with such intensity she immediately looked away. His voice was calm when he spoke, though the question was anything but. "Where were you last night?"

Her heart stopped. He knew.

But even as the belief crossed her mind she rejected it. How could he possibly know?

"What do you mean?" she stalled.

"It's not a difficult question. Where were you last night?"

He couldn't possibly know, she repeated to herself.

"I left your place, went home. I actually climbed into bed pretty early. I was beat."

Bethany could hear the lie in her words. Her voice sounded hesitant, softer than usual. Richard was certain to pick up on that.

She finally met his eyes again, hoping to see concession and trust, but they were still blank and cold.

"So, you didn't leave the building after midnight and meet Frankie Lioni in a seedy hotel."

She couldn't even attempt to hide her shock.

Before she could sputter an excuse, Richard continued his interrogation, "Why are you meeting a mobster in the middle of the night and lying to your best friend?"

Her voice shaky and soft, she said, "I don't know what you're talking about."

"What?" Richard practically screamed. "You're still lying? I saw you with my own damn eyes, Bethany! Do you think I'm so stupid you can talk your way out of this?"

The right thing to do was to tell the truth, spill everything and beg for pardon. But that was the exact opposite of what she did.

"You were watching me? You followed me?" she snapped. "How dare you!"

"How dare I?" Richard growled back. "You. Are. Lying. To. Me. I haven't done anything!"

"You followed me! You spied on me!"

Richard's face was a fiery red, and he was clutching the table with such force that it seemed he was seriously considering throwing it across the room. That was why his soft voice sounded so strange when he finally spoke.

"Recently, I've seen a lot of strange things. You've got secrets, Beth. Unexplained bruises. Long lost relatives. And the more you tell me, the more I can see there's a lot you aren't telling me. I'm not proud of what I did. But I'm glad I did it. Because the secrets need to stop."

His tone was having the desired effect. Her anger was fading, leaving behind painful sadness and shame for lying about it all this time.

"And what if they don't?" Bethany asked.

"If the secrets don't stop, I don't think we can continue being friends."

"So, this is an ultimatum?" Though she'd intended a challenge, the retort sounded more like a concession.

Richard only shook his head sadly. "If we're lying, the friendship I thought I had will disappear. If you don't understand that, it's already gone."

Bethany considered his argument. He was right, of

course. There was no excuse for trying to dupe him after she'd been caught.

It had been so long since she'd decided her quest was more important than his friendship, more important than her love for him. But with everything she'd seen in the past few weeks, she'd have to be a complete idiot not to see the value of what she had in this room.

Fearful of his response, Bethany began her confession. "I'm investigating my mother's murder," she said.

Richard ran a frustrated hand through his hair. "I know that. You told me about that."

"No, I mean that's what I was doing. That's what I'm often doing," she added, almost under her breath.

"What could you possibly have been doing in that hotel to investigate your mother's death?" Richard's face was looking less angry and much more concerned. There was a fear now. And it seemed to Bethany it was fear that he already knew the truth.

"Frankie arranged for us to meet someone who had information on Geoffrey's murder."

"Who?"

Bethany balked at the question. It was one thing to confess. It was another to allow him anywhere near this horrific part of her life. "Look, I told you the where and the why. The who doesn't mean anything. The who will only get you involved. I don't want you involved."

"It's someone I'd know?" he realized.

"Rich, I don't want you involved with this," Bethany repeated.

"Why? Because it's dangerous? No shit it's dangerous! That's why you shouldn't be doing it by yourself."

"Frankie's helping now. You need to stay out of this."

He met her eyes aggressively. "No."

Bethany scowled at him. He was just being stubborn now. "What do you mean no?"

Richard continued calmly, "You asked me to back off. I'm saying – No. I won't. Somehow I was too stupid to see what you were doing all these years. Now that I know what's going on I refuse to walk away. So, the answer to your question is no."

"It wasn't a question," Bethany stated through clenched teeth. "It was a statement. You need to stay out of this."

"I'm not giving up that easily."

Bethany considered arguing with him, but instead decided to take a different approach. "I'm not going to fight about this. You won't change my mind."

A small smile crossed Richard's lips at the declaration. He matched her smug tone and declared, "Okay then, I'll undertake my own investigation. I'd rather avoid staying out all night following you around, but if you can survive on that little sleep so can I."

Bethany's eyes widened at the threat. "You wouldn't dare."

"I'd dare. You know that as well as I do."

He'd backed her into a corner. A dark scary corner. Bethany realized she had two options. Tell Richard the truth – the whole truth. Or risk having him following her around.

Between those two there was only one answer. The alternative was just too dangerous.

"Tony Mirriani," she said, without any further explanation.

Richard obviously recognized the name, but couldn't place it. "What does he have to do with your mother's death?"

"Possibly nothing. That's what we're trying to figure out."

Suddenly, Richard sat forward, recognition in his eyes. "The hitman? Of course. You went to *talk* to the hitman? You went to a seedy hotel to chat with a hitman?" he continued sharply. "A place like that, anything could happen and nobody would step in to help you."

Even as he said the words, Bethany could see the pieces start to fall into place. The dark shadow in his eyes. The fear.

He sat back now, clearly thinking, gathering himself. His voice was so soft when he finally spoke that Bethany wondered if he was really just talking to himself.

"The martial arts when you were a kid. The private sessions in college. All those times you seemed so worn out for no reason. That awful bruise. You didn't go to that hotel to *talk* to the hitman, did you?"

Bethany wanted to answer. She wanted to explain. But she had no words. This was what she'd spent years trying to hide. She was going to lose him.

"Did you hurt him?" he asked, plainly not sure he wanted to know the answer.

"He's going to be fine," she replied without meeting Richard's eyes.

Richard's voice gained strength, making it clear he was no longer buying her evasion. "What did you do to him?"

"I applied the right pressure to convince him to tell me who hired him," she explained, trying desperately to separate her mind from this situation, distance herself from this moment that was about to become unbearably painful.

Richard's voice remained surprisingly even. "You know who hired him?"

Heart pounding, Bethany tried to match Richard's tone. "He didn't know who he was working for. But he gave us bank account information and the amount that was wired. Hopefully we can track the money that was used to pay him."

"We?"

"Normally, I'd use various private detectives to track something like bank account information. But I want this taken care of as quickly as possible. That means I need to rely on Frankie's connections."

"Normally?" he asked. But before she could answer, he took it back. "No, I don't mean it that way. I'm not judging. I just want to understand."

Richard took a deep breath and then said, "Do you think it's a good idea to trust Frankie with that information?"

Bethany's fears were easing a little. He was still so calm. How could he be so calm?

"I'm having one of my own private detectives look into the information also. But Frankie will get me the information more quickly. I'll rely on him until I learn I shouldn't."

"Do you really think that's a good idea?"

Bethany sighed and finished her drink. "I really think Frankie loved my mother. I really think he's willing to help me in any way he can."

Richard nodded.

"Do you need another drink?" he asked absently. "We'll need to call for a waiter if you want one. I told them we had a business meeting. They won't interrupt."

Bethany looked closely at her friend. There was such sadness in his eyes.

She didn't recognize her own voice when she spoke. "Tell me you're going to be okay. Tell me we're going to be okay."

He reached out and took her hand.

"It's never gotten better for you has it? You just pretended so the rest of us wouldn't worry."

In that moment, she realized he saw her, really saw her, in a way no one ever had. And amazingly, it looked like he didn't love her any less because of it.

Actually, she didn't think he'd ever looked at her with so much love before. The connection was like nothing she'd ever hoped to feel, an intimacy she hadn't dreamt she could achieve.

"You have to let me be a part of this," Richard said.

Still confused by his strange reaction, Bethany asked, "You're really okay with this?"

He seemed to consider the question.

"I'm pissed you've been lying all this time, but mostly I feel terrible that you felt you had to."

He paused, and added, "This is all going to take a little getting used to. But to be clear, we – as in you and I – we're fine."

"I thought you wouldn't understand," Bethany admitted. "I don't think I really understand it myself."

He leaned closer. "I know you, Beth. The rest of this doesn't change anything."

Bethany stared across the table at him and thought of the promise he'd made to her so many years before. She hadn't believed it at the time. She'd been wrong.

"You said there was nothing that could change how

you felt about me," she said, with a trace of awe in her voice.

Richard's face turned a horrified shade of purple and he looked away. "I'd had much too much to drink that night. There's no reason to bring it up now."

There was every reason to bring it up. A path was opening up before her. A path she'd rejected as too dangerous so many years before.

"I'm sorry I misjudged us," she said. "I was scared. I was wrong."

Richard met her eyes with confusion. "What are you saying?"

Her pulse was pounding in her ears now. The fear was still there. Even with all he'd shown her that night, it was still there. But she took a deep breath and said, "I'm hoping you'll give me another chance."

Richard stood and swept her to her feet. He paused only a moment to look in her eyes, clearly as incredulous as she'd been a few minutes earlier. And he kissed her. In an instant, all the questions, all the worries, faded into nothing.

His lips were perfect. His kiss strong and passionate, yet soft and protective. The feel of his hair between her fingers. The smell of his cologne. The taste of the martini on his tongue. Her knees melted as he eased her up against the wall. She was running her hand down his back when her cell phone rang.

The abrasive cords of Salsa Number Three chimed from Bethany's purse. It would be Frankie. He was going to call when he had some information on the bank account.

She told herself she could ignore it. As Richard's hand slid down her arm, she wanted to ignore it.

But she knew she couldn't. She needed that

information almost as much as she needed what was happening here.

Richard seemed to sense her decision. "Do you need to get that?"

Bethany had already let the call go to voicemail. "I don't want to."

He interrupted her. "But you have to. This will be here. I promise."

"I'm sorry," she said, leaning her head against the wall. "I'm really sorry."

Richard chuckled. "I understand."

She realized he did, a little, and that was more than enough. Bethany pulled him close, burying her head in his chest as he stroked her hair. She loved the smell of him. Underneath the scent of Polo was the scent of familiarity. It was the simple essence of Richard.

When he was holding her like this she felt as safe as she ever had. She wished she could just stay here. That she could just have this normal life and forget the rest of it.

But she knew it could never be enough. Too much had happened. Too much time had passed. Some things couldn't be changed.

~ 40 ~

Less than twenty minutes later, Bethany was a world away from her dinner with Richard. It was disturbing how quickly she found herself pulled from that place of happiness and peace and back into the world of revenge and violence she'd created.

She and Frankie were alone in her workroom, surrounded by her demons. He was as at ease as she was in the space, quickly relaying what he'd discovered.

"I didn't think things was going very good at first. One of my guys called me this afternoon. Said it was looking like the best he could do would be the originating bank. Not the branch, just the bank. And it wasn't some rinky-dink local bank."

"What bank was it?" Bethany asked.

"FTL."

"Federal Trust and Loan?" Bethany groaned. She'd passed at least four of their branches on the walk from dinner.

"Yeah, I know. Huge bank. That wasn't something we could work with. I told my guy to think regional. I figure – Manhattan – that's where the murder happened. And, on a chance, I had them run Staten Island and Brooklyn."

"Why there?"

"Just a guess. I mean we're figuring this connects to Rita. That means rewind a lotta time. Gotta go back to how things were then. Rita grew up on Staten Island. She was born in Brooklyn. Your father, he grew up in Brooklyn. I figure, let's run them, see what we get. Sometimes the neighborhood follows you no matter where you go."

Bethany nodded. More than thirty years after she'd left it and a quarter century since her death, Rita's neighborhood was still following her.

"Did they find something?" Bethany asked.

"They hit with Brooklyn."

The statement made her heart drop. Manhattan would've been acceptable. Staten Island was almost expected. But Brooklyn. Was there a connection to her father? It was too astounding to even consider. Wasn't it?

"What does that mean 'they hit with Brooklyn'?"

"It means we got our branch. It's a small one in Brooklyn."

Bethany looked around her workroom, wishing she'd taken more time to furnish the place. She needed to sit down. This was too much to absorb. Ignoring the rigid metal chair that was poised in front of her laptop, Bethany took a spot on the floor, leaning up against the wall.

"What exactly can we do with that information?" she asked after a minute.

"That's what I've been thinking about. My guy can't get anything more from a remote location. He needs to get inside."

"So where does that leave us?"

"I figure we got two choices. We start asking some questions, showing some photos. You know, standard police style."

Bethany thought that sounded slow. "Or?"

"Or we break into the bank. We get the codes to get into the system."

"I can't rob a bank!"

"No, but I got some people who could. If that's the way you wanna go."

The offer was genuine, and that only increased her anxiety. This was a man who could make almost anything possible. Moral and legal boundaries weren't going to stand in his way when he was doing his job. And, right now, his job was helping her.

Bethany had spent most of her life on the precipice. She recognized an invitation into the abyss when she saw it. She just hoped she was wise enough to decline.

But Frankie, it seemed, had more concern for her well-being than she'd believed.

"I don't wanna tell you how to do this. It's your thing. But I think we try this the legal way first. The bank, that's a federal crime. You don't wanna mess with the feds unless you have to."

Bethany nodded, relieved that somebody was thinking clearly.

He continued, "I'll put together a file with photos tonight. Map out the locations: the bank, the neighborhood where Aston grew up, the neighborhood where your mother's family was when she was born. The works. You let me check the place tomorrow.

We'll meet after work. I'll tell you what I find."

"Sounds good, but I'm going with you."

Frankie shook his head. "You gotta work. We can't be doing this at night. We need the bank open."

"I'll take the day off," Bethany replied.

"Don't you got meetings and stuff that need to be handled?"

Bethany smiled and fished her phone out of her purse. After only one ring she heard Emily's voice on the other end of the line.

"I'm sorry to call you so late, but I need to clear my day for tomorrow. Can you do that?"

Always efficient, Emily rattled off the day's scheduled events. Bethany told her to move two of the meetings and take the other two herself. In minutes, the call was completed and Bethany was ready for a day of investigation.

Frankie was dumbstruck. "Why'd you do that? You can't go with me. People, they know who you are."

"They'll talk to me," Bethany interrupted. "You'd be amazed what people will tell me."

"You can't be seen with me."

"Why not?"

Frankie stood over her. "Are you kidding me? Why the hell do you think? I work for Pietro Timminolo. People know that. Lots of people know that. You're Bethany Chase. Lots of people know that too. You and me, we can't be spending time in public!"

Bethany sighed. To some degree he was right, there might be buzz. It might start some rumors. But, when all was said and done, it seemed like a pretty minor problem.

"You let me deal with the gossip and the rumors and the public. Okay? What time should I meet you tomorrow?"

"You're unbelievable!" he shouted at her. "Reckless. Stupid!"

Bethany calmly rose and met his eyes. "You have followed me around my whole life. You knew my mother. I'm betting you know me pretty well too, as much as I hate to admit that. I am a lot of things – unbelievable is probably one of them. But I am rarely reckless and I am never stupid. So, what time should I be at your house?"

Frankie's face was growing redder by the second. He muttered something to himself about the impossibility of protecting her when she was acting like this.

Taking a deep breath, he said more firmly, "I don't like the idea of people knowing you was asking questions around that bank."

"I don't like the idea that somebody paid a man to kill my fiancé. And the same somebody may have hired someone to kill my mom. What I do like is the idea that I may be getting closer to the answers."

Frankie shook his head in frustration. "I'll meet you at your place tomorrow – around 9," he growled.

"I'm guessing you live on Staten Island with Pietro. That means you'd have to drive through Brooklyn and Manhattan to get to me, and then drive back. That's absurd. Write down your address. I'll meet you."

Frankie shot her a look that conveyed every foul word he wanted to say. But he said none of them. Instead, he snatched a pad of paper from the table and scribbled down the address. Handing her the paper, he added, "You gotta get all the way to the right off the exit. It's a bad merge."

Bethany smiled at her belligerent protector. "This

may surprise you, but I can be a little aggressive when I need to be."

The remark finally earned her a reluctant chuckle. She could see what he was thinking, plain as day. The situation couldn't have been stranger, but it was nice to be around someone who'd known her mother so well. It warmed her heart to know she shared so many similarities with the woman who was taken from her so prematurely.

After a moment or two, Frankie spoke again. "There's something else. A little problem you need to know about. I don't know what it means."

Bethany didn't like his tone. "What problem?"

"Your friend, the guy."

"Richard? What about Richard? Is he in danger?"

Frankie's expression grew more uneasy. "No. He's fine. You see, I still have people watching you. You know that."

"Yeah, I know."

"Well, they weren't the only ones watching you last night."

Bethany felt a flood of relief. This she could handle. She finished the story for him. "Richard waited outside the building last night and followed me. I know. He told me. We talked. I told him everything."

Frankie smiled. "Good. I was worried there might be something weird. Something we missed somehow over the years."

"No. Everything's fine."

"So, you told him the truth? Everything?"

"Most of it, yeah. It's actually a relief. He knows. And he doesn't hate me."

Bethany considered the revelation for the first time. It was astonishing.

Frankie shuffled his feet somewhat uncomfortably. "I'm not sure if you care at all what I think about this. But that kid, that Richard guy, he's the one for you."

Bethany smiled at his paternal tone. "Thanks, Frankie, I agree with you."

"Not to speak ill of the dead, but maybe you're better off."

The remark set off so many alarms in Bethany's head that she could only gape for a moment. "I'm sorry, what did you say?"

Frankie went back to shuffling his feet. "It's nothing. I shouldn't've said anything."

"No. No," Bethany replied, trying to keep her voice calm. "You absolutely should've said something. What are you talking about?"

Frankie turned away, staring in the direction of a blackened window.

"Your grandfather has been keeping an eye on you for years," he began vaguely. "In all that time, I never saw nothing that'd make me put a special team on Richard. We put a special team on your friend Annie once."

Shame hung heavily. Her friends had been spied on, "special teams" assigned to monitor them, because of her. She wanted to make Frankie stop, but she knew that was what he was hoping she'd do. He was starting slow, hitting unimportant stuff, wanting to show her it was awful to know other people's secrets, wanting her to ask him to stop.

"End of your freshman year in college, Annie was slipping out of your room a few nights a week. You had no idea. We got a little worried. Put a team on her. Turns out it was nothing. She had a girl she was meeting up with."

Bethany felt some relief. This was something she knew about. When Annie told them she was feeling very torn about her sexuality, she admitted there'd been a woman she'd been seeing secretly. That must've been what Frankie had investigated.

"We keep close tabs, you see. But even with that, your friends, they're clean. Not even an affair. Geoffrey was different, though. When you first started dating we checked him out. You know, the usual preliminary scan, everything seemed clean. But time passed and he was around people he shouldn't've been around. Going to places he shouldn't've been going."

"He was a prosecutor. He was probably checking out the crime scenes for his cases. He used to do that all the time. He told me it helped him paint the picture for the jury."

Bethany almost begged for this to be the answer. But she knew Frankie was more thorough than that.

"That explained a lot of it. Yeah. And actually, we backed off for a while, 'cause it seemed that was all there was to it."

Frankie took a deep breath, giving her plenty of time to stop him if she wanted. Then, he continued, "You see, my guys, they watch you. They don't watch your friends unless we think something's wrong. So, we only checked up on Geoffrey that one time. Other than that, I didn't know what he was up to."

"But you know something now?" Bethany prompted.

"The day he announced he was running for mayor, he dropped you at home."

Bethany could almost see the scene again in her mind's eye. The crowds. The cheers. Her praise of the candidate. How proud she felt to be helping him.

How proud she felt to be a part of a better future for the city. She could still see him, giddy about the response. So appreciative of her support.

In that moment, she'd almost felt it – or she thought she did. She'd wanted so badly to love him. To be in love with him. For that instant, she'd felt like she was almost there.

Bethany braced herself, knowing the image was about to be shattered forever.

"The guys that were keeping an eye on you in the park. They was heading home for the day. So, two new guys picked you up outside of your building and the original guys started to head home. It just happened they was still behind the limo when it stopped and let Geoffrey out."

"So?" Bethany asked, growing more impatient.

"My boys were stopped at a light. And they saw Geoffrey get out of the limo, turn around and hail a cab."

"That's not so strange," she protested, knowing it was incredibly strange. The only reason to abandon the limo was because he didn't want anyone to know where he was going.

Frankie ignored her objection. "My guys thought it was strange enough that they followed the cab. They stayed with him through the city traffic, but lost him in the Battery Tunnel."

Bethany sat silently, but her inner voice was screaming. The Tunnel could take a person any number of places: New Jersey, Staten Island, but before you arrived in any of those places you'd have to drive through Brooklyn. The very borough they were heading to tomorrow to investigate Geoffrey's death.

Frankie didn't fill in the gaps. They both knew she

was capable of doing that herself. "We thought about putting a couple guys on Geoffrey. But, I gotta admit, I didn't think much of it. It was strange, yeah, but we'd investigated him before. It seemed pointless to do it again."

"So, you didn't find anything out?"

"Wish to God I'd looked more closely."

Bethany only nodded. *What the hell had they missed?*

~ 41 ~

Bethany made a call on the walk back to her apartment. There was one other source of information about Geoffrey. She doubted he'd know anything more, but she'd be a fool not to ask. Though it was late, Bethany knew he'd still be awake. Aston Chase never slept more than six hours a night. He considered anything beyond that weakness and laziness. As she'd expected, her father picked up by the second ring.

"Dad, I need you to answer a question honestly," she began without greeting.

It didn't seem he even noticed the conversation began abruptly. "What can I help you with, honey?"

"Did you find anything when you had Geoffrey investigated?"

There was silence while Aston plainly attempted to assess the intent of the question.

"Dad, I need to know the truth," Bethany repeated.

"Bethany, what's this all about?" he asked.

"Will the purpose of my question change your answer? Just tell me the truth," she snapped.

"I'll never understand you. I thought we were breaking new ground today. It seemed like we might actually be learning how to talk to each other after all these years. Now you're calling me to provoke an argument. I won't let you do it."

Bethany took a deep breath. She was taking her frustration out on her father. It was natural, but it was unproductive.

"It's not an accusation," she explained as calmly as she could. "I want to know if he was hiding anything. Anything at all."

"I'm not sure we should have a conversation like this over the phone."

To Aston, it was Business 101 to make sure you had all volatile conversations in person. Bethany stayed silent, knowing he'd eventually respond.

After a moment, he answered, "I assigned a group of private investigators when you first started dating. They came up with nothing."

There was more, Bethany could hear it in his voice. "And then, when we got engaged, you looked again, but more closely," she suggested.

Aston muttered to himself, but answered, "Yes, I hired a couple more people to look into things. He was still perfectly clean."

"But?" Bethany knew she heard hesitation.

"Genuinely, there was nothing there. That was the problem. One of the investigators, when he gave me his report, he told me he thought things were too clean. He's a good investigator. And I trust his hunches. But, Bethany, he looked into every angle, and he finally gave up. There was nothing."

As her father spoke, a thought flashed through her mind. "Did the investigator find any evidence that Geoffrey had tried to track down his biological parents?"

"No. That was something that always bothered me, to be honest. It was a loose end. I hate loose ends."

Bethany wasn't sure why it would be important, but she agreed with her father about the loose ends. "Did your guys try to track them down?"

"They couldn't find any information. Frankly, if my investigators couldn't find any leads, I can't imagine Geoffrey could have."

Unless Geoffrey covered the trail up after he found them, Bethany thought. That was the flaw in the investigation. And perhaps that was the reason her father's investigator had the hunch there was more going on than met the eye. If Geoffrey had tracked down his biological parents, and if he'd wanted to keep their identity a secret, he could have.

Bethany, however, didn't consider sharing that theory with her father. "Thanks, Dad, I appreciate the honesty."

"Is there anything else?" he asked. She could tell by his tone he knew something was up.

Bethany was about to sign off quickly, hoping to avoid her father's questions, when she suddenly realized she'd been missing something.

"Actually, Dad, there's one more thing. Those men you told me about today, the ones who invested in your company. Where did you say they were from?"

Aston seemed slightly more comfortable with these questions. "The guys had some offices in Manhattan, but Rita told me the Family they worked for was from Brooklyn. I gathered they were one of Pietro's rivals and was why Pietro moved his family to Staten Island."

The coincidences were starting to pile up. She'd been worried that the bank being in Brooklyn might somehow point to her father's childhood. Maybe it was pointing to her mother's murder. Hadn't she just been telling her father that she couldn't believe his investors weren't somehow related to her mother's death?

"What's going on, Bethany?" Aston asked, the concern back in his voice.

"Not a thing. Have a good night," she replied, disconnecting the call as quickly as she could.

With only a moment's hesitation, she made another call.

"Hey, beautiful," Richard said in greeting.

The sound of his voice brought a small smile to her face, despite the circumstances. "I have a favor to ask."

"Sure, whatever you need," he replied, his voice matching her seriousness.

"With what just happened tonight, this may be creepy, and I'm really sorry to even ask, but can you possibly come with me over to Geoffrey's apartment? I want to look for something."

The pause on the end of the line told Bethany that Richard thought this was as creepy as she did. But he agreed.

She tried to push the discomfort from her mind. This wasn't about the unprecedented make-out session in the restaurant. This was about her friend helping her look into some tough things.

And besides, she wouldn't have had to do any of this if Geoffrey had just been honest in the first place. Of course, she was no better than him, but she couldn't think of it that way, at least not tonight.

~ 42 ~

As Bethany dug through Geoffrey's desk, Richard stood in the middle of the room feeling useless and incredibly uncomfortable. She hadn't said a word the whole walk over, which told him she felt as strange about this as he did. It also told him she must have been desperate to have called him in the first place.

"Can you tell me why we're here?" he asked, finally.

Bethany didn't look up from her search to reply. "I'm not sure. Geoffrey was investigated by my father and Timminolo and neither of them found anything."

The mention of Timminolo made one thing clear – Bethany was worried about the secrets they might be digging up tonight. That was why she'd asked him to help and not Annie.

"If neither of them found anything, why are you searching Geoffrey's apartment?"

"I don't really know. It's an instinct, I guess. Frankie said they saw Geoffrey behaving oddly right before he died. It's kind of hard to explain. But I realized I've been working on the assumption I know everything there is to know about Geoffrey. I never even thought to go through his things."

"Is it okay if I look around also?" Richard asked, feeling it would definitely not be okay, but knowing he was going to have to pretend it was.

"Sure, why don't you check the filing cabinet over there?" Bethany replied, pointing across the room.

Richard nodded and dutifully began his search. He was staring at the first file – Geoffrey's tax return from the prior year – when the obvious question struck him. "Are we looking for anything in particular?"

Bethany offered a half-smile in what was probably a failed attempt to appear optimistic. "Anything out of the ordinary, I guess. Isn't that what the private eyes on the bad television shows always say?"

Richard offered a similarly stilted smile in response. "Of course. Sorry, I didn't realize we'd entered the cops and robbers portion of our program."

After about a half hour of digging with no real success, Richard broke the silence. "Do you really think Geoffrey was hiding something?"

Bethany rubbed her eyes and looked up, seeming happy for a break. "Maybe it's just wishful thinking? I mean, if Geoffrey was killed over some secret of his own, then none of this has anything to do with me or my mother's murder. That would be a tremendous relief."

"Do you think this is about you?"

She shook her head. "Their murders are identical. I think this could be about the past as much as Geoffrey."

Richard considered the comment for a moment. "I

mean, it's odd. The similarities are obvious. But it really doesn't make a lot of sense. Geoffrey has nothing to do with your mother. There's no reason the person who wanted to kill her would want to kill your fiancé decades later."

"With all I told you tonight, do really think that?"

"Your investigation?" Richard asked. "You think someone might've done this to stop your investigation?"

"The threat's pretty clear."

All along he'd believed this had to be about Geoffrey, nothing else had made sense, but she was right. Having all the information changed the analysis.

"Have you told the police about this?"

Bethany stared at him, a mixture of shock and maybe fear on her face. "The police can't know about my investigation."

Richard knew Bethany well enough to know this was a fight he wouldn't win, but he wasn't ready to let it go so easily.

"Shouldn't they know? Don't you think this changes things?"

Her face hardened. Before she could say anything that both of them would regret, Richard stopped her.

"I know what you're going to say. I understand. Just think about it, okay. Promise me you'll think about it."

Bethany nodded vaguely and returned to her search of Geoffrey's desk. Knowing he couldn't stand the tension that remained in the air, Richard changed the subject. "Have you found anything helpful over there?"

"Nothing at all. Checkbook. Bills. Birthday card from his mom. It's all the basic stuff you'd expect to find. Though, I guess he wouldn't exactly keep a file with all of his deep dark secrets in the top drawer of his desk. You?"

He shook his head. "Not a thing."

It was almost two hours later when they spoke again. They'd finished looking through the office and come up completely empty. Though the rest of the apartment was just waiting for their perusal, it was late and they both knew they needed to give it a rest for the night. Neither of them had gotten much sleep the night before.

They walked home in silence. It wasn't until they reached the hallway between their apartments that either of them said a word.

"Thanks for coming with me," Bethany said. "I know it must've been weird for you, but I couldn't do it alone."

Richard laid a gentle hand on her cheek.

"It was absolutely weird. But I'm glad you asked for my help. We got a lot out in the open tonight. But it's good. I promise. It's all going to be good."

"I'm sorry I had to leave before," Bethany said after a minute.

For perhaps the first time in his adult life, Richard felt nervous. He'd laid his heart on the line ten years earlier and she'd stomped on it. She'd been kind about it, but he'd been so sure they were soulmates, so sure they belonged together, and she'd very objectively explained all the reasons he was mistaken.

He didn't know what had changed. But it didn't matter. When he'd kissed her, everything else faded away. He'd been right all those years ago.

"I totally wrecked your dinner plans," she went on.

Richard chuckled. "Dinner was really more about

talking and less about eating, to be honest."

"I'm glad we talked," she said.

Though he feared the answer, he knew he had to ask the question. "Are you glad about the rest of it?"

Bethany ran a hand through her hair. Richard knew that meant she was as nervous as he was, which oddly made him feel a little bit better.

"It was amazing," she replied, not meeting his eyes.

He tilted her chin up and smiled at her. "I think I told you it would be."

Bethany smiled back, relief in her eyes. "I should always listen to you."

"That's true. So, kiss me good night, Bethany."

~ 43 ~

Annie was pouring her morning coffee when her phone rang. The only thing stranger than getting a call this early in the morning was the person who was making it.

"Bethany? Is your clock broken or something? You shouldn't be awake yet," Annie joked.

Her friend's immediate laughter told her that bad news hadn't prompted the call.

"I have an early meeting, but I wanted to catch you before the day got away from me."

Annie settled in at the kitchen table. Karen was still in the shower. She'd have plenty of privacy if necessary. Laughter or not, there was no way a call at this hour could be mundane news.

But she tried to seem casual, sipping her coffee and asking, "What's going on?"

Bethany paused for a minute, and then just blurted it out. "I kissed Richard."

Annie wasn't sure what she'd been prepared for, but this wasn't it. If she hadn't already swallowed her coffee, she would've choked on it.

A thousand thoughts rushed through her head. Not the least of which was – it was about damn time. But she managed to keep her voice even, know that this was a potentially volatile situation.

"Really?" she said.

Bethany continued on as if Annie hadn't spoken. "It was amazing. Absolutely amazing."

The wistfulness in her voice was magnificent.

Relieved, Annie allowed herself a laugh. "Thank God. What did he do to finally convince you you were being a dumbass?"

"What makes you think I'm the one who was being a dumbass?" Bethany asked, with what was probably supposed to be indignation.

"Something happened between the two of you in college. Junior year I think it was. It was right after you broke up with that rugby player. I don't know exactly what happened, but I'm not an idiot. Suddenly you were trying desperately to make everything seem okay. About the same time, Richard began dating as if it was a competitive sport."

"You knew?"

Annie took a sip of her coffee. "Yup. Frankly, the first thing Karen asked me about you and Richard was why you weren't dating."

"Did you tell her it was because I'm a dumbass?"

"In so many words," Annie confirmed.

Though she hated to be a wet blanket, Annie knew she needed to ask some crucial questions.

"So, it was awesome?" she asked cautiously. "Meaning, you're okay?"

She was relieved to hear that Bethany seemed to welcome the question. "It was last night. And it was great. Seriously, it was fabulous. I was almost afraid to fall asleep. Like somehow I'd wake up and it would be different. Does that make any sense?"

Annie thought it made perfect sense. "Was it different when you woke up?"

"No. I can't get him out of my head. I'm walking to the car and my mind just wanders back to it. I just keep feeling it over and over. I feel," she paused, "like I'm lit up."

Yeah, Annie knew that feeling. The only person who'd ever done that for her was in the other room.

"Did you see him this morning?"

"Yeah, I stole his coffee before I left."

"He's good with all this?" She suspected he would be.

Bethany laughed. "He's almost smug about it. It's like he's known all along."

Finally reassured things were truly in balance, Annie said, "Honey, I am so happy for you."

She could almost hear Bethany smiling on the other end of the line. "I'm happy for me, too."

~ 44 ~

It was a couple of minutes before nine when Bethany turned onto Frankie's street. It was a small block, lined with enormous houses that overwhelmed the tiny plots of land. The street reached a dead-end at the largest house on the block. It was up a little higher than the others, as if sitting sentinel. The ornate home made it obvious just how lucrative it was to work for Pietro Timminolo.

Bethany pulled her car next to Frankie's large Cadillac. Taking one last gulp of her now cold coffee, she pushed thoughts of her personal life from her mind. Like a soldier on a mission, she marched up the stone walkway.

Two heavy oak doors with gold trim stood as the last line between herself and the day she didn't really want to begin. When she rang the bell, Bethany could hear the music chime through the house. The sound of high heels on tile told her she was about to meet Maria

Lioni.

The door was opened by a beautiful woman with dark brown eyes, flawless olive skin, and jet black hair, sprayed perfectly in place. She was probably in her early fifties, though she clearly worked very hard to make herself look younger.

Her appearance was stunning, not because of how she looked, but because of who she was.

It took a moment to place her, but Bethany was certain. The night of Geoffrey's murder, there'd been that woman in the bar. Bethany had brushed it off at the time, but the staring had been more than the usual gawking. Though she wished she had Annie there to confirm it, Bethany was certain that the woman from the bar was standing in front of her right now.

Unlike that night, Maria now offered a broad, inviting smile. With a wave, she ushered Bethany into the vaulted entryway of her home, barely giving her a moment to register her recognition.

"Please come in. Frankie's running a little late. He's not a morning person."

Bethany followed her over gorgeous Italian tile into a formal sitting room done in immaculate white with silver accents. It looked like something out of a design catalog. The stark perfection of the room only made Bethany feel more uncomfortable than she already was.

Unable to resist, Bethany asked, "Have we met before?"

Maria laughed politely. "I know who you are of course. But no, I'm afraid we've never met."

Before Bethany could say anything more, Maria offered her coffee. Bethany didn't even consider declining the perfect homemaker's offer, which sent Maria scurrying into the kitchen and left Bethany to worry over the idea of drinking coffee on the spotless furniture.

The kitchen was just off the living room. Maria raised her voice so she could be heard in the other room. "It's really a pleasure to finally meet you. I've known your family for years."

It took a few moments to realize she was talking about Timminolo. Of course to Maria, that man was Bethany's "family."

The sound of heels on the kitchen tile forced Bethany's attention back to her hostess. She was emerging from the kitchen with a silver tray carrying two cups, along with cream and sugar.

"I didn't know how you took yours," Maria explained.

Bethany accepted the coffee and took a seat on the couch, trying very hard to stop thinking about her new "family." She was so focused on her inner demons she didn't realize she was staring at a photo on the coffee table.

Apparently thinking Bethany was just focused on the picture, Maria picked it up and handed it to her. Her voice filled with pride, she asked, "Have you met my Joey?"

In her mind's eye, Bethany could only see Joey pointing a gun at Richard.

"I met him briefly," she said instead. "Graduation?" she asked, feigning interest.

"Yes. Six years ago. It's hard to believe my baby is going to be twenty-five."

Maria's voice was adoring and a little possessive when she spoke about her son. It left Bethany to wonder if the woman really knew what Joey did for Timminolo, what her husband did.

"Do you expect to be working with Frankie for a while?" Maria asked, returning the photo to its place of honor and taking a seat opposite Bethany.

"It's hard to say," Bethany replied. She resisted the urge to explain that she intended to spend as little time as possible with anyone associated with the Timminolo family.

"Your grandfather is very good to him," Maria said, as if she thought Bethany misunderstood something.

The unsolicited explanation was strange, as was the flash behind Maria's eyes. There was something going on, but Bethany couldn't quite tell what. Maybe the woman did know what her husband and son did for Timminolo. The comment almost sounded like a mantra, the type of thing you're trained to say in stressful situations. Did she think Bethany was somehow a part of it too?

Instead of commenting on the remark, Bethany said, "Frankie seems like a good man. He's been very kind to me."

But her efforts didn't have the intended effect. Again, there was the strangest look in Maria's eyes, and what almost looked like a grimace in response.

Before either of them could say anything else, Frankie hurried into the room. "I'm sorry. I hope you was getting to know each other."

"Yes, we were," Maria said quickly. Then, rising and making a graceful exit she added, "It was a pleasure to meet you, Bethany."

She was again the solicitous hostess, all anxiety gone from her face, causing Bethany to wonder if she'd misconstrued the look in her eyes moments before. Maybe this was merely the act reserved for the Family. The thought made her feel more than a little nauseous.

Plainly unaware of Bethany's confusion, Frankie asked, "You ready to go? I'll drive. I know the neighborhood. You can leave your car in the driveway. Maria's is in the garage. She'll be able to get out once I move mine."

Bethany placed her coffee on a coaster and followed Frankie. It was time to focus, time to visit a bank and find out who paid a hitman to kill her fiancé. It was becoming very clear her day had taken a dark turn. She shuddered to think what was awaiting her in Brooklyn.

~ 45 ~

Frankie allowed the drive to pass with very little conversation. In what was clearly his general practice, he parked his car illegally in front of the FTL branch.

He looked intently at Bethany and asked again, "You sure you won't let me do this on my own?"

Bethany didn't dignify the question with anything more than an eye roll. Without a word, she slipped out of the car and into the bank with Frankie trailing reluctantly behind her.

It was a very small branch. Only one person sat at the customer service desks – the assistant manager (as the placard indicated). Two others waited in the teller windows.

The man sitting at the desk was in his mid-forties. His eyes were hidden behind thick horn-rimmed glasses. And he looked about as plain as a person could look – receding hairline, slight paunch, round face.

Despite the wedding ring on his pudgy little finger,

he noticed Bethany the moment she walked in. While the ogling was rude, it provided a helpful way to begin the conversation.

Bethany flashed a smile and approached. He stood immediately, smiling brightly back.

"Good morning," Bethany said sweetly. "I'm…"

"Bethany Chase," he finished for her.

Bethany extended her hand in greeting, and then reading the nameplate on the desk she said, "And you would be Robert Dranti?"

"Please, call me Bob," he replied, taking her hand with a look that practically screamed *I will never wash this hand again.*

"Hi, Bob. This is my friend, Frank," Bethany continued, gradually extricating her hand from his vice-like grip.

Frankie smiled as kindly as he could, clearly trying to look more like a doting uncle and less like a henchman.

Bob, however, barely glanced his way. "Miss Chase, how can we help you today?"

They all took their seats and Bethany leaned in a little as she spoke, hoping to create a conspiratorial effect. The more he felt like she was inviting him into her world, the more likely he'd help.

"I'm trying to find someone. I think they frequent this bank."

Bob wasn't sucked in as easily as Bethany would've hoped. He looked at her uneasily, plainly concerned about his customers.

She laid it on a bit thicker. "You know who I am, Bob. So, you must know how closely I work with the police."

He nodded like a child. "You've helped them with community programs and stuff, right?"

Bethany smiled flirtatiously. "That's right."

"But you do all that with Central Park, don't you? You don't usually work with Brooklyn police, do you?"

Bethany's heart skipped at the question. She couldn't help but notice that she wasn't as good at sweet-talking as she would've expected. It was harder than it looked.

"I'm actually not working with the police currently," she admitted, hoping the honesty would get her back in with him. "I'm just looking for a little justice."

Bethany was startled to hear Frankie's voice chime in. His tone was perfect. "Mr. Dranti, I really hope you can help us out. I mean, you know the tough time this girl has been going through lately."

Bob turned his attention to Frankie. "Is this about Geoffrey Quinn?"

"We're just trying to get some answers, Bob. The police are doing their investigation. We're looking around a little ourselves. Many hands make light work, you know," Bethany offered.

It was a relief to see the intrigued gleam in Bob's eyes. Clearly, this sounded exciting to him. He looked as if he couldn't wait to get to the questions.

Bethany reached into her oversized purse and pulled out a file folder. Inside were pictures of anyone either she or Frankie thought could possibly have wanted to hire someone to kill Geoffrey. The photos were of everyone from Aston Chase, to aides to Mayor Wilson, to Leo Snell and his weasely friends, to Bethany's own close friends.

Bob looked through the photos earnestly. After an intense examination, he handed the file back.

"I'm sorry. I don't think I've ever seen any of those people here in the bank. I recognize a couple of them from the news, but none of them are from around here."

"Are you sure?"

"Well, no, I'm not sure. I mean lots of people come in and out every day. I can't say I'd recognize all of them. But, I can tell you I know the regulars. And none of those folks are regulars."

Bethany reluctantly put the file back into her purse; she couldn't help thinking this man was probably their best chance at an identification. "Would you have any problem with us showing the photos to the tellers, also?"

"That would be just fine with me," Bob stated amiably. He seemed to hesitate for a moment, as if there was something he was going to say, but then thought better of it.

"Bob, if there's anything at all you can think of. Even the tiniest little thing. I'd love to hear it. Sometimes the little details are the key to what's really going on," Bethany urged.

Bob blushed and looked away uncomfortably. "Oh, I wish I could help, genuinely. I mean, Mr. Quinn was such a good customer and he always spoke so highly of you. I really wish I could help."

Bethany didn't even hear the last part of the sentence. *Geoffrey was such a good customer? Geoffrey was a customer?*

~ 46 ~

Instead of staring at the assistant manager with slack-jawed shock, Bethany found her voice to be unexpectedly calm and even, with barely the smallest hint of surprise.

"He loved you guys, too. It's a little funny to be here actually. I can almost hear him telling me about you."

Bob's blush deepened. "Oh, please, I'm sure it was nothing like that."

"No, sincerely," Bethany replied, swallowing the bile rising in her throat. "He loved you guys. I mean, how long did he have an account with you? It seemed like forever."

"Gosh, it must have been five years."

The wave of nausea grew stronger, as she realized he'd been visiting this strange bank the whole time they were dating and she never knew it. Feeling almost lightheaded, she slid a cool hand over the back of her neck, hoping to regain some balance.

Bob stood. "I've taken up enough of your time. Why don't you let me introduce you to the tellers."

It was all she could do not to scream – *No. Wait. Tell me everything. Tell me why my fiancé had a bank account here! Tell me how the payment to the hitman came from this very location!*

But, instead, she remained calm. Knowing she had no other choice, she stood slowly, hoping her legs were steady enough to follow Bob to the tellers.

It wasn't until a half hour later, when they were safely back in Frankie's car, that she was able to discuss her astonishment. But before she could say anything, Frankie growled at her.

"I can't believe you'd set me up like that. I mean, I know you don't like me or the boss so much, but that was low."

"What the hell are you talking about?" Bethany snapped back. "You think I knew about that?"

"I think you skipped work today to show me up. Yeah, that's what I think."

Bethany laughed at the accusation. "And I thought I had trust issues. Frankie, I'm as surprised as you are about all of this."

Frankie's brow furrowed. "You said he told you about those folks. You said Quinn had an account there for five years."

"I said it had seemed like a long time, hoping the manager would tell us exactly how long. I lied. If he'd realized I had no idea about Geoffrey's account he would've stopped talking to us."

She watched Frankie replay the conversation in his mind. "You didn't know," he said slowly.

Bethany smiled, feeling a little proud of her acting

skills. "I guess it would be pretty ridiculous to ask if you knew about the account."

Frankie offered a small smile in response. "I didn't know."

"I guess Geoffrey has some connection to Brooklyn?"

Frankie started the car and pulled out of the spot.

Taking advantage of his distraction, Bethany asked, "Does Pietro have enemies around here?"

Frankie's eyes remained riveted on the road. "Pietro has a lot of enemies. That's why we keep a close eye on you," he replied.

Bethany heard the avoidance and she remained quiet, hoping he'd add more.

Eventually, Frankie added, "Pietro started out in this neighborhood. He moved the family to Staten Island right before your mom started school."

Bethany didn't push any harder. She knew Frankie had probably already said more than Timminolo would have wanted.

She had her answer. It was safe to assume money coming out of this part of town might point in the direction of one of Pietro Timminolo's enemies. Thinking about what her father had said about his investors, Bethany knew that a mob connection could just as easily point to him.

But the real question was Geoffrey. As far as she knew, Geoffrey Quinn had no connection to Brooklyn. Yet he had a bank account there. And for some unexplained reason, it was a bank he visited often. In the whole time she'd known him, Bethany couldn't think of one time Geoffrey actually went inside a bank. He was a strict ATM user, as were most people she knew. None of it made any sense.

"How could I not have known about this?" Bethany muttered, as much to herself as to Frankie.

"People keep secrets. Sometimes they keep them to protect others. Sometimes to protect themselves. Just because he was hiding things don't mean he was up to something bad."

Bethany nodded in agreement, but she didn't believe it. Geoffrey wasn't like this. He was the perfect boyfriend. The perfect fiancé. The perfect man.

As naïve as that sounded, she really believed it was true. She'd never loved him, but she'd stayed with him all those years because she believed she'd change her mind eventually. She'd believed she would because he'd been perfect – at least on paper.

When she didn't say anything more, Frankie spoke. "You of all people should understand about secrets."

"I guess." Bethany shrugged. "How about you, Frankie?"

"What about me?" he asked.

"You love your wife, right? Does she know the truth? Does she know what you do?"

Frankie sighed deeply. "When we first met, she didn't know. And I gotta say it was weird. I was crazy about her. But I didn't know how to handle it. I mean, I dated a couple girls after your mom. They was all from the neighborhood. They all knew who I worked for. But not her. She didn't know. She thought I ran a bunch of restaurants in Staten Island and Jersey. Which I did. But she didn't know who I ran them for."

Bethany was surprised to see the genuine look of remorse on Frankie's face. Just thinking for a moment about the betrayal and confusion she'd seen on Richard's face in the past few days gave her an inkling of how hard it must have been.

"How did she find out?" Bethany asked.

"I guess you could say I got caught. We was married about six months. She was pregnant, not too far along. Maybe two months. We wasn't telling people yet. Anyways, I got shot. Bullet to the shoulder. I was lucky. Went right through. But it did land me in the hospital. And it did force me to make a decision. I told her the truth."

"What happened?" Bethany asked. The tone of his voice told her it hadn't gone well.

"She was furious. I love the woman, but boy she's got a temper. Like no other. And she certainly had a reason to be mad that time. She always knew about me and Rita dating. She knew how much I'd loved her as a kid. She thought Rita was the reason I hadn't been straight with her about my job."

The betrayal, Bethany realized, must have been devastating. To find out Frankie had been lying about who he worked for was one thing. To discover his employer was his ex-girlfriend's father. That was even worse.

"Did she find a way to forgive you?"

"She was pissed a long time. A good stretch. Three, maybe four months. Yeah, probably about four months. I remember she was really starting to show, you know with the baby, and I wanted so bad to be there with her. I was worried she'd take the baby and leave me."

Frankie eased the car into his driveway. He put it in park and turned to face Bethany. "Take it from an old man who's done a lot of screwing up. If you find the one for you, you gotta tell him everything. If you can't trust him with the truth, then you can't be with him. It don't work unless you're honest."

Bethany heard the truth in his words. And it left her to wonder, how much was enough?

Richard knew the basics. He knew the implications. Did the details really matter? The loft? The weapons? The walls covered in her own writing?

"Thanks, Frankie," she said simply, still uncertain how to deal with her mountain of secrets.

Instead of focusing on the troubling question, she shifted gears. "Do you think your people can dig up anything more on the bank account?"

"I don't know. I got a couple thoughts. Let me run them down. Call you tonight?"

Bethany nodded. "Give me a ring on my cell."

She climbed out of the car, the question of what to tell Richard weighing more heavily than the questions about Geoffrey. By the time she made it back to Manhattan, she knew what she had to do. It was time to call Master Jung and make an appointment.

~ 47 ~

Richard had only been home for five minutes when Bethany knocked on his door. He knew immediately there was a problem.

She wore no makeup, her hair was in a messy ponytail, and she looked like she could sleep for two days and only barely catch up.

He invited her in and asked, "Can I offer you a beer or something? You look like you need it."

Bethany sunk onto his couch, but refused. "I made the mistake of taking a nap this afternoon. Seriously, I must've been running on adrenaline the past few days because I crashed hard. I woke up about an hour ago."

"Was your trip to the bank helpful?" Richard asked, joining her on the couch.

"It was interesting," Bethany replied, telling him about the branch manger and the discovery of Geoffrey's account.

"I don't even know what questions to ask after all

that," he said, running a hand through his hair. "Did you guys have any thoughts?"

Bethany shook her head. "Frankie's looking further into the account. But, no, nothing yet. Honestly, I have no idea what to make of it."

"Hey, wait a second!" Richard exclaimed, hopping to his feet. "If Geoffrey had this account, there'd probably be bank statements. We should be looking for bank statements. If there are cancelled checks or – I don't know – something should tell us about his account activity. That might give us the answers we're looking for."

He was thrilled to see Bethany smile.

"I don't think I've ever loved you more, Richard Marshall, Private Eye. I should've brought you in on this years ago."

Richard offered a sarcastic grin. "That's what I've been telling you. It's bad to keep secrets from me."

"I know, honey. I know." Bethany replied, gently taking his hand.

Richard slid back onto the couch and looked at her more seriously. "I'd like to take you out. You know, on a date, like a formal date. I don't want to just back into this. I want to do it right."

Bethany nodded, though her eyes were strangely distant.

Before he could say anything else, she asked, "Rich, do you trust me?"

With all that had been going on the past few days, it was a tougher question than it used to be. "What do you mean?"

"Do you trust me enough that you'll do something, no questions asked?" she clarified, still not meeting his eyes.

Even with all that had happened, the answer was obvious. "With my life."

"Then I need you to come with me."

Bethany took his hand, allowing him only enough time to grab his keys off the table by the door. Without a word, she led him outside. They were three blocks away from their building before he spoke.

"I'm guessing I'm not supposed to be asking any questions? Because, Beth, I have about four thousand," Richard said, somewhat winded by her brisk pace.

Bethany didn't answer. In fact, it didn't look like she even heard him.

"Beth?"

She turned to face him briefly without slowing her pace. "I can't," was all she said, before turning her attention back to the sidewalk.

They passed the remaining two blocks in silence and entered the building that Richard recognized as Master Jung's studio. They stopped at the large reception desk in the front of the main room.

A petite, wiry woman greeted them with a smile. "Good evening, Ms. Chase. He's ready for you. You can leave your friend with me."

Bethany nodded at the woman and then turned to face Richard. There was a hesitancy in her eyes, a look of almost fear. She squeezed his hand tightly and, for a moment, Richard was sure she was going to cry.

"I love you so much," she said in a whisper, her voice breaking slightly. "God, I hope…" But as the tears pooled in her eyes, she lost the ability to speak. Instead, she embraced him tightly.

Before he could say a word, Bethany disappeared through a door behind the reception desk, leaving Richard to stare blankly at the woman behind the counter.

She smiled reassuringly at him. "He'll be with you in just a moment," she said.

"I'm sorry, who will be with me?"

The look he received told him the woman was wondering if he was a complete idiot. "The Master. Master Jung," she clarified. "He'll be with you in a moment."

Richard only nodded, trying to pretend he had some idea what was going on. All he could figure was he was about to meet Bethany's long-time trainer for the first time and she was obviously nervous about it, though he had no idea why.

It wasn't long before an Asian man entered the lobby through the door Bethany had used earlier. He was an average height, probably about five inches shorter than Richard. Very lean, but obviously strong. He walked with a grace that made Richard wonder if his feet were even touching the ground.

Though his face was unlined, Richard could tell he wasn't a young man. His head was shaved completely bald. So, there was no sign of any gray hair. Despite that, Richard estimated the man was probably over seventy. Both his age and demeanor told Richard this was Master Jung.

Richard stepped forward to greet him and waited somewhat impatiently as the Master gave him an obvious once over.

"You are Richard." The man spoke slowly and precisely, his speech slightly broken by an Asian accent. "It is an honor to meet you, Mr. Marshall," he added with the slightest of bows.

"What's going on here?" Richard blurted out, unable to hold his tongue any longer. "I mean, Beth brought me here, but she didn't tell me anything and I just don't understand."

The words were tumbling out of his mouth. Though he knew he wasn't making any sense, he couldn't stop speaking.

Master Jung put a firm hand on his shoulder. "You will see. First, you follow me."

"Follow you where?"

The Master smiled slightly at the snippy retort. "You are very impatient, Richard Marshall. You will see soon enough. Follow me now."

Richard followed. But he didn't want to follow. He didn't want to wait. He was sick and tired of secrets and waiting and patience. He wanted answers. And he wanted them now. Not five minutes from now.

But the tirade occurred only in his head. And he followed the Master through the door behind the front desk, past two offices and into another at the end of the hall. This room was larger than the others, but without any windows. The Master closed and locked the door behind them.

As Richard began to take a seat in front of the large desk, Master Jung stopped him. "We are not done. You must follow me."

Before Richard could ask what the hell he was talking about, the old man moved two books on the floor-to-ceiling bookshelf, revealing a knob. With a swift motion, the shelf swung out like a door. Behind it was a narrow staircase leading down one level. Master Jung descended the stairs without even looking back at Richard. The man was confident he'd follow obediently. Though Richard was dying to protest, he knew he had no alternative.

The stairs were dark, but the absence of any dust told him they were frequently used. They led into a hallway that opened into a large room. Three of the walls were mirrored. Mats lay stacked in two corners. The room was clearly a martial arts studio. And based on the path they had to take to get here, Richard was certain only one person trained in this room.

"Bethany has asked me to explain the room," Master Jung said, finally turning to face Richard. "Her father did not want people knowing about the training. He bought this space and renovated it. That must have been twenty years ago."

"Why the secrecy?"

"She was a little girl. The cameras were always watching. He did not want to attract attention. There had been enough attention."

Richard nodded solemnly. He'd been there too. He remembered. Bethany had mentioned at some point she had a private studio. She hadn't mentioned it was not only private, it was very clearly secret. "Aston is very protective of her," he said simply.

The Master seemed to agree. "Bethany wants you to sit here. I will join you in a moment. You must stay right here, though, and I have to insist, no matter what occurs, you must stay where you are. I will address things if there is any problem. You must stay."

Richard wasn't given an opportunity to answer. Master Jung left him alone in the room, sitting where he was told to sit, all the while muttering complaints to himself about the repeated order that he should stay where he was. Did he think he was some kind of moron? He heard him the first time.

He stared at the door on the opposite side of the room where the Master had disappeared. There was no indication of the door's purpose. Just a door. At the opposite end of the same wall was another door. Again, nothing distinctive, just a door. And between the two was a third.

It was a few minutes before the Master rejoined him. The man gracefully squatted on the floor next to him. He had a black baseball cap in one hand. A large-framed pair of sunglasses in the other. He handed both to Richard.

"What exactly do you want me to do with these?" Richard snipped.

"She says you may be recognized without them and she does not want that," the Master replied.

Richard assumed the "she" in that sentence was Bethany, but that was the only part that was making any sense at all. "Recognized by who? What the hell is going on? If *she* wants me to put this stuff on, *she* should come out here and ask me herself. And, you know, here's a crazy idea, *she* could explain what the fuck is going on."

Master Jung was completely unruffled by the flare-up. "She says to wear the hat and please also the sunglasses. You will see why soon. But you must do this."

Richard considered arguing further, but he knew it was pointless. He snatched the hat and sunglasses, donning both and growling, "Okay, they're on. Now can we get on with this?"

The Master stood and retrieved a long bamboo stick from the corner. Taking a spot in front of Richard, with his back to him, he tapped the rod solidly to the ground three times in rapid succession. As if on cue, the door through which the Master had previously disappeared opened and a very thin man dressed entirely in black entered. Richard craned his neck so he could see the man better.

He moved much like the Master, very light on his feet, with obvious agility. Despite his thin frame, he looked very strong, very intimidating, which might have had more to do with the black hood-like mask that covered his face and less to do with the man himself.

Slowly piecing together what was going on, Richard realized Bethany wanted him to see the truth, to see what it was she did here in her training. While on some level he agreed, he had to wonder if this was a good idea. Maybe she could've just told him about the training sessions.

The Master rapped the floor again, and this time four men – all of them significantly bigger than the masked man – entered. They were all wearing white. And none were wearing masks.

Richard stared at the five men and then looked to

the third door. Was Bethany planning on fighting all five of these guys? Was one or more of them on her "team"? Did they have "teams" in martial arts?

The Master rapped the floor a third time, and Richard's eyes were locked on the door waiting for her to emerge, braced for the sight of her like this, in this place, among this violence. But to his surprise, the door didn't open, and the four men in white began slowly circling the man in black, clearly assessing the competition.

The single man stood perfectly still, almost as if he was unaware of the other four. Also, Richard thought, he seemed to be staring right at him. Maybe there was a reason to worry people would recognize him. Funny, he never thought of himself as recognizable.

The Master settled on the floor next to him, leaving Richard to wonder where the hell his girlfriend was and why this seemed to be making less sense by the minute. Richard was about to ask the Master for some clarification when the tallest of the four sprung on the single man.

He charged forward, initially appearing as if he was going to go for the other man's feet, hoping to strike and knock him off balance. But the charge was a bluff. At the last second the man leapt in the air, aiming a kick directly at the masked man's face. The blow was dodged as if the masked man had known it was coming.

Almost simultaneously, the smallest of the four men attempted to sweep the man's feet. Not only did he fail, but the masked man delivered a vicious kick to his throat, sending him flying back against the wall.

What happened from that point was a blur. The four men attacked the single fighter swiftly and violently, showing no restraint. The thin man in the mask deftly evaded their attacks, frequently landing sharp blows of his own. After only five minutes, the tallest of the four men went down and stayed down. The other three were harder. But after two went down back-to-back, the remaining man was quickly dispensed with.

Richard had all but forgotten the reason he was brought to the secret room. The masked man was amazing. The battle had been so graceful that it had looked more like a dance and less like a fight. It was almost hard to believe the men still lying on the floor were anything other than actors in a choreographed production.

The man bowed in the direction of both Richard and the Master and then rigidly turned towards the door. It wasn't until the man began to walk toward the exit that Richard realized what he'd seen.

Despite the black. Despite the mask. Despite his initial assumptions. Richard knew that walk. He'd known it for decades.

Taking a closer look at the slim line of the masked figure's back, he realized it wasn't a thin man he was looking at. It was a woman. A tall woman. Wearing baggy clothes, maybe even some additional padding under those clothes.

When she exited the room, Richard looked desperately to her trainer for some confirmation. He merely nodded solemnly.

"You go to her," he said in a hushed voice.

Richard was on his feet and about to run for the door when the old man grabbed his arm. In that instant, the years were showing on his face.

His voice was still hushed, clearly not wanting to be overheard by the others in the room. "For more than twenty-five years, I have tried to help her. I have tried to make this right, tried to guide her. I have failed. I fear you are the last hope. I pray you are up to the challenge."

Richard stared in shock. *Was it really this bad?*

"She needs something," he continued. "Maybe it is you that will help her find it. You go to her now."

Richard had more questions swirling through his head than he could consider, but he knew they'd have to wait. He practically sprinted through the door Bethany had used a few moments before.

~ 49 ~

Inside, he found a very typical locker room. Tile covered the walls and floors. A narrow hallway led to a wide-open space containing a row of lockers and two benches. Beyond these were three shower stalls encased in glass. But Richard barely noticed any of it.

Bethany was sitting on one of the benches in front of an open locker. The black mask was on the floor at her feet, but otherwise she was still dressed as she'd been earlier.

She didn't look up when he entered. Though a braid held her hair back, the lighting in the locker room was poor enough to obstruct his view of her face.

He stood silently over her for a moment, hoping she'd look up. When it became clear she had no intention of meeting his eyes, he squatted on the floor in front of her. Still receiving no response, he tilted her face toward him. It was only then that he realized she was silently crying. Actually, weeping might have been a better word.

Taking her face between his hands, he gently kissed her forehead. "Please don't cry," he whispered.

Bethany smiled weakly at him, as if the gesture would help.

"Beth," he said, kissing the tip of her nose this time, "I'm here. Please, please stop crying."

She took a deep breath, trying to gather herself. "You can go. It's okay."

"What are you talking about? Go? Where would I go?"

"Anywhere. Anywhere else. Thank you for staying and for watching, but it's okay. I understand."

Richard held her face a little tighter, trying to get more of a binding eye contact. "You think I'm going to leave you? Leave you about this?"

"It's okay. I understand," Bethany replied.

Richard sighed deeply. "Last night. You sat across from me in a restaurant; you looked me straight in the eye and you lied to me. A couple of days ago, you were the reason I was snatched out of my home by mobsters. About two years ago, you threw a martini in the face of the first girl I thought I loved. A few years before that, you crashed my car because you were so upset about a fight you had with your dad that you didn't see a stop sign. Need I say more?"

The blank look on Bethany's face told him that he did, in fact, have to say more.

"Every couple of years, one or the other of us does something stupid and the other person is mad for about three seconds and then we get over it."

"You think you can get over this?"

Richard shook his head. "I'm saying even if I was mad, I'd get over it. I love you too much not to. But, sweetheart, I don't see how there's anything to be mad about. I'm not mad. I can't believe you let me see this. It's amazing."

Bethany's brow furrowed deeply. "You don't find all this troubling?"

Richard smiled and kissed her hard on the lips. "You, my dear, are an angry young woman. And I hope to hell someday you'll make peace with that. I've never thought fighting was the way. But it doesn't really matter what I think. It's your decision."

She continued to look at him skeptically, but the tears were beginning to slow.

"I have one question," he said. "Why the lies? Why would you keep this from me?"

Bethany took a deep breath. "I'm pretty good at this."

Richard almost laughed at the understatement. "I did notice that."

"No, I mean I always have been. My father was afraid people would talk. So he pulled me out of public classes, made the sessions private, told me not to tell anyone the truth. The more time passed, the harder it was to fill in the blanks. What was I supposed to do? At sixteen I could beat up grown men. How could I have told you that? You would've totally freaked out."

Richard thought of himself at that age. Thought of Bethany's friends who'd come and gone through the years. And then he thought of the headlines, pictures in the paper, and the near obsession with her mother's murder. The public would have eaten her alive. Aston had been right about that.

"There's more," she said after a minute.

"You don't think fighting four guys is enough for one night?"

"What?"

"You said there's more. How many more guys can you fight in one night?"

Bethany shook her head. "No, I mean there's more to this. More to me. More you need to see. It's worse," she added softly.

Richard tried his best to conceal his concern. He couldn't imagine how things could be worse.

Bethany opened her locker to retrieve the clothes she'd been wearing earlier. "I just need to change, then we'll go upstairs."

She was out of her workout clothes and into other clothes in a flash. Or at least it felt that way to Richard, who was immediately distracted by the heavy Kevlar vest Bethany removed. Once she was completely dressed, he couldn't resist the obvious question.

"Is that what I think it is?" he asked, pointing at the vest.

Bethany nodded. "I train in it so it doesn't feel awkward when I need it."

Richard wanted to ask her what she was talking about, but the fear in her eyes stopped him. Without comment he accepted her extended hand and followed her to a dark corner of the locker room where an elevator was very subtly placed in a nook between two lines of lockers. It was entirely clear this was how she typically entered and exited the building without anyone realizing where she was going.

They entered what looked like a freight elevator. The walls were a scratched battleship gray without any embellishments. The push button panel had two floors listed – one labeled ground, the other basement.

Above the two buttons was a keyhole. There was no writing anywhere near it. Richard wasn't sure he would've even noticed it if he hadn't seen Bethany place a small silver key in the slot.

"Are you sure you don't want to just go home?" Bethany asked, as the elevator began to rise.

"Based on the look on your face, I'm guessing that would be a lot easier," Richard kidded, trying to lighten the dark mood that was descending.

The look he received told him this was neither the time nor the place.

"Beth, I can deal with anything you want to show me. And I think it'll only be better if you can be completely honest with me about all of this."

Richard wanted to believe it was true, but he suspected that whatever was waiting at the end of this long elevator ride was going to be worse than he could imagine. He could feel it. And he could certainly see it in her eyes.

This was a test. He hoped he was up for the challenge.

~ 50 ~

The sight that awaited him when the elevator opened was like something out of Richard's worst nightmares. Only a crazy person would exist in a place like this – could exist in a place like this.

It was a huge open loft with stark white walls, which were blackened by a very familiar scrawl. Bold block letters formed names. Not the least of which were Rita Chase and Geoffrey Quinn.

Black lines shot off from Rita's name, leading to other names Richard didn't recognize. The only things that broke up the horrible black web were a series of sharp red lines that slashed through name after name. He prayed the lines meant a dead end and not a more literal death. Days ago he wouldn't have even questioned a thing like that, but he was quickly realizing he should be questioning everything.

The only thing more disturbing than the writing was the photos – black and white blow-ups of what had to have been crime scene photos. Rita Chase, a woman he'd loved almost as much as his own mother, was lying at the top of a grassy hill. Her face pale, eyes vacant, hair matted with what must've been blood. And if that wasn't enough, there was the tiniest handprint on her white shirt, suggesting what Richard had often feared – Rita Chase wasn't the only one who'd been irreparably damaged that day.

"This is where I work," Bethany whispered. "It's kind of crazy, I know."

Kind of? Richard practically screamed. But instead he simply said, "It's an unusual approach."

Seeming to notice his attention was on the photos, Bethany added, "The police think I turned her body. That's why she was on her back."

Richard wondered if she actually thought he was staring because the ballistics and the body position didn't match up.

He knew he didn't have the words to respond, so he began to wander around the room. He was drawn to a large cabinet in a dark corner. Bethany followed, flipping a switch, illuminating a single bare bulb over the cabinet, casting more shadows through the loft.

Richard didn't even try the doors before he looked to Bethany for assistance. Without a word, she pulled a small gold key out of her pocket and inserted it in the lock. She opened both doors broadly and then stepped to one side, providing him with an unobstructed view of the arsenal inside.

He stared at the weapons in disbelief – everything from shotguns to handguns; nunchucks to Chinese stars; knives to machetes. The silver sparkled in the room's stark light; even the jet-black weapons seemed to glow incandescently. It was like the light was coming from inside them, like they had a life of their own.

"Most of the weapons, I've never used. It just makes me feel better to know they're available," Bethany explained, her voice only a whisper.

Richard was certain he didn't feel any better knowing they were available. Still unable to say anything even remotely constructive, he nodded and returned to the main part of the room.

He took a seat at the desk. He noticed the chair was the only one in the room, but he didn't consider offering it to Bethany. He needed to sit, needed to try and comprehend this, needed to consider if anything would ever be normal again.

After a while, Bethany spoke. "I know it must seem like I'm completely insane."

Richard couldn't tear his eyes away from the black scrawl, from the red slashes. It certainly did look like she was insane.

"I painted the walls white when I moved in. I was going to order whiteboards, but this just seemed easier," Bethany offered meekly.

"Do you want the truth?" Richard asked, finally facing her.

Bethany was clearly struggling to keep her voice even. "Yes, I think I need to hear the truth."

"This doesn't just look crazy."

Bethany nodded, fighting the tears, avoiding his eyes.

He leaned forward and took her hand. "Which is exactly why we need to stick together."

The tears were falling now. "I don't understand."

Richard brushed the tears from her cheek. "I think you've been a little crazy ever since you lost your mom."

"Rich?" she asked in confusion.

"The strain of the loss of your mom. That trauma did something to you. I was only a kid, but I saw it even then. And I've seen it just about every day since. Occasionally, you have these moments of peace, moments where the anger isn't right at the surface. But they're rare."

Bethany was staring at him now, looking more lost than he'd ever seen her look.

He smiled at her, hoping she could see the truth in his eyes. "I've never understood why you train, never understood how beating somebody up could help any of this. I don't know if this is the right thing. But, Bethany, I can see that this is how you're working through it. For better or worse, I'm with you."

"You're okay with this?" she asked.

"I think okay may be a strong word. I'm here. I'll support you. But on one condition."

She looked suddenly nervous again. "What's the condition?"

"When you find the asshole that did this, it has to end. That has to be your closure. Do to them whatever it is you need to do to them, and then walk away. Walk away and be the woman your mom would've wanted."

"I can do that," Bethany replied through fresh tears.

Unable to resist any longer, Richard grabbed her in a tight hug. "I love you so much," he murmured.

He resisted the need to add – *I wish I could fix this for you.* His whole life he'd made that wish. And his whole life he'd never been able to do anything more than he was doing right now. It would always be his greatest regret.

~ 51 ~

Bethany couldn't believe everything was okay. Richard looked a little freaked out, but he was still standing there next to her, which was more than she dreamed possible.

On the walk home, he did something even more amazing.

"You have to eat," Richard ordered. "I'm betting you haven't had much more than coffee in the past couple of days. I think we should grab some take-out and then head to Geoffrey's apartment."

The last part of the sentence caught Bethany completely by surprise. "Geoffrey's?"

"You need to follow up on that bank thing, right? I mean, hell, I'd rather go anywhere else, but you probably need to move on this. Don't the TV cops always worry about the trail going cold?"

Bethany laughed at the reference. "You're the most perfect man in the world. Yes, it would be better to look into this bank thing as soon as possible. But you said you wanted to take me out. I'd love to go, Rich. Frankly, you've dealt with enough for one night. The bank statements can wait until tomorrow."

Richard took her hand. "We're a team. Whatever you need to do, we'll do it together. That's always been how we've done it. No more secrets. The date will keep. Consider it a standing invitation."

Bethany gave him a kiss, stunned by the selfless gesture, almost overwhelmed by her emotions. "If we get in and out quick maybe we can grab some dessert after?"

Richard ran a thumb over her chin. "I'd like that."

~ 52 ~

Richard still felt weird being the one helping Bethany search Geoffrey's apartment. With everything that was going on between them now, it just seemed disrespectful. But he knew Bethany needed answers the way most people needed air.

She was dying inside. The haunting questions were pushing her further and further away from a normal life.

Answers, though, were never as simple as one might expect. They'd already searched Geoffrey's desk, finding several bank statements, none of which were from FTL. A search of a nearby file cabinet yielded similarly poor results.

They eventually made their way to Geoffrey's bedroom. Richard found himself in charge of pulling boxes out of the back of the closet. Bethany was sorting through them. It wasn't long before he came across a very heavy shoebox.

"This one feels interesting, but it certainly doesn't sound like bank statements," Richard said.

As he handed her the box, there was a distinct sound of metal against metal. He couldn't initially see the contents of the box, but the expression on Bethany's face as she opened it told him more than he needed to know.

Devastation.

Quick as it had appeared, the expression faded. Bethany folded back in on herself. She was all business as she carefully examined two handguns and a box of bullets.

"What the hell is all that?" he asked.

"Nine-millimeters. Hollow point bullets," she replied, as if he'd asked something other than a rhetorical question.

Richard tried to remain calm. "He was a prosecutor. He probably has a license, right?"

Bethany's eyes were locked on the guns. "He didn't have a license."

"How do you know that?"

"I investigated Geoffrey when we started dating. So did my father. So did Timminolo. We all managed to miss this hidden bank account, but I seriously doubt any of us would've missed a publicly filed gun license," Bethany replied, her voice disturbingly flat.

Richard stared in shock at how calmly Bethany looked at each gun and the box of bullets, gently placing them on the floor next to her.

"The guns are loaded," she warned, as she moved on to the remaining contents of the box.

Emotionless, she withdrew an envelope with the familiar crest of FTL Bank. He peered over her shoulder as she removed the statement. The postmark was recent.

Even the unlicensed guns couldn't have prepared Richard for the contents of the statement. Two million dollars, in a checking account.

Who kept two million dollars in a checking account? Which brought Richard to an even more important question; where would Geoffrey have gotten two million dollars?

Before he could say anything, Bethany was at the phone. Using the speaker so they could both hear, she connected them to the automated line for the bank. As she punched in the relevant numbers, Richard wondered what the hell she was looking for.

An automated voice informed them that Geoffrey's current balance was one million five hundred thousand dollars.

Before Richard could ask what had happened to the other five hundred thousand, Bethany was pressing a series of buttons. The same flat computerized voice relayed numbers and something about a transfer. Though the information meant little to Richard, it clearly meant something to Bethany. Without a word, she disconnected the call, dropped her head in her hands and, for the second time that night, began to weep.

~ 53 ~

Bethany sat on her dead fiancé's bed, her new boyfriend's arms around her, feeling nothing. No sting of betrayal, no remorse about moving on so quickly. Nothing. A half an hour ago, such a display of affection would have been so inappropriate she would've been disgusted. But now, everything had changed.

Her pain was giving way to anger, she could feel that. The shock giving way to a familiar need for vengeance. The humiliation giving way to rage.

In the anger, she began to think more clearly. There was more going on here, more she wasn't seeing.

As she focused, she rose to her feet and began to pace the room.

Richard watched her with obvious anxiety. He spoke hesitantly. "I'm sorry, but I really don't understand. There's a shitload of money in that account. Like way more than Geoffrey should've had.

And then you called the bank, and, well, then everything kind of went to hell. Could you possibly clue me in?"

Bethany didn't stop her pacing. In a clipped voice, she replied, "There was a withdrawal made from the account, through an electronic transfer. The amount and the date of the transfer match the money the hitman was paid for the killing."

Richard stared with continuing confusion. "Are you saying Geoffrey paid some guy to shoot him in the head?"

"No," she said coldly. "I'm saying Geoffrey paid some guy to shoot *me* in the head."

Richard recoiled. "How? How could that happen?"

Bethany shook her head. "How could my fiancé be secretly planning to kill me? Hell if I know. Turns out I'm a worse judge of character than I would've thought."

"No." Richard looked more focused now. "Are you sure it makes sense that it was supposed to be you?"

"It's the money, Rich. I can call Frankie now and have him work on the account number, but come on. He just happened to transfer five hundred thousand dollars on the exact same day?"

Richard stood and joined her pacing. "So what if it's the money? Why would you think he paid to have you killed?"

"There were only two people there that night – him and me. The man who fired the shot was paid by Geoffrey. Unless you think this was the most ornate suicide ever, the answer is obvious."

Richard still didn't look convinced. "I guess."

"And oddly, it sort of makes sense. We could never

figure out how the killer knew where we'd be that night. It seemed like we'd just randomly decided to walk, randomly picked that place. When the police asked about that night, you all agreed it had been Geoffrey's idea to walk. It didn't make sense as a lead before. No one thought he could've been the one who hired the hitman, not since he was the one who ended up dead."

"So, what? The guy missed?"

Bethany sat back down on the bed. Closing her eyes, she tried to remember the details, picture things as they happened. Geoffrey had asked if she'd heard something. Only then did she lift her head. An instant later came the shots. The thing was – Geoffrey hadn't moved.

The killer wasn't aiming at her. He couldn't have been. If he'd been aiming at her and missed, he would've hit Geoffrey in the arm, or the stomach, but not in the head. It couldn't have happened that way.

"Or someone told him to miss?" Richard suggested.

Bethany looked up. Richard was standing over her. He placed his hands firmly on her shoulders. "Think about it," he urged. "Hitmen don't make mistakes, do they?"

As he stared at her knowingly, it slowly came together. "The men who follow me around didn't make a mistake that night," she realized.

Richard shook his head. "No. I don't think they did. You want to take a trip to Staten Island? I think there's a guy there who might be able to answer some of your questions."

"I'll call Frankie on the way. I'm anxious to hear what he has to say for himself."

~ 54 ~

As Richard pulled Bethany's car out of the parking garage, she dialed Frankie's number.

The more she thought about it the angrier she got. Pietro had been lying from the start, making it seem like he thought Geoffrey's murder had something to do with her mother's death. The bastard had known the truth all along.

Most painful was the realization that Frankie had double-crossed her. He had to have known. Didn't he?

It was that final question that was turning over and over in her mind when Frankie picked up his phone. His greeting sounded distracted and distant.

Bethany got straight to the point. "Richard and I are on our way to Timminolo's house. I suggest you be there as well."

"That's good, Bethany," he replied, though his tone made it clear he didn't think any of this was good.

"There are a couple of things your grandfather would like to explain to you."

"Wonderful," Bethany sniped, "then it should be quite a fluid conversation, because I have a couple of things I'd like to 'explain' to him, as well."

"Okay," Frankie said simply. "I'll see you."

Bethany disconnected the line before she had to really consider the resignation in Frankie's voice. If she'd been a less skeptical person, she would've been inclined to believe Frankie was discovering all of this for the first time himself. But, she didn't believe in such fairy tales. She couldn't afford to.

"You okay?" Richard asked, merging into traffic. "You look weird."

Bethany wished her laugh sounded less bitter. "Why would I look weird?"

Richard reached over and gently squeezed her hand. "You wanted answers. That's what you're getting. When this is all figured out, you'll finally be able to put this behind you."

"Maybe I was wrong. Maybe I was better off not knowing."

"Don't do that," he ordered.

"Do what?" Bethany replied. She could feel him staring at her, but she refused to look his way.

"I'm your best friend in the world, right?"

Bethany murmured something that resembled a yes.

"I know you better than anyone on the entire planet." Though Richard paused for her answer, he didn't stop when she ignored him. "You're smart. You're steadfast. You're also stubborn, sometimes to a fault. And your temper does, on occasion, make you quite a bit more spontaneous than you should be. But I can tell you one thing you've never been – stupid.

Don't start now."

"What the hell is that supposed to mean?" Bethany snapped.

"Don't start second guessing yourself. You made a decision ten years ago. Hell, I think you made a decision the day you stepped into that gym with Master Jung. You've pursued it with a tenacity that's nothing short of extraordinary. You're close. And you're scared. I get that. Jesus, I'm petrified. But you can't stop now. You can't run away. Face it. Get your answers. You'll never forgive yourself if you don't, and you'll never forgive me if I let you."

Bethany was speechless. He was right, of course. She had to continue. Deep down she'd known that, but to hear someone else say it, for someone else to believe it.

He knew everything. All the insanity. All the violence. And with all that he was standing by her. He was actually encouraging her. She squeezed his hand tightly in response.

"My God, I love you so much. I don't know how I could even get through a day without you." The words tumbled from her lips before she could even consider the meaning.

Richard smiled. "Well, then it's a good thing you'll never have to."

After a moment he added, "I love you, too."

He'd said it a hundred times before, as had she, but it was different now. The reality of that didn't escape either of them. And for a moment she thought that maybe, just maybe, this could all work out.

~ 55 ~

The gates to the Timminolo house were open, but on that dark night nothing about the house looked welcoming. Matching black Cadillacs stood at the top of the circular drive. If she hadn't been too tense to get the words out, Bethany might've wondered aloud if crime syndicates got family discounts on cars.

Shutting off the engine with a certain determination, Richard turned to her and asked, "You ready to kick some ass?"

The ridiculous suggestion brought a small smile to Bethany's lips. And as she got out of the car she realized she was, in fact, ready.

She strode to the house with Richard walking about a half a step behind her, looking every inch the protector. Knocking, Bethany straightened to her full height and vowed to use every trick she'd learned from her father to be the most intimidating person in the room, despite the questionable morals of the two men she was meeting.

Her resolve slipped a little when she saw Frankie. There was a new strain on his face that told her he hadn't known the truth. He'd been snowed by his boss and felt he'd betrayed the memory of the woman he'd loved.

The signs were obvious, but they had to be ignored. As did the ache in Bethany's heart that was growing more painful by the minute.

"Is he here?" she asked without a greeting.

"He's in the office, waiting for you," Frankie explained, holding the door open wide.

Bethany expected him to comment on Richard, to make a big deal about it, but Frankie seemed to barely notice him. Without a word they crossed the great hall and entered the dimly lit den.

Pietro Timminolo was sitting in his high-backed chair, his dominating presence filling the chair in a way his tiny frame couldn't. He was a lot like Aston actually. Bethany wondered if her mother had realized that.

"I am glad you have come. There are things that need to be discussed," Pietro said. Then, noticing Richard, he added, "I would prefer to keep this in the family."

"Richard is more family to me than you'll ever be," Bethany snapped.

Pietro nodded passively and then turned a hostile eye to Richard. "My granddaughter is a good girl. You must treat her with respect."

Richard didn't flinch. "I've never treated Bethany with anything other than respect. You, on the other hand, have had your moments."

Bethany suppressed a smile. Richard's confident

sarcasm gave her even more courage. "I want an explanation of what you did and how you did it."

"I think you should sit down," Pietro replied, pointing to the chairs in front of his desk.

Holding her position over him, she said, "I'll stand, thank you. I want an explanation."

Pietro looked between Frankie and Bethany. "He said you would be angry. That is something I do not understand."

"You had my fiancé murdered," Bethany answered icily.

"If you know that, then you know why I did it. He hired a man to kill you. That man was someone who worked for me many times. He knew who you were. When he got the contract he called me. There was only one thing for me to do," Pietro replied in a matter-of-fact tone.

"There were a thousand things you could've done!"

"You tell me one," Pietro ordered, his voice showing his growing anger.

"You could've gone to the police."

"That is absurd. I turn in one of my men? A man who is just being loyal? I cannot do that. The police were no use in this situation. You know who I am. You know who Geoffrey was. A call to the police and I would have been in jail."

Bethany began pacing the room. "You could've told me."

"You did not know our relationship. You did not even believe I was your grandfather at first. You would not have believed the story about Geoffrey."

"My father. You could've told Aston."

"And what could he have done?" Pietro snapped. "This is enough now! There was no other way. He wanted you dead. You are safe if he is dead. That is it."

"That's not it!" Bethany shouted back. "That can't be it!"

Frankie stepped between them. "You're upset. I get that. But what's done is done. I'd never have put you through this if I'd known the truth."

His interjection had the desired effect; it diverted Bethany's anger. And it focused that anger directly onto him.

"How stupid do you think I am?" she growled. "Do you expect me to believe this is news to you? To you, the man who leads the team that stalks my every move? That's ridiculous! Of course you knew. You knew and you patted me on the head and led me on a wild goose chase."

"He did not know," Pietro stated flatly. "And if you will stop shouting we will discuss this properly."

"I don't discuss matters with murderers!"

Richard placed a gentle hand on Bethany's shoulder. In barely more than a whisper he said her name.

On instinct, Bethany spun around to face him, feeling only rage, hatred, and the fire of her vendetta. At first, she couldn't even hear him. She was certain if anyone other than Richard had touched her at that moment she would've knocked him on his ass.

She saw a flicker of panic in his eyes, but it faded quickly. "You came here to get answers. Ask the questions. Get the answers," he whispered.

She wanted to lash out. In fact, she was surprised to discover that all she actually wanted was to kill someone. To commit cold-blooded murder and end this. End all of it. And there was a tiny, very insistent, and very vocal part of her mind that was screaming for her grandfather's head.

Fortunately, Richard's voice broke through the din.

He was right, of course; the rage wasn't helping. And whether his methods were appropriate or not, Pietro Timminolo had saved her life, saved her life from a man she'd thought loved her.

It wasn't Timminolo she wanted dead. It was Geoffrey. That was part of the reason she was so angry. The old man stole her opportunity. He'd fought the battle for her.

Bethany willed herself to regain control. She stared at Richard's eyes, focusing on the color, noticing how dark they were. Maybe it was the lighting, maybe it was fear, but they looked almost black they were so dark.

"Beth?" he whispered, clearly uncertain where she was, clearly worried.

"Thanks," she whispered back.

Then she turned back to her grandfather and Frankie. Frankie's face was awash with remorse and concern. Pietro was stoic.

"I don't agree with what you did," she said, her voice now calm. "I hate what you did. I hate that you murdered someone. And maybe even more, I hate that you did it before I had the chance. And that, Grandfather, is the reason I'm the most angry with you."

Pietro nodded. "I am sorry you do not agree with my methods," he replied through gritted teeth. He was plainly trying to harness his temper also.

"You really didn't know?" Bethany asked Frankie.

"I'm sorry," Frankie replied. "If I'd known I wouldn't have let you go through what you did. When we found the account today, that's when I started to wonder. I assume you found independent confirmation of the payment?"

"Bank statements," Bethany said simply. "Do you know why? Why he did it? Why he wanted me dead?"

Frankie looked to Pietro for the answer, clearly not knowing himself.

"My men have been looking into the situation. They have found nothing. But we did not know the Brooklyn connection until I talked with Frankie tonight. That may be a help."

"You've been looking since his death and you've found nothing?" Bethany hoped her voice didn't sound as defeated as she felt.

"One of the reasons I had Frankie bring you here originally was I had hoped by talking to you I would discover more information. I hoped you knew why he would do this. But you thought it was about your mother and your investigation. It was clear you did not know Quinn wished you harm."

"That was the reason for our meeting?" Bethany asked, beginning to understand.

"When I was told about the contract, I immediately ordered it reversed. The man who ordered the hit is to be taken out in the way of the original contract. That is how these matters are handled. It sends a signal to the others. You do not come after my Family."

"So you killed him without asking any questions?"

"I am a man of action."

"You're a fool. You killed our only lead. You murdered the only person who could tell us why!" Bethany shouted. She was trying to keep a handle on her temper, but her frustration was only growing.

"The why does not matter! I do not care why. We made an example of him. I brought you here to make sure you did not know why he wanted to harm you, that way we could make sure any remaining threats could be eliminated as well."

"You killed the only person who knew if there were remaining threats. Now we have nothing to go on."

Pietro's back stiffened. "How dare you question me! I saved your life. I protected you."

"You aren't protecting me any better than you protected my mother," Bethany growled back.

That, Bethany realized even as she said it, was possibly the cruelest thing she'd ever done in her life.

Despite his life choices, despite questionable parenting skills, her grandfather had loved his daughter. Even in the story Aston had told, she could tell he'd seen the love between father and daughter. There was disagreement, without a doubt, but there was love.

The tears that pooled in her grandfather's eyes only confirmed the love, and proved Bethany was even more vicious than she'd previously believed. She wished she could take the words back, wished she could at least apologize, but she knew she couldn't do either.

And she also knew she was on her own again. Frankie wasn't going to help her. While her grandfather would certainly continue to send his men to protect her, they wouldn't be socializing for a very long time.

Bethany's voice was soft when she spoke again. "I think I have to leave now. I only ask that you tell me if you find anything out about Geoffrey. Please."

Pietro remained silent. However, Frankie spoke, his voice hesitant. "I'll make sure you're kept up to date."

"Thank you," she replied.

Then, taking Richard by the hand, she rigidly exited the room, marched through the great hall and out to her car. She slumped into the passenger seat and began to shake with anger and remorse, but the worst of it was simple despair.

She'd failed. She'd spent her whole life focused on one thing. She'd been sure it was the right thing, sure it was the only thing that really mattered, but the truth was, it didn't matter. It had all been a terrible mistake.

Richard took her hand. For a moment, she allowed herself to feel the gentle warmth of his touch and pull some strength from it. He was amazing. Perhaps most astonishing was that after all he'd just seen, he could still look at her with such love. It was clear he could see something in her that she couldn't see in herself. And she wondered, as he drove her home, exactly what that was.

~ 56 ~

Richard didn't like any of this. They'd passed the entire drive in silence. And now, as they stepped off the elevator, she'd still only managed a few words. He'd just witnessed a showdown worthy of the Wild West. He couldn't tell if Bethany was unfazed by the experience or devastated. Either way, he figured they needed to talk about it. At a minimum, he needed to talk about it.

He led Bethany into his apartment. The way she allowed him to guide her inside and over to his couch without comment or objection only increased his worry.

Sitting next to her, he took her hand. Uncertain what else to say he asked, "What are you thinking?"

Bethany's eyes shifted away from his, but not before he saw the tears in them. She fought against them as she spoke, "I was thinking about my mother."

He said without hesitation, "She would've been

proud of the way you stood up to the old man tonight."

Bethany laughed ruefully and roughly wiped a tear from her eye. "Proud? I was thinking of a lot of words. Proud wasn't one of them."

"Of course she would've been proud of you. From what you tell me, she worked her whole life to stand up to her father. And she eventually managed to get herself out from under his thumb. I think she'd be really proud of the way you handled yourself with him tonight."

Bethany slipped her hand out of his and walked to the other side of the room. She stood staring silently out the window for so long that he was surprised when she finally spoke.

"My mom hated his life, hated his world. She stood up to that man and made it on her own. It's amazing really, absolutely amazing. All she wanted was a normal, quiet life. A life without secrets, without lies, without violence, without hate."

Richard felt her pain with every word. She wasn't talking about her mother's life anymore, at least not entirely.

"You aren't your grandfather," he said.

Spinning on her heels, Bethany's eyes flashed with rage; rage he knew was directed solely at herself.

"I use violence to get what I want. I lie to my friends. I lie to my family. Maybe my reason's a little more noble than his, but that doesn't change what I do. The ends can't justify the means."

"You're just trying to find out what happened to your mother. It's understandable," he insisted.

"Tell that to Angelo Bria."

It took a minute before he could place the name. "That mob lawyer? The one who was mugged in the park?"

"I broke every finger on both of his hands. I'd have drowned him in that pond if I'd had to. If you aren't really willing to hurt them, the threats don't matter. I learned that pretty early on."

Richard felt a little sick to his stomach, but that was most likely her point. She was doing it again. She was trying to scare him away.

"Why?" he asked.

"He had information about my mother's murder, information about the man who was hired. I tortured him until he told me everything. Just like my grandfather would have."

"You did what you had to do," Richard said.

"Tony Mirriani."

This time, Richard interrupted. "Mirriani shot Geoffrey. You had every reason in the world to be angry about that. You did what you had to do," he repeated.

Bethany shook her head and laughed cruelly. "I crushed his hand. Ruined his shoulder. The shoulder I did because I had to. It was the only way to get the information. But his hand – I did that just because I could, because I hate him."

Richard stood and walked to the window next to her. He didn't face her, but instead stared into the night at the darkened park below them.

When he spoke, he spoke slowly and deliberately. "You want me to tell you that you're a monster. You want me to judge you and tell you to leave. But I'm not going to do that. I'm never going to do that.

"Bethany, if you don't like what you've made of your life, then change it. Stop straddling these two worlds. Stop being the person who loses sleep over all the unanswered questions. What's in the past is in the past. Let it go. You broke some bones, you made some people suffer, and from what I can tell most of them had it coming."

Richard could feel her staring at him in what he imagined was disbelief, but he didn't turn to face her yet.

In a whisper, she said, "I'm just like him. Don't you see it?"

Neither of them needed to explain who he was. It was obvious, just as obvious as it was that she was lost on her own.

Richard turned to her now, wishing he didn't see the self-hatred on her face. "You're both powerful people. He uses power to gain influence and wealth. You use power to help people, to empower others. I've always seen you that way. Nothing you've told me in the past few days has changed that, nothing could, because, Bethany, that's the truth."

"You're wrong," she said, but the protest was a whisper.

Gently, he wiped away the tear that slipped down her cheek. "I'm right," he replied.

And then he kissed her. Softly at first, barely brushing her lips. She wrapped her arms around him as if he was the only thing in the world that could keep her safe.

He could feel her tears on his cheeks as he pulled her close, getting lost in the scent of her, the feel of her body so close to his.

Her eyes were closed as she kissed him almost desperately. And he realized he'd never felt as important as he did now. She needed him, maybe as much as he needed her.

He found his hands trailing over her body, exploring curves he'd only ever fantasized about. As he slid her shirt over her head, he paused at the bruise that still stained her ribs. He traced his fingers over it ever so lightly, and he felt her shiver in response.

He promised himself he'd help her with all of this. If it was the last thing he did, he'd make sure she made it through.

~ 57 ~

Bethany awoke slowly, the haze of sleep melting into reality. If you could even call it reality, because this was like nothing she'd ever known.

Richard's heavy arm was slung across her stomach and one foot was wrapped around her leg. All her life she'd felt claustrophobic having another person this close, but with Richard it was different. With him it wasn't like there was another person at all, but more like an extension of herself. She felt a new insight into the concept of someone being your other half.

Yet even with the sense of peace, there was an electricity between them. She'd known there would be. She'd felt it innumerable times when his hand had brushed against hers, or she'd touched his arm. Actually, when life had seemed particularly tough through the years, she found herself looking for excuses to be closer to him, because even for an instant, his energy refreshed her.

Now, as he shifted his arm, his hand sliding across her stomach, she shivered with the memory of the night they'd had together. It had been better than she could've imagined. And with all the years she'd had to consider it, she had imagined.

She felt like she did after a good workout: tired and sore, but inspired and invigorated.

She was considering just how sore she really felt, when she realized Richard had turned his head ever so slightly and was watching her with a warm smile.

"Good morning, gorgeous," he said, chastely kissing her cheek.

Bethany grabbed the nape of his neck before he could slip away and kissed him more intimately. Flashes of the night before had her heart pounding faster than she would've expected.

After a moment, she reluctantly pulled away. She was pleased to see Richard's eyes looked as glazed as she felt.

"I don't think that'll ever get old," he grinned.

Bethany was certain she couldn't agree more.

"How'd you sleep?" he asked.

Richard had heard many stories of Bethany's bedroom claustrophobia. She could see in his eyes a fear that he'd broken a golden rule. She wrapped her leg around his and pulled him closer.

"I don't think I've ever slept as well as I did last night," she assured him.

Relief lit up his eyes, but he passed it off with a joke. "Well, I am that good."

Bethany laughed and felt compelled to join in the teasing. "Some might say you've been training your whole life for this."

Richard shifted, sliding his body over hers, touching

just enough to drive her crazy. "There was never anyone but you. I knew that before. I'm certain now."

Bethany stretched her neck just enough to catch Richard's lips with hers. She trailed her tongue across his jaw line to the edge of his ear.

"You're obviously the smartest person I know," she whispered.

Tilting his forehead against hers, Richard smiled. "I'm glad to see you're finally catching on."

For a moment she just laid with him, staring into his eyes and enjoying what it meant to be there. For all these years, he'd been right and she'd been wrong – and not just about this.

"I need to seriously change things," she said softly, not really knowing what she meant.

Seeming to sense her tone, Richard gave her a little space. "What kind of things?"

It was an obvious question with a far less obvious answer. "I've always said I was hunting this killer for my mother. I think it's pretty clear my mother wouldn't have wanted this."

Running a soothing hand over her hair, Richard replied, "Probably not."

"So if I decide to keep doing this, there's no confusion now, I'm doing it for me."

"And no one could blame you if you decided you had to do it for yourself."

Bethany wasn't sure that was true, but either way, she didn't like what she saw when she looked in the mirror anymore.

"Continuing is self-destructive. If my grandfather and his goons couldn't figure out what happened to my mother, it's pretty damn unlikely I'm going to."

Richard only nodded, telegraphing one very

important message. He'd support her – even if she picked wrong. And that was possibly the most important reason she had to let it all go.

"This obsession of mine is the reason I almost missed out on being here with you. As many mistakes as I've made, that would've been the worst."

Richard cocked his head. "How does this relate to you and me?"

Bethany shifted uncomfortably. As good as it felt to confess all of her sins and finally get them out in the open, she hated to dump so many things on him in such a short period of time.

"That night in college, when you asked me about us getting together, I wanted to say yes. I was attracted to you. I knew that. I had for while."

"I'm a pretty hot guy," Richard said with a wink.

She was relieved by his humor and again astonished at his strength. He was her rock, always had been. She really hadn't understood what that meant until now.

"I knew what I wanted to do to find out more about my mother's death. And I knew I'd have to do things I wouldn't be proud of to make that happen. Though I was wrong about a lot of it, I was right to know I couldn't do any of it if I was sharing a bed with someone, at least not on a regular basis. With other guys I could maneuver, demand space. But with you it never would've worked. You knew me too well. And I knew I couldn't lie to you like that."

Richard leaned in and kissed the top of her head. It was a few seconds before he spoke.

"You could've told me," he said.

Bethany shook her head. "It was wrong, Rich. Part of me has always known that. It's also crazy. I've always known that too. I couldn't confess to the most important person in my life that things had gotten so wrong and crazy. And I couldn't let you stop me."

Richard ran a finger down her nose and over her lips. "None of that matters anymore, Beth. We're in this together now. If you're ready to close the book, I'm ready to help you."

Bethany breathed a sigh of relief. That was the end of it. There were no more secrets. No more lies. She could just be herself now. They could start fresh.

"I love you, Richard Marshall," she said, believing the words more than she ever thought she could.

"I love you too," Richard replied, pressing his lips to hers.

She sank into his embrace, feeling safe and completely protected from everything, including herself.

~ 58 ~

Bethany knew her vow to move on with her life was essential to her sanity, and that meant she needed to move on as soon as possible, before she talked herself out of it. The first step was closing the door on a very dark chapter - Geoffrey.

She'd promised Geoffrey's mother she'd box up his belongings and send them to the Quinn house in Westchester. Though spending more time among Geoffrey's stuff was the last thing she wanted, Bethany knew she had to. She'd made a promise when things had been different. And unless she was going to explain what had changed, she had no alternative but to follow through.

She was actually able to tell Emily the truth when she called to find out if another day's worth of meetings could be cleared so she could take care of Geoffrey's apartment. Emily was, of course, accommodating. People were more than willing to give her time and space. No one needed to know the time had nothing to do with mourning.

More importantly, Richard cleared his day too. He understood how much she was dreading this. Frankly, if she hadn't thought the process of cleaning out the apartment might be oddly cleansing, she would've paid someone to do it for her.

She was boxing the contents of Geoffrey's desk while Richard packed plates and glassware when the insistent and annoying ring of her cell phone interrupted their work. She glared at Richard as she finished what she was doing. The call could go to voicemail. She'd check it in a minute.

"Seriously?" Richard snorted. "You're just going to make me listen to that. You could pick it up you know."

"You could volunteer to change it back to something that isn't so annoying it could cause brain damage," Bethany snarled back.

"I'm trying to teach you a lesson in how to work your phone. I think you just need the right motivation."

"You tried to change it back, didn't you?" Bethany realized with a laugh.

"Yup. A couple of days ago. The stupid ring is honestly going to drive us all insane. You're an heiress for God's sake, please, go get a new phone."

The ringing had stopped, but a follow-up beep informed her she had a voice message. Bethany sealed up her box and retrieved the call. But she didn't miss the opportunity to toss a balled-up piece of newspaper at Richard's head as she walked by.

"That's for ruining a perfectly good phone," she teased.

Richard smiled his most charming grin in response.

The voicemail was from her father. His message was vague, as his messages often were, but he picked up immediately when she called him back.

The tension in his voice surprised her.

"What's going on?" she asked, immediately worried.

"I was calling to ask you that question. Emily said you took the day off. It sounded like there was more to the story. Is everything okay?" Aston asked.

"Why do you ask?" Bethany prodded.

"Can't I just call my daughter?"

"You can call me anytime you want, but clearly something's up."

"You're one of the most suspicious people alive, do you know that?"

Bethany grinned a little at the remark and the note of pride she heard in her father's voice. "You trained me to be skeptical, Dad. Did the old man call you?"

"Pietro?" Aston scoffed. "No. He isn't one of my bigger fans. Frankie called. He was worried about you."

"Did he tell you what we found?" She hoped he had. Bethany dreaded going through the whole story to catch him up.

"He told me about the bank account, told me about the payment to the hitman, told me about the switch Timminolo made. Where are you, honey? I really need to see you, make sure you're okay."

His tone was not unlike one he would've used when she was eight and had a scraped knee. And part of her wished she could just trust, as she did then, that he could make everything better. It was a tempting fantasy.

"I'm at Geoffrey's," she confessed. "Richard's here

with me. I decided it was time to box things up. I'd just like all this to be over."

Bethany wished she didn't hear the resignation in her own voice.

"I'd like to join you," he father said. "I can be there in fifteen minutes. If you'll let me."

"I'd like that," Bethany admitted. "The more of us working on this, the faster it'll be done."

"I'll be there as soon as I can," Aston assured her.

Despite herself, Bethany found herself believing – if only a little – in the fantasy. Her father was coming. And he was going to fix this. Just as sure as a kiss and a hug made a scraped knee feel better.

Aston arrived less than ten minutes later. He was wearing a crisp navy suit, a starched white shirt and a conservative tie. He'd plainly just come from a meeting. For the only time Bethany could remember, Aston seemed entirely unconcerned at the prospect of wrinkles. He grabbed her in a tight bear hug the moment he entered the apartment. He stripped off his jacket, laid it across the back of a chair and immediately rolled up his sleeves.

"What's the system?" he asked.

He smiled at the helpless look she exchanged with Richard. There wasn't a system. Bethany had to admit that. She was mostly just packing as she found stuff.

"How about I take over the kitchen? The toughest part is going to be the bedroom. Why don't you two team up on that? Richard can pull things out. Bethany, you can pack it away."

On any other day, she would've resented the orders, but this wasn't any other day. Without a word, she gave her father a kiss on the cheek and led Richard back into Geoffrey's room.

Her father was right. Packing Geoffrey's room was a massive endeavor. Somehow, in three years of dating, she'd never noticed his wardrobe was actually bigger than hers. As she folded another Armani tie, her mind was drawn back to the bank account. He had millions sitting in a checking account, his clothes rivaled the rich and famous, but he was a prosecutor. His family was well-off, but not this well-off.

Her instincts were driving her, begging her to investigate, ask questions, find answers. How easy it would be to fall back into old habits.

Fortunately, Richard was on his game, protecting her as only he could – with humor.

"You seriously thought this many shoes was normal for a guy?" he called from the closet.

Bethany rolled her eyes. "I suppose all lying boyfriends have large shoe closets?"

Richard emerged arms laden with shoes, which he

dumped on the floor next to her. "You said it. I didn't," he said with a wink, before disappearing back into the closet.

She was considering how best to pack the shoes when there was a crash from the closet, followed by a string of muttered curses and something about stupid shoes. She was about to make fun of his clumsiness when Bethany realized it had suddenly become very quiet.

"Hey, Rich, you okay in there?"

He was slow to respond and when he did, his voice didn't carry any humor. "Beth, there's something you need to see."

She found Richard squatting on the floor next to what initially looked like a broken shoe rack.

He looked up when she entered. "I tripped over one of his goddamn shoe racks. But it wasn't a shoe rack, I mean, not really. It's a storage compartment." He held up what looked like a stack of photos. "You should look at these."

A sense of dread settled over her. She took the pictures he handed her, wishing she could just walk away, but knowing she wasn't built that way.

They looked like old family photos. The pictures were primarily of two people – a man and a woman. As children, they were photographed alone; as adults, there were several pictures of them together.

"Did you look at these?" she asked Richard.

He nodded, a look of pity on his face.

"That man couldn't look any more like Geoffrey." They both knew the truth, yet somehow she felt it might not be real until she said it.

Richard said it for her. "They've got to be Geoffrey's parents."

Pictures in hand, Bethany sank to the floor. "The man isn't in the more recent pictures."

Again, Richard nodded. He'd put the pieces together, like she had. He was just waiting for her. "I'd estimate the pictures of him stop about twenty years ago."

This time Bethany found the strength to say the words herself. "He's dead."

Richard pointed to a picture of the woman on the front step of a house. "Based on the houses, the yards, I think that's Brooklyn, don't you?"

Slowly, the anger began to creep back. That was the thing about anger, rage, it was empowering, energizing. Without it she was left helpless in the face of these assaults. Years of practice taught her the power of her rage. And it wasn't letting her down today.

"Is this all that's in there?" she asked, her voice sounding stronger.

Richard gave her an odd look she couldn't quite decipher. "There are some papers too."

He pulled them out for her and then leaned over her shoulder to read as she did. The paperwork confirmed their suspicions. A birth certificate. Adoption papers. Louis DeAmanto and Celeste Vicetti.

"Do you recognize his parents' names?" Richard asked.

She didn't, but there were a couple of people who might. One of them was in the other room. "Maybe my father will."

Again, Richard gave her a strange look, almost as if he didn't recognize her. She dismissed the thought as ridiculous, even though part of her knew the truth. She was shutting down again, abandoning the normal life she'd promised herself hours earlier.

Bethany brought the new bundle of information to her father, who was efficiently packing a box of dishes. She laid the pictures and papers on the table next to the box.

"It looks like Geoffrey did find his biological parents. I'm guessing the reason you couldn't track them was that he covered it up."

Her father looked between Bethany and Richard, then turned his full attention to the new information. He skipped through the pictures quickly and focused on the paperwork. As he read, the color drained from his face.

When he finally met her eyes, Aston looked distant and withdrawn. "We're going to have to call your grandfather."

Bethany's heart was pounding now. "No. You're going to tell me why you look like that."

Aston's eyes turned to Richard, who was standing silently at Bethany's side. It seemed he was trying to determine if he could be trusted. Bethany was a little surprised at how quickly he dismissed his hesitation.

"I know that man," Aston explained. "I told you about the men who fronted the money for my company. I told you Pietro set them up in a different business. He set them up in DeAmanto's shop."

From the corner of her eye, Bethany could see the confusion on Richard's face. In another time and place she might have explained, but she knew Richard well enough to know he'd roll with whatever she did.

She simply asked, "Are you sure?"

Aston sank into a chair. "I'm certain. We need to contact Pietro. We need to find out what happened to that man."

Resignation and sadness threatened to undercut her

resolve. She'd really believed she could let all this go.

She'd been wrong of course. The path was set. She had no choice. She never had.

~ 60 ~

By the time they reached the Timminolo house, Bethany felt completely numb. In the past few days with Richard there'd been moments when she'd felt alive again, whole for maybe the first time in her life. But she had to shut that down, shut it out. Just like in any fight, she had to ignore the blows, ignore the pain, and simply attack. It was the only way to survive.

Richard pulled her aside as Aston knocked on the heavy oak door.

"I think I should wait in the car," he whispered.

"What are you talking about?" she replied, more focused on the closed door than anything else.

"This seems like a family matter. I mean it's one thing for me to stay with you for moral support when you're by yourself, but your dad's here. I'm not sure it's my place."

Suddenly realizing what he was suggesting, Bethany shifted her attention to Richard. "You're seriously talking about skipping out on me?"

His eyes grew wide at the accusation. "Skipping out? No. I'm just saying I'm not sure you really want me in there. Seems like there are a lot of Chase family secrets to go with the Timminolo family secrets I've already heard so much about."

"If you want to wait out here, that's your choice. But if you're asking me if I want you in there, the answer is yes. If you catch this whole story live then I won't have to rehash it later."

Richard smiled with surprise and relief and, for just a moment, the strange look that had been on his face since Geoffrey's apartment vanished. Before he could say anything more, Frankie appeared in the doorway and ushered them inside.

Greetings were short and clipped. Frankie knew nothing was going to get done until they got in the room with Pietro. They all did.

They followed Frankie into the now familiar den. Bethany and Richard took seats in front of the desk. Though there was a third chair, Aston chose to stand.

Pietro's chair was in deeper shadow than usual that morning. But even the darkness didn't conceal his disdain for his son-in-law.

"Aston Chase, it seems you only appear in my midst when you need something."

Bethany looked between her father and her grandfather. She'd never seen Aston allow someone to treat him so patronizingly, yet the look on his face told her he was going to stand there and take it.

"Yes, it does," he replied.

"It has been more than two decades since we last saw each other, correct?"

"Yes."

"And now the same story. You come to me needing help."

Bethany had watched the interaction as long as she could without saying anything. "We're here because it seems you didn't do such a great job of *fixing* things twenty-five years ago."

Pietro glowered. "I was not talking to you."

"Really?" Bethany snapped. "How about you start?"

"This is what you raised?" Pietro accused, his hostile eyes focused on Aston.

Bethany was pleased to see a slow smile cross her father's face. "I can't take much of the credit really. Rita was a wonderful influence on her. But, yes, that's what I raised. Astonishing. I agree."

That was the sarcasm Bethany had been looking for.

"If you two are done catching up, I'd like to get down to business and get the hell out of here," she suggested.

Extending the photos and papers toward Frankie, Bethany continued, "We found these in Geoffrey's things. Photos of his parents. We're all fairly confident that looks like Brooklyn."

Frankie took the pictures and handed them directly to his boss. Pietro gave each a thorough examination and handed them back to Frankie as he finished. Bethany was pretty sure he was purposely dragging it out – making them squirm.

"Do you know who this man is?" Pietro asked finally. His tone indicated he remembered; he just wanted to know if Aston did.

"He owned the company you sent those men into," Aston replied.

"You know the story?" Pietro's question fell to Bethany.

"I got the background from my father. I know about the investors in the company. I know when things became a problem, you helped by relocating them. What I don't know is what you did to that man."

"I did nothing to Lou," Pietro growled at the implication. "Lou DeAmanto owed me a great debt. I gave the debt to the family that was bothering your father. They used DeAmanto's company instead. It was a small company. Not fast growing. Lots of boxes and shipments. It was a better fit for them. For DeAmanto it was nothing new. He had worked for me three years already. Just a new boss now."

"You make it sound so simple," Bethany replied.

"It is simple. You take a favor. You pay your debt. This is how it works."

"Yet, somehow DeAmanto ends up dead?" Bethany challenged, assuming they were right about the gap in the photos.

"And you think I had something to do with it?"

"I think the men you sent into his business had something to do with it."

Pietro sat back in his chair smugly, and Bethany realized she'd miscalculated. The connection had seemed so obvious, but now it was more obvious she'd been wrong.

"Lou DeAmanto was a weak and stupid little man. That is why he is dead. It had nothing to do with me, nothing to do with the men who used his company. He took a bottle of pills and then shot himself for good measure. He was not a man. *That* is why he is dead."

Bethany could only stare in disbelief while she reevaluated the situation. She'd been so certain all the pieces fit, so certain the men that had weaseled their way into her father's business had caused DeAmanto's death. That made sense. Mostly because it explained why Geoffrey might've been angry enough to want her dead. It was a neat little package. This, however, was anything but.

"He committed suicide?" Richard voiced the thoughts that were racing through her mind. "Are you sure?"

Frankie spoke up. "Yeah, he killed himself. Guy was a loser. There's something else yous need to know. The lady in the pictures. She's a good friend of my wife – Celeste Vicetti. She and Lou, they was a couple for years. My Maria, she was always telling Celeste to drop him, to move on. I gotta say this information about the baby, maybe that's why she always stuck by the guy."

"You know Geoffrey's mother?" Bethany didn't know how it could be important, but it seemed like it had to be.

"She and my wife, they grew up together."

"Where did they grow up?" Aston asked.

"Brooklyn. About two blocks from the bank where Geoffrey had his account."

"Did you know this woman had a child who was given up for adoption?" Aston's voice was steeped in allegation. He was clearly thinking the same thing as Bethany – if Frankie had known about the child, the location of the bank should have tipped him off.

"This is the first I heard of any of this. I didn't know Maria when the baby would've been born."

"Do you think you can stop with the accusations now?" Pietro said, his eyes sharp with sarcasm.

"We didn't come here to fight with you," Aston replied. "We came here to give you this information and to ask you what you know. These people – DeAmanto and Celeste – they're the link to all of this. They're the reason Geoffrey Quinn wanted my daughter dead. If you have nothing more helpful to offer, I guess we'll be on our way."

"Actually," Frankie said quickly, "I think I could help, if that's okay, boss."

Pietro merely nodded.

Frankie continued, "I'll talk with Maria tonight. See if we can arrange dinner tomorrow with Celeste. Maybe she'd be willing to help us understand what's going on."

Bethany looked to her father for confirmation. She was back in the thick of things. Richard or not, there was no turning back.

~ 61 ~

Dinner was an awful idea. Bethany knew it almost immediately. And the more she thought about it, the more certain she became.

It was simply too civilized. Was she supposed to sit down with Celeste Vicetti and discuss her son's murder plans over a glass of Merlot? Nothing about this was normal. Efforts to make it into something it wasn't would only make it worse.

Bethany spent the day wondering if she should just walk away. She had Richard now. She didn't need to know the details, didn't need to know the reasons.

But the truth was, she did need to know and she couldn't walk away from the answers. So, at six o'clock, when Debbie told her Richard was downstairs waiting for her, she went without hesitation into certain disaster.

She found Richard waiting next to his car in the Chase Electronics parking garage. He was still dressed from his work day, in a starched gray shirt that accentuated his strong, broad chest. He opened his arms to her when she got close and enveloped her in a tight hug.

For a moment, she was tempted. They could go home. Just the two of them. In his arms, she thought of all the ways he could distract her. All the ways he could make her forget the endless questions that never seemed to lead to any answers.

Bethany pulled away just enough to look closely at his face, see his loving smile and the sparkle of adoration in his eyes. He would protect her from anything. She only had to let him.

He ran his hand over her hair and asked, "You sure you want to do this?"

Bethany chuckled. "I'm sure I'd rather do anything else."

Richard shook his head, knowing the truth. "But?"

And, of course, he was right. There was always the but. There always had been. It felt like there always would be.

She didn't answer. Instead, she pulled him into a long kiss, allowing herself a moment to feel the simple warmth without all the thinking.

When she finally pulled away, she didn't need to say anything more. Neither of them did.

Climbing into the car, Richard asked, "Are you ready for some bonding with your almost mother-in-law?"

"You're kidding, right?"

"At this hour, it's going to take us a while to get to Staten Island, so we've got some time to strategize."

"I've been thinking about this all day and I don't have a clue what to do."

Richard strummed his fingers thoughtfully on the steering wheel as he maneuvered out of the parking lot and into the dense traffic. "I suppose locking her in a room and beating the information out of her is out of the question?"

It was stunning that he could make her smile at a time like this, but she immediately fell into the banter. "Well, it was my plan A, but I think it might be an inappropriate way to behave at a dinner party."

Richard continued, his eyes twinkling with humor, "Well, if we're going to follow the rules of etiquette, that'll eliminate violence and general name calling. I guess that leaves us with sweet talk. How are you at that?"

"To be honest, not very good."

Richard grinned. "Ah-ha! I think we may have finally hit upon a way I can be useful. I have quite a way with the ladies you know."

"I did notice that."

"Well then, it's decided. We go with the Marshall charm and we'll get all we need. I'll need a little background. Do you know anything about this woman?"

"Nothing more than you do."

"Do you think she knew Geoffrey's little plan?"

Only Richard could make a murder plot seem funny. "You mean his plan to have me killed? I think we're going to have to assume she knew and possibly even encouraged it."

"So, I'm thinking she's not one of your bigger fans."

"It wouldn't seem that way."

Before Richard could ask another question, Bethany's cell phone rang. He rolled his eyes at the obnoxious ring.

"I am begging you, Beth, please, please, please, get a new phone."

Bethany only shook her head. "I don't want to hear it. This is entirely your fault."

A glance at the caller ID revealed it was Annie, reminding Bethany she hadn't talked to her in days. She told Richard who was on the line as she picked it up, greeting her good friend somewhat hesitantly.

"Oh, don't try to be all remorseful to make up for the fact you've been completely out of touch," Annie snipped, feigning anger. "You have serious crap going on with your life these days and I've heard nothing. Zero."

Bethany tried to think back to the last time they talked. Before she'd gone to the bank, before she'd found out about Geoffrey. There was so much, too much to discuss over the phone.

"I'm sorry, honey. It's been crazy."

"Hi, Annie," Richard shouted.

"Crazy like you two are going at it every moment or crazy like a problem? More family stuff?" she asked.

"Crazy like family stuff," she admitted. "It's way too much to get into now. Lunch? My office? Tomorrow?"

As they agreed on a time, Bethany heard the worry in Annie's voice. She wished she could tell her it was fine, that she was fine, but it would've been a lie. Though she hated that her friend would be left with hours to fret about undisclosed horrors, the truth was undoubtedly worse than anything Annie could imagine.

They said their goodbyes as Richard entered the tunnel. Bethany watched as the stunningly bright day turned to night in the tunnel's darkness. She could see the light at the exit and wondered if there was a figurative light awaiting her as well.

It had been a long journey. It seemed like forever since she'd last seen the light. In fact, she almost wondered if the last time hadn't been that warm spring day when she and her mother took their last trip to the park.

Her memory of the day was spotty at best. Even worse, she had nothing more than the memories of a six-year-old, which meant they were largely skewed by her own vision of the world.

She remembered they were making a game of hurrying through the streets. Looking back, it seemed odd, maybe even a little suspicious, but it could've been nothing more than an attempt to get rid of some excess energy.

Bethany had only one truly troubling memory before the shooting. While she was off gathering wild flowers and bringing them to her mom, she'd swear she remembered her mother looking around the park. It was almost as if she'd been waiting for someone, as if she'd expected they'd be there when they arrived.

If those memories were accurate, it meant the hit was set up through a meeting. The hitman hadn't just followed them to the spot in the park. He'd been waiting. He'd known where they would be. That meant Rita Chase knew the person who'd set her up, knew them well enough to be willing to meet them, trusted them enough that she'd brought her daughter.

~ 62 ~

They were driving through residential Staten Island when Richard saw Bethany's eyes finally refocus.

"Where have you been?" he asked. "You've been staring out the window the whole trip. The look on your face made it pretty clear you weren't checking out the scenery."

"Do you need help finding the place?" Bethany asked, without acknowledging the question.

"No, I got it," Richard replied, pointing to the navigation system. He considered asking her again if she was all right, but he knew it was a stupid question. She wasn't.

They turned off the winding road and onto Frankie's block. Richard knew immediately which house it was. He would've known even if he hadn't known the address. The monstrosity was as subtle as he would've expected from one of Pietro's close associates. Richard pulled the car behind a small Ford and a large Cadillac.

"Are you ready?" he asked.

Bethany took a visible breath and said, "Let's get this done."

Richard squeezed her hand. "Now don't forget. Tonight is all about me charming the ladies; you just sit back and watch the information flow."

She offered a small smile at the weak joke, which was clearly more to tell him she appreciated the effort than an expression of humor.

And then Bethany got her game face on. Richard wondered if he'd ever get used to seeing her close off like she did in situations like this. In an instant, the visible anxiety was gone; she looked calm, composed, and completely unconcerned. In those moments, he felt like she was gone. It made him worry that someday she'd shut down and never come back.

She started to reach out for his hand, but stopped herself. Before he could ask why, he realized the obvious reason. Walking hand-in-hand into a meeting with her former fiancé's mother was no way to curry favor.

As they approached the house, the front door swung open revealing a woman who he assumed was Maria Lioni.

She was the picture of the perfect Italian wife. There wasn't a wrinkle, not a hair out of place. But her eyes glowed with a hatred Richard had never seen in his life.

It was all he could do not to grab Bethany and drag her away. There was nothing they needed from this woman, nothing worth the price of admission those eyes promised.

But he couldn't. No matter what he wanted,

Bethany needed answers. And despite the certain cruelty that would come from their hostess, she was the only person who could give them access to those answers.

Maria's voice was oddly rich and inviting. She greeted Bethany and added politely, "This must be your friend Richard?"

It was obvious she didn't think much more of him than she did of Bethany.

Richard wondered why her tone was so light. Did she actually think she was fooling anyone?

Since pretending to be civil seemed to be the approach everyone was taking, Richard used his most charming voice for greetings and followed Maria inside.

"It's a beautiful neighborhood," he offered, hoping to shift the focus from Bethany.

"Thank you, that's nice of you to say," she replied. This time her voice was stiffer, the false welcome slipping a bit. "The others are in the living room, follow me."

The room she led them to was bizarrely immaculate, designed in a virginal white. It was simultaneously beautiful and disturbing. Not unlike their hostess.

When Richard saw the solitary woman on the couch, the room became an afterthought. He felt bile rise in his throat, and he bit back against the anger and fear.

He hadn't been prepared for this, for her. In the shape of her nose and the curve of her chin, he could only see the man who'd tried to kill his best friend.

Frankie stood and made the introductions, as if this was a normal dinner party and not some kind of twisted nightmare.

Richard kept his attention focused on Geoffrey's mother. She was dressed in widow's black from head to toe. Her eyes red-rimmed from lack of sleep.

He no longer wondered if the woman had been involved in Geoffrey's plans. Without words, her face conveyed her belief, her pain. Illogical as it was, it was clear she thought Geoffrey was a martyr and Bethany was a killer.

Celeste spoke first; her words betrayed none of the emotions that were so obviously written on her face. "I agreed to do this because I had to see you for myself. I'm glad I did. You're different in person. I've seen many photos, but now I can see much more."

"Geoffrey showed you pictures of me?" The question seemed to have escaped Bethany's lips before she realized what she was saying.

"Of course he showed me pictures. He was my boy," the woman snapped. "You were supposed to get married."

It almost seemed she believed it was that simple.

Bethany settled into a chair across from Celeste. Her eyes never leaving her face. Richard knew she was calculating her next move and he wished her luck. He had no idea what to do.

Bethany finally said, "Geoffrey never told me about you."

If Bethany had been trying to get a rise out of the woman, she failed.

Celeste said simply, "Geoffrey knew about your mother's family. Knew about his father and the troubles he had with the Timminolos. He didn't want you to know about that."

The room was silent; everyone watching the back and forth, no one wanting to interrupt the exchange.

"What kind of troubles did Geoffrey's father have?" Bethany asked.

Celeste glared at her. It was obvious she was certain Bethany already knew the answer and was trying to embarrass her. Richard suspected that was why she turned her attention to him.

"So, you're Richard. I told him to keep an eye on you. I read the papers. I see what they say."

Her tone suggested Celeste had somehow just found the proof she needed for some unspoken allegation.

"Ms. Vicetti, you'd be amazed at what garbage they report in the paper. Beth and I have been friends since we were little kids, nothing more scandalous than that."

Celeste snorted at the response. "My poor boy was too trusting for his own good."

Now he was getting angry. "Bethany never cheated on Geoffrey."

"Then why are you here with her?"

"I'm here because I have been Bethany's best friend for our whole lives. She needed someone to accompany her," Richard replied.

His response was met with an icy stare. Richard felt his anger rising. He was about to protest further when Bethany put a hand on his arm, as if she was considering restraining him. The look she shot him reminded him of all he needed to know. Celeste most likely believed Bethany was guilty of far worse sins than infidelity.

Bethany took a deep breath. Her voice was even and calm, her face stoic when she spoke. "I've been working with the police to find Geoffrey's killer. They haven't had much luck."

Celeste's tone was far less civil. "I read they had

somebody in custody. Then they lost some evidence. I'm just wondering what it cost you to get them to misplace it? Are you paying in political favors or was it just cash?"

Richard could think of only a couple times in his life when he'd lost his temper, but he burst to his feet without even a thought.

"You have a hell of a lot of nerve!" he practically screamed. "How dare you! Bethany has done everything in her power to find out who killed your son. Everything! And you sit here and accuse her of cheating and then of trying to protect the man who murdered her fiancé?"

Frankie stepped between them. His eyes locked desperately on Richard, silently begging. "Everybody needs to take a deep breath. Otherwise somebody's gonna say something they'll regret."

"Regret?" Celeste sneered. "There's nothing I could say to that woman I'd regret. Wasn't it enough her family killed my Lou? She had my son murdered!"

Frankie put a forceful hand on Richard's chest, keeping him from lunging at the woman on the couch. He didn't know what he would've done had Bethany not spoken.

He realized she, too, had risen to her feet, but not in the aggressive way Richard had. Her voice was soft when she spoke, smooth and powerful.

"I have no idea what happened to Lou. I know he owed the Timminolo family a debt. And whatever happened, there was something between my grandfather and him. My mother didn't want to have anything to do with that family and neither do I. And I want one other thing to be entirely clear…"

Before she could say anything more, Maria spoke

up, "Are you still singing that song?"

Frankie looked at his wife, an expression of surprise and fear crossed his face. "Maria, this isn't the place," he threatened.

"What're you gonna do, Frankie, have me knocked off? You're not gonna shut me up. It's about time somebody told the truth. Rita Timminolo never left the Family, not really."

"Maria, I swear to God, this is not the time."

"Rita Timminolo was living like the princess she'd always been. Daddy's men protecting her, happily helping her whenever she needed anything taken care of."

Frankie turned his full attention to his wife. "You know that's not true."

Maria thrust her chin out defiantly. "Really? Then you weren't working for Pietro when you were spending all that time *taking care of her?*"

~ 63 ~

Richard watched the color drain from Frankie's face as he stared at his wife in disbelief.

Maria didn't pause even a moment. She simply focused her naked hatred toward Bethany. "I know who Rita Timminolo really was."

"It's because of her my Lou is gone," Celeste added. "And it's because of you my Geoffrey is gone,"

"I didn't kill Geoffrey!" Bethany growled. "Your precious son hired that hitman to kill me! I didn't do anything."

"How dare you," Celeste hissed.

Bethany shook her head, again the rage that had been so apparent only a moment before vanished. "It's the truth. I had the hitman tracked down. He was paid by money that came from Geoffrey's bank account, a bank account no one knew anything about, at a bank about a block from your house. Any idea how he ended up with millions in that account?"

Frankie nodded at the two women who'd turned to him for confirmation. "That's why we're here. Bethany deserves to know why."

Celeste glared at Frankie. "If Geoffrey hired that man to kill *her*, then how is it he's dead?"

"Let's just say this hitman knew better than to kill Pietro Timminolo's granddaughter," Frankie replied.

There was the slightest shift in Celeste's expression. After a moment, she turned to her friend, as if looking for guidance. But Maria's face was impassive.

Richard lowered himself back to his seat. He watched as Bethany did the same. Her face was expressionless. It was now clear they'd been wrong – Celeste had no idea about the murder.

It was Bethany who spoke first. Her voice was still soft and even, but it was different now. She was furious, possibly even more than he was. The soft voice was just a cover, probably had been all along. Now, though, her eyes gave her away – they were practically glowing with rage.

"I'm sorry to put you through this, but I have to know. Clearly, you hate my family. Clearly, you hate me. It seems Geoffrey did too. Then why the relationship? Why did he spend years convincing me to marry him? I think I deserve to know."

The look on Celeste's face made it clear she didn't think Bethany deserved much of anything. But she answered anyway, probably out of spite. "It was about the money."

Maria took her friend's hand. "Don't fall for it. She'll say anything to get you to tell her what really happened. Then they'll kill you."

"I promise you, no one will hurt you," Bethany

swore. It was the first time all night Richard was sure she was speaking sincerely.

She looked to Frankie and asked, "Can you make sure of that? No matter what. I don't want any of this taken out on her. Enough is enough."

Frankie nodded. "It all stays here."

Though Maria looked unconvinced, the answer seemed to satisfy Celeste. "The account you found, the money in that account, it was yours."

"Geoffrey stole two million dollars from me?"

"That sounds about right," she replied without any remorse.

Bethany seemed at a loss for words. She finally sputtered, "How?"

"It was something to do with a charity scam. I didn't really understand the details."

Richard's heart broke. The jackass hadn't even been man enough to steal family money. He'd stolen from the Foundation. Richard knew the money didn't really matter to Bethany, but to have failed in her job of protecting the Foundation was devastating.

"If this was just about stealing my money, then why the relationship?" Bethany asked. Her voice sounded broken now. Even with all of her efforts to remain stoic, the news was proving too much.

Celeste sounded like a proud mother as she explained, "It was always about the money, but not in the way you think. We wanted all of it. The money, the power. That meant a marriage, a high profile marriage. That was his plan. He was confident he could do it. He made his way into the D.A.'s Office. He built a reputation for himself and got involved with your work in Central Park. You bought the act hook, line, and sinker."

Richard put a hand on Bethany's shoulder. He wished he could just take her away from all of this.

Cruelly, Celeste continued, "The bank account. The charity scams. That was just a plan B. You know, in case he didn't get you to fall for him. But my boy was a charmer. When you accepted his proposal, we thought we were home free. At least we did at first. After a while, Geoffrey became worried. He said you were getting more distant. You kept putting off setting a wedding date, kept delaying any discussion of your marriage. As time passed, he realized you never actually intended to marry him."

The remark seemed to catch Bethany completely off guard. "What do you mean? Of course I intended to marry him."

"You've been engaged nine months. No date. No discussions of specifics. Just evasion. You didn't even want to move in with him. Geoffrey moved up the timetable on his candidacy.   He thought he could convince you to finally walk down the aisle because a married candidate would be more likely to succeed."

Richard looked between his friend and the others in the room. Maria looked like she was savoring the victory. Frankie looked like a man who'd just been run over by a truck. Richard prayed someone would stop this, but knew no one would.

"Obviously, the mayor plan didn't work either," Celeste noted. "He was discouraged at first, but the last time I saw him he was very excited. Told me he had a new plan. He just kept saying he was done trying to piggyback off the Chase family. Now, wait, let me get this right. He said – 'Mom, why should I use them for an easy ride when I can use them to launch me beyond their power and control?' He was vague, told me I was better off not knowing much. But he was certain this was his ticket into the mayor's office."

Bethany shook her head slowly, in what looked like stunned amazement. "For a candidate whose platform was crime control, the murder of his fiancée in Central Park would be just the thing," she stated dully. "And he had to know my people would make sure the Foundation funneled money into his campaign and any other projects Geoffrey wanted to use to make him look like the big hero."

"I guess that was the plan," Celeste agreed. "I wish he'd told me more. It was a bad idea."

"A *bad idea?* Murder's a little worse than a bad idea," Richard snarled.

Celeste looked at him as if he was the greatest fool that ever lived. "You misunderstand. I don't care about her. I only worry about my boy. No one is going to successfully put a hit on Timminolo's granddaughter. It was a *bad idea*," she repeated.

Richard couldn't sit there any longer. Bethany had her answers now, but that was it. "You talk about all of this like it's okay. Like fraud and murder are no big deal. Like the lies and the deceit were nothing."

"For a Timminolo, fraud, murder, lies, deceit, *are* nothing. It was time to fight fire with fire," Celeste snapped.

"Bethany Chase is not, nor has she ever been, a Timminolo. Her mother made sure of that. And nothing you people do will make her one now. You can bet your ass I'll make sure of that," Richard declared.

"Look, I think everybody needs to calm down," Frankie urged.

"At the mention of the sainted Rita Timminolo

everybody needs to calm down? Funny how that's always the case," Maria pointed out.

Bethany's voice quickly silenced the room. She wasn't speaking softly anymore, plainly having no interest in concealing her anger. "My mother's name was Rita Chase. She changed it the moment she had the chance. And I would thank you to remember that."

"Anybody can change a name. It doesn't change who you are," Maria countered.

"If you're still jealous of the relationship your husband had with a woman who's been dead for twenty-five years, I can't help that," Bethany replied.

Maria's expression of shock and anger confirmed what everyone had already believed, though she quickly disputed the allegation. "This has nothing to do with Frankie. Those thugs should've been hassling your father, not Lou. Instead, Aston ends up a billionaire and Lou ends up dead. All those years ago, Rita chose her family over the family Celeste never got the chance to have. Today, I choose my best friend over you."

"Enough!" Frankie roared. He jumped to his feet and for a moment Richard was very concerned he was going to hurt his wife. "Nobody wants to hear this, but Lou was a bum. Celeste, I'm sorry, God rest his soul, but he never would've married you, never would've looked out for your little boy. You know that. And you," he thundered at his wife, "you know that, too. I remember when we was first dating, you told me about your friend Celeste and her boyfriend. You told me he was no good. That she should dump him. Now Lou's the victim?"

Frankie looked back and forth between the two women, neither one met his eyes. "Lou was in debt to Pietro big, huge, in fact. He had outstanding loans, big time loans. He hadn't paid them in months. About a week before Rita asked her father for help, Lou got into a fight. You girls remember that? I think he told yous he got jumped and somebody robbed his place. There was no robbery. That was a warning. Things was bad. There was talk about a contract going out if he didn't get some money paid up soon. Instead, Pietro forgave the debt. In exchange, Lou agreed to work with some guys from another family. Those guys imported some things through his business. That was all."

"That's not true!" Celeste insisted. "My Lou was being pressured by those men. They were threatening him."

"They was threatening him because he owed them money, because he ran up a debt with them too. Just like he'd owed the Timminolos years before. Rita's decision gave Lou another chance. It's not her fault he made the same stupid decisions all over again," Frankie replied.

Richard looked between them and tried to decide if they were listening. Before anyone could say anything else, Bethany took his hand and helped him to his feet. She shook her head sadly, her eyes conveying more grief than he'd ever seen.

She turned to the others and said very calmly, "I think it's time for us to leave."

Frankie looked like he was about to protest, but he decided against it. "I'll show yous to the door."

Celeste looked away as they left, but the glare they received from Maria spoke for both of them.

When they reached the entryway, Frankie offered a weak apology, "Maria told me this wouldn't go well. I'm sorry. I shouldn't have done this. I really thought she was over the stuff with your mother."

Bethany shrugged, clearly wishing he'd just let her leave.

Frankie didn't catch the hint. "I told you she was mad when I told her about my job. She never understood we was just friends. Rita was like us, you know, from the neighborhood, but also not like us. She was living in the city, living a very sophisticated life. It was fun to hear about all the things she was doing. And I think Rita missed us in the neighborhood a little, as much as she would've denied it."

Richard thought the explanation made perfect sense. Unfortunately he was pretty sure Maria Lioni didn't really care what made sense.

"Rita was my childhood sweetheart, but Maria is the love of my life. I don't know how to get her to understand that," Frankie continued.

Bethany only nodded, looking back toward the living room uneasily.

Seeing her glance, Frankie ended the conversation. "Anyways, I'm sorry. You guys drive home safe. Bethany, I'll call you tomorrow."

Bethany agreed, and they took the opportunity to slip out of the house. Richard was relieved it was all finally over. Maybe now the dead would rest in peace.

"So, that's all there is to it. My grandfather had the hitman kill Geoffrey, but only because Geoffrey had already hired the hitman to kill me, because he wanted to punish me and my family for the harm he believed we'd caused his family," Bethany summed up, peering over her sandwich at Annie, who was sitting on the other side of her desk, her own food completely untouched.

After a moment without even a peep from her friend, Bethany prodded, "Now come on, I talked for like fifteen minutes straight, you have to say something."

Annie just shook her head in amazement. "Words are failing me, and words never fail me. Are you really okay?"

"It was touch and go in the middle. Honestly, Richard really helped me. A lot. I don't think I could've done it without him. Actually, I'm sure I couldn't have."

"So, you met his mother?" Annie asked, clearly processing what she'd heard.

"Yeah."

"She was the source of all this?"

Bethany considered the question. It was tough to say who the source was. "I guess. She was angry, very angry. And she clearly blamed the Timminolo family for all that had happened to her. More specifically, my mother. My mom helped my dad out early in his career. It indirectly caused problems for Geoffrey's father. And that was a big reason Geoffrey's mom was so obsessed with my family. It kind of seems like she believed she was entitled to the success and wealth my father had obtained because of all she'd lost."

Annie slowly shook her head. "Wow, that's carrying around a lot of anger for a really long time."

Bethany thought of her own anger. How long had she clung to it? Geoffrey's mother wasn't the only one who'd done crazy things in the name of revenge. She'd already gone online and ordered two cans of primer and a can of white paint. She had some walls that needed to be painted over, and a property to sell.

"What is it?" Bethany asked, realizing Annie was staring at her.

Annie smiled. "I was just thinking you look happier than you've looked in a long time. I know that's a crazy thing to say, but there's something different about you. Less strained, more peaceful."

"It's over," Bethany said, more to herself than her friend.

In answer to Annie's quizzical look, she explained, "This all started with my mom. All she wanted was a new life for herself, something quiet, less public, no more violence. Funny how life ends up giving you everything you never wanted."

"Do you think Geoffrey's crazy mother will just let it go now?"

Bethany thought of the women she left last night. She didn't think either of them would let it go. Ever. The hatred was just a part of them now, but that was something they'd have to deal with on their own.

"What about you? What do you do now?" Annie wondered.

Bethany shrugged. "I'm still here. I know a bit more about my family than I ever wanted to. I know a lot more about Geoffrey than I could've imagined. I think I'm just going to try to live a normal life. Do you think that's possible?"

Annie laughed. "Honey, you've never had a normal life. Are you worried the stuff about your grandfather will come out?"

"It's bound to happen eventually, don't you think?"

"I'm astonished it hasn't happened before now."

"I'm seriously considering just going public with it. You know, clearing the air on my own terms, finishing it. But I need to talk to my father about it and, though I hate to admit it, I need to talk to my grandfather about it too."

"Just let me know. I'm here if you need anything at all. Karen, too."

"You know, I could totally go for a fancy, fun dinner with friends tonight. I'd like to think of it as the first day of the rest of my life."

Annie picked up her sandwich and finally started eating. Bethany was settled back into her own lunch when she realized Annie's eyes were fixated on her, as if she was reading her mind. Bethany paused mid-bite, watching as a slow grin spread over Annie's face.

"You slept with him," she said. "The peaceful look, the calm. Here I was thinking it was just all the stuff that happened last night, but no. I've been waiting for you to sleep with him for ten years and you didn't even tell me?"

Bethany laughed and carefully returned her sandwich to her plate, narrowly avoiding choking on it.

"You do have a way with words, you know."

Annie hit her hand on the table. "Don't bullshit me. Spill. Now. Richard. You. When? How was it? Details! I want details!"

As Bethany relayed the experience, she couldn't help but realize just how normal things were. A lot had changed. A lot was bad. But all in all, it felt like this was just the type of bad you had to go through to get to the good. She didn't have any delusions it was going to be easy, but it felt like she was finally on the right path.

They were finishing lunch when Bethany's cell phone rang. Seeing that it was Frankie, she excused herself and found a quiet conference room to take the call.

Remorse still tinged his voice, but he sounded better than he had the night before. "I want to say sorry for last night. Maria and me, we talked, and I think she understands now. I just can't believe she said those terrible things about your mother."

The call was nice, but unnecessary. Bethany just wanted to put the whole thing behind her. "Thanks. And thank you for organizing the meeting last night. Despite everything, it was helpful."

"At least now you know what happened with Geoffrey. It didn't have nothing to do with your investigation."

"Speaking of my investigation, you should know that I decided there are things better left unsaid," Bethany explained.

"You really expect me to believe you're going to drop it, just like that?"

Bethany chuckled. "You don't have to believe me, but it's true. I've learned a lot about my mom in the past few weeks. She wouldn't have wanted this. And if this whole ordeal with Geoffrey has taught me nothing else, I've learned sometimes the answers only make things worse."

Frankie seemed to consider her words very carefully. "Are you sure? Because if you're still trying to pursue this, I can talk to the boss about helping you out. I know you two don't get along so well, but I think with all the circumstances we got here, we could work something out."

"I don't think Pietro is the only person who'd rather you stay far away from me," Bethany pointed out.

Frankie sighed deeply. "I don't know why Maria hates you so much. I mean, she hates Rita, and it's crazy, but I get it. You, what'd you ever do?"

"Look, Frankie, it really doesn't matter. I'm done. It's over. I'm just going to work on accepting that my mother's murder was a horrible, unsolved violent crime. It sucks, but continuing with my search is pointless and, frankly, borderline suicidal."

"I don't disagree. Promise me one thing though?"

Bethany smiled at the sincerity in his voice. "Anything."

"You ever need backup, you call me first."

"I wouldn't consider doing anything else."

~ 65 ~

Bethany arrived at the restaurant a half an hour early. She'd called ahead to have their table changed to a private room. She was in no mood for the general public.

The restaurant was a trendy, popular one. That meant lurking photographers and gossip columnists. It meant keeping her hands off Richard all night. While she had no intention of sitting on his lap, she hated the idea of worrying about what might be printed, what might be said. After all, no one knew her fiancé wasn't worthy of a typical mourning period.

Bethany was in the back room, fussing over place settings, when a familiar and frightening voice filled the room. "I think you and I still have some matters that need to be discussed."

Bethany turned to see Maria Lioni closing the door behind her. The hatred was completely unmasked now, making Bethany long for the times when the woman was at least pretending to be civil.

It was a conversation Bethany didn't want to have, but since Maria was standing between her and the door, there wasn't much she could do about it, at least not yet.

Bethany shrugged. "There's no reason to hash this out. Can't we just agree to disagree?"

"You're so much like her," Maria growled. "Always easygoing and carefree. What's it like to get everything you ever want?"

Bethany was stunned. Maria had to know what she'd been through since her mother's death, at least generally. Hell, most of Manhattan had an inkling.

"What do you want me to say? Do you want me to tell you that you're right? My mom has been dead twenty-five years! Why does it matter to you what kind of person she was? Why do you even care what kind of person I am?"

"Why does it matter?" Maria practically screamed. "It matters because she was trying to take my Frankie from me."

"They were friends! That's all there was to it. Nothing else."

"You aren't so naïve that you believe that."

Bethany considered the accusation for a moment, and then continued, "You know what, I do believe it. I believe it because I trust the relationship my mother and father had. And you know why else? Because I've seen Frankie with you. He loves you. He wouldn't be unfaithful to you."

"She's the reason he lied to me. The reason he lied about his job. The reason he lied about them seeing each other. He kept it from me because he didn't want me to know about the affair."

Maria had a violent rage radiating off her, the kind of rage Bethany had only experienced right before a fight.

She was standing on the other side of the room, and Bethany wished she'd step closer. From that distance, Bethany would have trouble defending herself if Maria had a gun. Though it would have seemed unfathomable at the beginning of the conversation, Bethany was seriously worrying Maria was here to do her physical harm.

"You need to be having this conversation with Frankie," Bethany stated, inching towards the door.

"Come on now. You're the little Nancy Drew, right? You should know all the answers. I just figured you'd be more likely to tell me the truth than my husband. Obviously I was wrong."

"I am telling you the truth. There was no affair. Why are you so sure there was?" Bethany couldn't have cared any less about her theories, but the more time Maria talked the more time Bethany had to get to the door.

"I caught them."

The single sentence was enough to stop Bethany in her tracks, her curiosity overpowering her sense of self-preservation. "You caught them? When?"

"Frankie was supposed to be at work. I found them in a coffee shop here in the city, holding hands. Your mother was crying about something, and Frankie was wiping her tears away."

Bethany still thought that sounded more like two friends meeting for coffee than a love affair, but she also thought this was the wrong time to argue about it. "When was that?"

Maria eyed her skeptically. It seemed she could tell

Bethany wasn't believing her story. "It was during my separation from my husband."

Bethany thought back to her talk with Frankie, his little pep talk that had encouraged her to come clean with Richard. He'd said he and Maria had separated for a few months, during Maria's pregnancy. As she considered the circumstances, the implications of the fury in Maria's eyes suddenly became clear.

Joey was going to turn twenty-five this fall, hadn't that been what she'd said? That meant Frankie and Maria's separation had to have been right around the time of her mother's murder.

"When were you two separated?" Bethany was hoping she could confirm her memory.

The ghost of a smile appeared on Maria's face. Bethany was certain it wasn't her imagination. "Now let me think, it had to have been almost twenty-six years ago, not too long after New Year's. We got back together in April. I had little Joey in September."

Maria stared at Bethany fixedly, daring her to make the accusation. Bethany could only stare back with a mixture of sorrow and confusion. This was the moment. This was all she'd worked for practically her entire life. This was supposed to be nirvana.

Yet, it was agony. Her mother had died because of petty, unfounded jealousy, nothing more. Instead of the rage she'd felt her entire life, Bethany only felt gaping sadness.

"Couldn't you have just hired a private investigator to tail him like a normal jealous wife?" Bethany asked.

"I didn't need an investigator. I know what I saw."

"You saw nothing! You saw two friends having coffee. My mom was probably crying because she was sorry Pietro's business was such a problem in your marriage. Don't you see?"

"Don't you dare judge me! Rita Timminolo was a slut. She was trying to destroy my family. I couldn't allow that to happen."

"Stop calling her that!" Bethany snapped.

"Don't raise your voice." Maria seemed to have suddenly remembered exactly where she was.

"Look, I think this conversation is over," Bethany replied, turning and taking a distinct step towards the door.

What happened next was a blur. All at once, Bethany heard a soft ping and the sound of rushing air, followed immediately by a fiery pain in her left shoulder.

~ 66 ~

Bethany was still about ten feet from the door when her legs buckled. Out of the corner of her eye, she saw Maria holding a 9 mm handgun with an elongated barrel – a silencer.

"This conversation isn't over," Maria retorted.

"You shot me?" Bethany was incredulous. It was one thing to hire a hitman to murder a rival. It was entirely another thing to shoot her daughter in cold blood. "Why would you do that?"

"I don't have the connections I once did. And you need to be stopped."

Bethany fought off a wave of dizziness. The pain was searing. She could feel the blood running down her back, dripping off her fingertips. She had to focus. *What the hell was she talking about?*

"What do you mean – connections?" Bethany asked, trying to take the questioning one step at a time.

"Lou DeAmanto helped me last time. Put me in

touch with the Family he was working for. Ironic, isn't it? If your mother had just left things with Lou alone, I wouldn't have had any way to put the contract out on her. I certainly couldn't have gone through the Timminolos."

The pain Bethany felt at the explanation was so severe she barely felt the gunshot wound anymore. This would kill her father, absolutely kill him.

"Lou helped me learn my way around the crime families. I tried to tell Geoffrey things were too interconnected now. There was no way to find a hitman willing to take out Pietro Timminolo's granddaughter."

"You knew?" Bethany gaped.

"I knew Geoffrey very well. He was a wonderful boy, but he was stubborn. I met him at the restaurant the night he died. I begged him to call it off, but he refused. He was so sure he'd found someone who was trustworthy."

Bethany thought back to that night. The woman in the bar, glaring at her. It hadn't just been a coincidence Maria Lioni had been in the same bar as her.

Maria smiled at the memory. "It was a shame really. His plan was so good otherwise. He recited part of his speech to me that night, the one he planned to give at your funeral. He would've been more than a mayor – he would've been a god."

Her legs were rubber now. The image of Geoffrey's near victory, the understanding she should never have survived, swept over her in a wave of nausea.

"You know, it's funny," Maria continued. "I was always so worried about getting caught. For more than twenty-five years, I lived in fear of the police, of the Timminolos. I never worried about you, until last night."

"What happened last night?" Bethany could hear her voice getting weaker.

"After our little meeting, Frankie was so mad. He was shouting at me, furious at how I'd talked to you. He'll always take your side, you know. Just like he always took *her* side."

"Why did that make you worry about me?" she asked, hoping to get back to the original point.

"He told me everything. He was trying to explain why I should treat you more kindly, trying to explain how you had it so rough. He wanted me to feel sympathy for you," Maria snarled.

"What did he tell you?" Bethany asked, though she feared she already knew.

"He told me about your vendetta. Told me he thought you'd see it through to the end, or take it to your grave. That was when I realized I had to make sure I took you to the grave before you had a chance to find the answers."

Bethany took a heavy breath. Only the sound of her own blood tapping on the tile floor could be heard in the silent room. She would've screamed, if only to drown out the sound, but she couldn't get the air.

She was trying to decide what to do next – if she was capable of doing anything at all – when she heard voices in the hallway. Annie and Karen and another voice, most likely the hostess.

Maria heard the voices too, and she moved two steps closer to Bethany. She looked manically between Bethany and the closed door, clearly realizing she'd taken too long. This wasn't going to be the simple job she'd thought it would be.

Outside, Bethany could hear Annie commenting on the closed door. She asked the hostess if anyone else had come back to the room. Bethany thought it sounded like Annie suspected Richard might have snuck in for some private time, but her tone was light enough Karen was probably the only one who'd notice.

The hostess rapped sharply on the door and called in. Bethany said nothing. Maria did little more than stare, eyes wide with shock and confusion. She didn't think to order Bethany to send them away. Of course that was the way out of this, but Bethany had no intention of sharing the strategy.

The trouble was, Bethany feared Maria might be crazy enough to turn the gun on Annie and Karen. She knew even if she could get her legs back under her – a prospect that seemed almost impossible at the moment – Maria was still too far away. There'd be another bullet through her body before she could get to her.

There was another knock at the door. This time Annie called inside, "Hey, Beth, what's going on?"

Still there was only silence as Maria and Bethany exchanged uneasy glances.

Maria spoke in a whisper, her eyes desperate. "This isn't the way I wanted to do this, but I'm not going to just sit in here and wait for them to catch me. First you. Then your friend in the hall. Then anyone else who stands in my way."

Maria cocked the gun for effect and moved closer. Standing over Bethany she said, "Say hello to your mother for me."

Knowing this was her last chance, Bethany dove into action, praying her body wouldn't fail her. She launched herself into Maria's knees, knocking her backward, slamming her arm into the tile floor. The gun slid away, but not as far as Bethany would've liked.

At the sound of the struggle, the door swung open. There was a shrill scream – most likely the hostess. She could hear Annie bark at the woman to call the police. Karen was calling her name. But the voices sounded distant and tinny. Bethany could see them in her mind's eye, standing in the doorway completely helpless, not knowing if there was anything they could do.

Unfortunately, Maria was regaining some balance. She bit viciously into Bethany's right forearm, bringing forth a new stream of blood.

Years of training had taught her to not to flinch. Only to proceed forward. Take down the enemy.

Despite the burning pain in her left shoulder, she drove her fist into Maria's face, wrenching her good arm free from Maria's locked jaw. Maria's eyes rolled back slightly, the blow leaving her stunned.

And that was Bethany's chance. She flipped Maria onto her stomach and pulled both arms behind her back. Using her right hand to secure Maria's arms, she dug her knee strategically into the small of her back.

It was then she heard Karen again. "I've got the gun!" she said, her voice shaking too much to sound threatening. "You freeze. I'll shoot."

Bethany cringed at the threat. She couldn't have sounded any less capable of using a gun.

Maria made one last attempt, twisting sharply, hoping to throw Bethany off balance. But Bethany expected the move, and was able to hold.

"Calm down, everybody," Bethany said firmly. Out of the corner of her eye, she could see Karen standing about five feet away from them, holding the gun, her hand shaking so badly she couldn't have hit anything with precision.

Making a decision she hoped she wouldn't regret, Bethany released Maria's arms and simultaneously threw her own weight forward. She ignored the squish of her bloody shirt against Maria's back and wrapped her good arm around the woman's neck. Using only her legs for balance, she applied the appropriate pressure. In less than a minute, Maria's body went limp.

Bethany released the woman slowly and checked her pulse to make sure she was okay. It was steady, but she'd be out for at least a few minutes. As she tried to stand up, Bethany was shocked to discover just how weak her legs were.

As the adrenaline wore off, she was again feeling the effects of the blood loss. Her shoulder was throbbing, each heartbeat bringing an ever-deepening pain.

Annie hurried to her side, catching her as Bethany swayed unsteadily on her feet. Karen held her spot, still clenching the gun in an almost comical way.

Once Bethany was seated and began to feel a little less lightheaded, she said to Karen, "You should give me the gun."

Karen was more than happy to oblige, though she seemed skeptical Bethany would know any better how to handle the weapon. She looked uneasily at the woman lying on the floor.

"Is she dead?"

"No," Bethany assured her. "She's going to be fine. She should be out for a few minutes. If she comes around before the police get here, the gun will hold her."

It was then that Annie found her voice. "Who is that?

"That's the woman who had my mother killed," Bethany said. "Obviously there's more to the story, but for now, I think that's enough."

"What happened to you?" Annie looked between Bethany's saturated shirt and the trail of blood on the floor, her face growing pale. "Did she shoot you?"

"Aren't we supposed to put pressure on that or something?" Karen asked nervously.

"Of course, right," Annie exclaimed. "Get her some towels or something!"

Karen fled the room, practically knocking Richard over on the way out. Though Annie and Karen were somewhat muted by the shock, Richard showed no ill effects.

"What the hell is going on in here?" he asked as he entered the room. Before anyone could answer the question, he was at Bethany's side, ripping off his suit jacket and balling it up to put pressure on the wound. "My God, what happened? Were you stabbed?"

"Shot," Bethany explained, holding up the gun. Her head rolled a bit at his touch, relief and exhaustion pulsing through her. Strangely, the pain was starting to fade a little. Edges of the room were starting to dim. She drew in a breath and tried to stave off the inevitable. "You may need to put pressure on the back; the bullet went through, I think."

Annie leaned over her, clearly taking a closer look at the situation. Bethany knew she was in trouble when she saw the look on her friend's face. "Take off your shirt," she ordered Richard. "We can use that for the pressure on the other side."

Richard quickly complied. They were both

applying pressure to her shoulder and discussing whether or not she should be laying down when Richard noticed the woman on the floor.

"Holy God, is that Maria Lioni?"

"That's the woman who had Rita killed," Annie explained, before Bethany could say a word.

Richard was looking to Bethany for confirmation when the police came crashing into the room with the paramedics close behind.   Everything else was a complete blur.   The only thing Bethany remembered was telling Richard to call Frankie and explain what had happened.

~ 67 ~

The light was blinding. Sharp. An assault. It burned her eyes. She struggled to fade back into the dim world of sleep.

But part of her insisted. It was time. It was past time.

She slowly blinked through the pain and grit of her dry eyes. Gradually it became clear they were fluorescent lights she was seeing. And they really weren't that bright. Actually, they were fairly dim. There was one right over her though, nestled among the panels of one of those drop ceilings with the funny holes. The kind you can throw pencils into and make them stay for days.

Bethany was feeling amused by the prospect of tossing pencils at the ceiling when she began to notice that her left arm felt funny.

It wouldn't move. Actually, all of her limbs felt very heavy. And her mouth felt uncomfortably dry.

She fought through the haze. Where was she? How did she get here? What was wrong with her arm?

The last question brought the most concern and caused her to focus on the limb with more precision. After a moment's concentration she was able to force the arm to move. She regretted it immediately.

The pain shot from her shoulder to her fingertips. The electric sensation seemed to wake her arm up and it explained why she had so much trouble moving it. It was fastened to her body. A sling.

Why was her arm in a sling? As the question crossed her mind, so did the answer. The restaurant. The shooting. Maria.

The flash of memory forced her to sit up in bed. Actually, it forced her to try to sit up. The quick movement caused the blood to rush from her head and she immediately flopped back, again jarring her painful shoulder.

The burst of movement had given her a better view. She was in a hospital. There were flowers everywhere and her father was standing on the other side of the room, staring out the window.

Bethany again tried to sit up, this time more slowly. She was surrounded by pillows. If she moved slowly, very slowly, the pain wasn't unbearable.

"Dad," she said, her voice raspy and softer than she'd intended.

The small sound was enough to get her father's attention. There were tears in his eyes as he raced to her bedside.

"Honey, you're awake. Oh, thank God. Are you all right? I should page the nurse," he gushed, rapidly tapping the call button next to the bed.

"I'm okay, really," Bethany replied, though the

sound of her voice made her question that a little.

Her father quickly grabbed a plastic container from the table next to the bed. "Ice chips. Your throat must be so dry."

"Dad, what happened?"

"You lost a lot of blood. A lot. You had us all a little worried. But they seem to have patched you up." Aston's voice broke, making it very clear he'd been more than a little worried.

Before Bethany could ask another question, a nurse swooped in. For the next few minutes there were all sorts of vital signs that had to be checked. Bethany waited not so patiently for the woman to leave. As she left, she informed them the doctor had been paged and should be there momentarily.

Aston spoke before Bethany could ask another question. "Richard will be furious I was the one who was here when you woke up. We've been alternating. They didn't want us both in here. They said it was essential you were able to sleep."

"You've been alternating? How long have I been out?"

Aston glanced at his watch. "Almost twenty-four hours."

"Jesus. No wonder you were worried."

As if on cue, Richard came bursting in the room. "I heard the nurse on the phone. I waited until she left the desk and then snuck in." Richard's speech was as frantic as Aston's. The two of them were exchanging looks that demonstrated a new camaraderie.

Richard gently took Bethany's good hand. "Are you okay?"

"I think so," Bethany replied, looking between the two men. The desperation on their faces made her wonder if maybe she wasn't as okay as she thought she was. "I've really been out for a day?"

Richard looked at Aston. "A very, very long day."

Bethany was afraid to ask the question, but she knew she needed to know. "What happened?"

"You lost a lot of blood," Richard began.

"No," Bethany interrupted, her voice cracking as she spoke. "What happened with Maria?"

Richard looked at her uneasily and consulted her father. Though he said nothing, his question to Aston was clear – *should we tell her?* She was pleased when they silently seemed to conclude that answers were better than fighting with her.

"The police brought her here to get checked out, but she was released pretty quickly. She was only a little bruised. She told them everything, told them what she did to you, what she did to your mother," Richard explained.

"It seems she was so afraid of retribution from Pietro she thought jail was a better option," Aston explained. "The police tell me she's not only confessed, but she has indicated she plans to plead guilty. Against her lawyer's advice, she's begging them to hurry the process up."

"What about Frankie?" Bethany asked.

"Frankie's devastated. He sent those flowers over there," Aston reported, pointing to the biggest arrangement in the room. "I spoke with him on the phone. I think he'll get through this, but it'll be tough on him. He told me he resigned from his job."

"You can resign?" Bethany asked.

"It seems that under these circumstances you can."

"Is Pietro going to do anything crazy?" Bethany was afraid to even consider the possibilities.

"Who's to say what that man will do. But Frankie said he thought Pietro would leave things alone."

"So, this means it's really over?" Bethany wondered, speaking as much to herself as to the others.

"It's over," Richard agreed.

As Bethany let out a deep sigh of relief and exhaustion, Annie slipped into her room. She had Karen by the hand and was dragging her behind her.

"We had to come and see for ourselves," Annie explained. "I haven't seen the doctor around, so if we're quick we might not get banished from the hospital."

She swooped over to Bethany's bedside, pushing Richard aside.

"You've had your moment. My turn," she insisted. Then looking down at Bethany very seriously she said, "I swear to God, if you ever, *ever* do that to me again, I will kill you, actually kill you. Smother you with a pillow while you lay unconscious in the hospital."

If she'd had more energy, Bethany would've laughed. "I'll try my best not to piss off any other homicidal maniacs."

"I am serious," Annie threatened. Then, laying a gentle hand on Bethany's good shoulder, she added, "You scared me to death. They say you're going to be alright. Are you sure you're alright?"

Bethany reached up and placed her hand on top of Annie's. "I think I'm going to be fine. My shoulder hurts. And I feel kind of fuzzy in the head. But I'm going to be just fine."

Annie looked away, wiping a tear from her cheek. "Seriously, you scared the crap out of me," she said, as if to defend her tears. "Once the paramedics showed up, you faded out on us. I swear, it was like you were just gone. I thought you were dead."

Richard wrapped his arm around Annie's shoulder. The look on his face said he'd seen the same thing, and he wasn't going to forget it anytime soon.

Karen gave Annie's shoulder a squeeze and then leaned in to give Bethany a kiss on the forehead. "I am so glad Annie convinced me to sneak in here to see you. Beth, you're going to be fine. I can tell just by looking at you."

Bethany looked up at the group gathered in her room. Her father smiling proudly and paternally. Richard grinning that classic Richard smile. Annie looking protective as always.

This was what life was about now. It was about life, living, no more murder and death. She was going to have the life her mother wanted for her – a life of peace, surrounded by family and friends.

The image brought a smile to her lips, because even with all of that, she couldn't give it up. Not entirely. There'd have to be a little fun, the occasional masked tournament. Four on one was really the only way to make it a fair fight.

There wasn't anything wrong with that, was there? Everybody needs a hobby.

~ Acknowledgments ~

The past year has been a whirlwind and I would be extremely remiss if I didn't take a few moments to thank all the people who have provided the support I needed to survive this process.

It's a funny thing, really, the process of sitting down and writing a story is relatively easy for me (I actually started writing as a form of stress relief). But the process of editing and getting a book to print is another matter entirely. And forget about the difficulties in the process of book promotion (I shudder just typing the word!).

The first people that must be thanked are the folks that provided the last rounds of editing for Vendetta and The Sinners – Megan, Anne, and Robin. I'm quite convinced that editing is the closest I've ever come to a truly infinite process. The mistakes you'll find are only limited by how many times you look. These three fabulous women help me strike the balance between thorough and compulsive. I'd be lost without them. In fact, when I drafted the dedication in The Sinners I planned to not ask them to proof what was essentially a brief thank you to them. Not surprisingly, the draft that I was ready to send to print had not one, but two typos.

I should also take a moment to single Megan out. She is with me from beginning to end with each story. And is the person who most often has to suffer through my interminable musings as I try to figure out how to deepen characters or stories. Her balance of patience, encouragement and criticism is key to this process.

And of course, Stephen, whose beautiful art graced both the cover of Vendetta and The Sinners. He's embarrassed already that I've even mentioned him. But this needs to be said, so he's just going to have to deal with it. Stephen and I trudged through Central Park last August on what was possibly the hottest day of the year, carrying a three-hundred pound camera (okay maybe it was only five pounds), and taking pictures of everything in sight, hoping to catch the right shot for the cover. In spite of everything, I somehow remember laughing more than sweating.

I also have to thank Michelle, who setup and maintains the website that I so seriously neglect. I honestly wouldn't have even dreamed of undertaking that process without her. In fact, I can't think of any other job that has been so completely delegated! Her generosity with her time is amazing.

So many people have read drafts of my stories over the years. Because of them, I learned countless crucial things. The criticism and praise, as well as the endless "book reports," given by my friends and family have been invaluable to this process. There are too many to name everyone, but I'd like to single out a few: Mary, John, Barb, Ruthie, Gina, Jody, Laurie, Michelle, Priya, and Trish. And I must say a quick word of thanks to my friend Allyson who trudged through the Nevada heat – while pregnant! – taking the pictures that we used for the cover of The Sinners.

Finally, I want to thank everyone who has been so supportive of The Sinners and so encouraging about the release of Vendetta. I have loved the book clubs, the interviews and preparing for the library appearances. I would be remiss if I didn't send a special thanks to Christine, Anne, Chris, and Joyce for all you've done to promote The Sinners on my behalf.

Ultimately, these are an awful lot of words to make what should be a relatively simple point:

Thank you, to all of you.

I couldn't have done it without you.

~ Liz